PENGUIN BOOK

HALF A DARK HEART

Other titles by H. F. Askwith

A Dark Inheritance
A Cruel Twist of Fate

H. F. ASKWITH

HALF A DARK HEART

PENGUIN BOOKS

PENGUIN BOOKS

UK | USA | Canada | Ireland | Australia
India | New Zealand | South Africa

Penguin Books is part of the Penguin Random House group of companies
whose addresses can be found at global.penguinrandomhouse.com.

www.penguin.co.uk   www.puffin.co.uk   www.ladybird.co.uk

First published 2026

003

Text copyright © H. F. Askwith, 2026

The moral right of the author has been asserted

Penguin Random House values and supports copyright.
Copyright fuels creativity, encourages diverse voices, promotes freedom
of expression and supports a vibrant culture. Thank you for purchasing
an authorized edition of this book and for respecting intellectual property
laws by not reproducing, scanning or distributing any part of it by any
means without permission. You are supporting authors and enabling
Penguin Random House to continue to publish books for everyone.
No part of this book may be used or reproduced in any manner for the
purpose of training artificial intelligence technologies or systems. In accordance
with Article 4(3) of the DSM Directive 2019/790, Penguin Random House
expressly reserves this work from the text and data mining exception.

Set in 10.5/15.5pt Sabon LT Std
Typeset by Six Red Marbles UK, Thetford, Norfolk
Printed and bound in Great Britain by Clays Ltd, Elcograf S.p.A.

The authorized representative in the EEA is Penguin Random House Ireland,
Morrison Chambers, 32 Nassau Street, Dublin D02 YH68

A CIP catalogue record for this book is available from the British Library
ISBN: 978-0-241-73842-9

All correspondence to:
Penguin Books
Penguin Random House Children's
One Embassy Gardens, 8 Viaduct Gardens, London SW11 7BW

Penguin Random House is committed to a
sustainable future for our business, our readers
and our planet. This book is made from Forest
Stewardship Council® certified paper.

For Mum

Prologue

The horrors gain strength when things in our world are broken.

A bone. A promise. A heart.

So much of what happened took place on the page, in words typed, or scrawled, or carefully composed. I've gathered up all the remnants I have, and it seems only right that I finally document everything that happened in between, even if my heart aches to write it. The record must be kept. There is a gap in the archive where this story belongs.

I could start with the horrors. But I won't.

For me, this story starts ...

With him.

Prologue

1

The evening was creeping in. Mother, weary and drawn, leant against the counter, her eyes fluttering shut. She had just collected the keys and payment from an elderly couple who were taking their leave of our guest house.

'Turn the sign, will you, Alice?' she asked, her voice fragile.

I nodded and went to turn the sign in the window so that it read *Vacancies – enquire within* and made a note to myself of a thin crack in the windowsill corner. It didn't matter how hard I worked to keep the Honest Opal clean and welcoming, there was always more to do. Everything inside was getting tired, and it was full of furniture that complained of its aches and pains in spite of how hard we tried to take care of it. We were doctors of our belongings, using ointments made of glue and bandages made of thread. Mother hated it when anything broke, and believed deeply in fixing things with haste, but I didn't understand the real reason why; I'd always assumed her motive was financial. Mother's preoccupation with mending and preventing breakages made me feel as though there were something wrong with me, because I was the heavy-handed one, the unlucky one, the one who always seemed to be breaking things, even when I didn't mean to.

Returning to Mother's side, I noticed that she was breathing heavily, standing with a slight sway.

'Do you need to rest?' I asked. She blinked her eyes open as though she were surprised to see me. I put my hand on her arm. 'I can take care of things if you need to go to bed early.'

Mother looked at the desk, and I could see her responsibilities tugging at her. Originally opened by her father, the Honest Opal had a reputation for clean rooms, good food and reasonable rates, but we were mostly known for our service being second to none. Mother was always ready to meet the whims of any of our customers, no matter the hour – even if her health was beginning to make that harder and harder.

Her decline had been gradual, the sickness that was engulfing her strange and not responding to any treatments. It sometimes seemed as though she was decaying, a strange smell on her breath and skin, her joints creaking and her hands wrinkled like those of a much older woman. I was certain that she was hiding other symptoms from us. But it would come in waves, and some days she was like her old self, with her usual intensity of focus and attentiveness to our guests. Other days she would crumple in on herself as if she were made of paper.

'Don't worry about the guests. I'll sit at the desk in case anyone needs anything,' I said, and Mother's eyes welled up with gratitude. She nodded, finally accepting my help and heading up the stairs to her room.

On a normal evening, I would keep to doing housework and preparing food for the next day, leaving my sister, Lucille, to take care of anything that required her confidence and charm and easy smile.

But that evening was different. Lucille had taken herself away to our room early, her silent tears more worrying than any big display of sorrow or anger. Lucille was prone to great performances of whatever emotion had swirled her into a storm, but that night she'd quietly retired without eating, her face pale and washed out. It was so disconcerting that I was at a loss as to what to say to her, while Mother seemed too weak to address Lucille with her typical vigour.

With both Mother and Lucille incapacitated, it was up to me to keep things running smoothly. I was determined to try my best, despite the fact I'd rather not have to be sociable. Not that I didn't like to be around people... just that it would take so much of my energy, having to think so hard for the right thing to say. It always came so naturally to Lucille. She made navigating conversation look so easy, while I picked my way through it like I was trying to avoid broken glass scattered across my path.

It would be fine, I reassured myself, even as dread settled in my stomach. It would be quiet. We weren't expecting anyone to arrive, and our existing guests surely wouldn't need to ask for much. I just had to be seen to be available.

So I fetched the novel I'd been reading and positioned myself on the stool behind the front desk, flinching as it creaked. The last thing I needed was for my propensity for unintentional destruction to rear its head.

But then a shadow appeared in the stained-glass panels of the front door. A tall, slender silhouette made its way up the seven stone steps to the guest-house entrance, outlined by the glow of the street lamp.

The door swung open with such a great clatter that it rebounded off the wall, the glass panels quaking. I winced at the *almost* and felt my breath catch at the narrowly avoided accident.

A young man wedged himself into the hallway, hefting his wooden trunk across the threshold as the door bounced against him and the harsh September wind rushed in, desperate for any opportunity to get inside. He had a slight, expressive mouth, a slender nose and huge eyes the colour of the sea on a dark day. I guessed he was around eighteen years old, like me, though possibly a little older. The stone-grey coat he was wearing was thick and looked expensive, with gold buttons that winked in the light.

I hurried out from behind the counter to help him, my ears echoing with Mother's well-repeated lectures on excellent service.

'Let me,' I said, restraining the door. 'Sorry about that.' I don't know why I felt the need to apologize, when the behaviour of the door was entirely the result of his own exuberance – perhaps it was because he was so disarmingly dishevelled, in spite of his wealthy appearance. His dark hair was ruffled by the wind and his trunk was so heavy that his brow creased and his arms looked as though they might snap with the effort of dragging it.

'Welcome to the Honest Opal. Delighted to meet you. I'm Alice Everglass,' I recited. The young man had successfully lugged the trunk fully into the reception area now, the rug in faded jewel tones crumpled in his wake. And then he properly looked at me, and I flinched slightly as I noticed his eyes inevitably draw to my hair, the striking white of it. I bristled, suddenly feeling self-conscious. 'Are you looking for a room?'

He nodded eagerly.

'How fortunate. We've just had one become available. How long were you wanting to stay?'

He pressed his hand against his throat and attempted to speak. No sound escaped, and his expression was pained, his eyes squeezed shut. He tapped his throat with a shake of his head. It seemed that while he had brought plenty of personal effects, the one thing he had not brought was his voice.

As I absorbed this information, he reached into the pocket of his fancy coat. The palm-sized leather notebook he pulled out had a worn and creased cover, with thumbed-through pages, as though it were in constant use. He brandished a short pencil with a blunt end in need of sharpening, which he now used to write a message with tidy, graceful penmanship. When he was finished, he held up the page for me.

My name is Austin Parker. I'm an actor from London,

seeking accommodation for the rest of the year. I'm here to get my voice back.

People did often come to the seaside to take the air and recover when they had been unwell. I assumed that was what had happened in order for him to lose his voice – some kind of malady. I looked from the note to his face. His smile was incredibly charming, but I had my reservations. Actors were known to be dishonest, weren't they? And flighty.

We had never had an actor stay at the guest house before. In fact, we didn't tend to have any young men, let alone ones in fancy coats. The Honest Opal was more the domain of elderly widows who liked to sit on the pier, couples in their autumn years visiting Whitby to enjoy the sea air and, sometimes, as was the case that week, honeymooners. We were also currently housing a retired doctor who happened to be an old family friend, and an aspiring writer who'd heard this town had been an inspiration for several successful authors. Perhaps he was hoping he'd cross paths with one of them, or maybe he thought our town was the key to finding his creativity. But he was sullen and insular, with fraying clothes and a disillusioned expression, and I feared he might struggle when it came to settling the bill in a timely fashion. He seemed rather lacking in imagination to me.

Mr Austin Parker was not our usual type of guest and, truthfully, I was also lonely a lot of the time and did not get smiled at by young men my own age. I wanted him to stay, the feeling sudden and surprising. But that didn't mean I trusted him.

'Let me just double-check our books,' I said, my voice hushed as I returned to the counter to go through the ledger. The Honest Opal might have been an ever more exhausted place, but we had our regulars who often returned to us on account of Mother's excellent attentiveness, so even with a room just opened up, I couldn't necessarily promise Mr Parker a room he could keep for several months, even in the descent towards winter when we tended to be less busy.

He turned the page of his notebook and began to write again.

You don't need to whisper.

A soundless laugh played across his lips. My cheeks flushed.

'Of course.' I shook my head, but my voice was still quiet. I opened up the ledger, and remembered what Mother always said about asking guests about themselves. 'I imagine being an actor is quite the adventure. Living another life on stage every night.'

His pencil scratched once more. I glanced up to see his tongue protruding slightly in concentration as he wrote.

It's exhilarating. An escape.

He had a dreamy, far-off look in his eye as he showed me the page, and I thought perhaps he was on a stage somewhere in his memory.

The notion of escaping into a night at the theatre was as glamorous as it was intoxicating. The closest I got was sinking into the fictional worlds of my books. I imagined that watching a performance might be like reading a novel – a safe way to eschew the repetition of the guest-house schedule, to abscond from responsibilities like cleaning rooms, without taking any of the risks.

'I've never had the chance to see a theatre performance,' I said, a little wistfully.

It wasn't being busy with work at the guest house that prevented me from going, or that there had never been anyone to take me, though of course these things didn't help. We did have a local theatre. But the fact was, I didn't leave the guest house any more than was absolutely necessary. For a long time, my heart had been struck through with terror at the very idea of venturing out, in a way it seemed like nobody else's was. I retreated into the safety of our guest house.

Austin Parker felt like a window.

One day. You absolutely must.

His enthusiasm made the words he'd written seem alive, made *me* feel alive. It was the strangest thing.

'Well, I've read several plays,' I told him. 'I find I like the tragedies the best.'

Me too. I played the role of Benvolio in Romeo and Juliet. *'I do but keep the peace.'*

'One of the few to survive by the end!' I said with a smile. He began to write again, filling the silence between us with the sound of his words forming on the page.

I would prefer the tragic hero . . . maybe next time.

My smile faltered. Next time. His voice would need to recover before there could be a next time. He noticed my hesitation, and immediately began scribbling again.

Enough about my stage dreams. Tell me about this place.

I cleared my throat. 'Well, we have four rooms for guests. Three of them have a view of the abbey on the East Cliff headland,' I began, crushingly aware of how stilted and boring I sounded. 'The attic is an apartment in its own right, but all the other rooms share a bathroom. Breakfast is served in the basement dining room from seven until nine, and rooms are cleaned every day. You are to let me know the night before if you want me to make up a lunch for you and . . .'

I trailed off, noticing that he was scritch-scratching with the pencil again.

Not the rules. The interesting things. I've heard this town is haunted?

His sea-blue eyes took on a feverish shine. I gave a small inward sigh. Another superstitious ghost hunter, then, drawn to the town's reputation. It had only become worse since the publication not so long ago of the vampire book *Dracula* set here.

'I don't tell ghost stories,' I said, more firmly than I intended. Lucille would have entertained the notion, told a ghoulish tale or two. But the truth was, I found stories about the spectres of the town settled in my gut too long after the telling.

I'd seen how fearsome the shadows could be, even while the sun hung high in the sky.

He arched one eyebrow, looking at me with an expression I'd never seen before – one that made me feel interesting, worthy of attention. I was slightly alarmed at how much

I liked it. Most often, I shrank myself, allowing the guest house and its quirks, or Lucille and her charm, to absorb the attention of visitors. And with good reason.

Not a believer?

'Too much of one,' I replied grimly.

2

'There is a room,' I said, diverting the actor from his talk of ghosts. 'It's not our largest, and you'll have to use the shared bathroom. But it's the only one available for as long as you'd like. And it does have a wonderful view overlooking the abbey. It's only just been vacated, though, so I'm afraid you'll have to wait while I get it prepared.'

Not all of this was *entirely* true; I would have to write to a weekend booking we'd agreed for the first week of November to cancel them, and somehow try to keep that a secret from Mother.

But it seemed of the utmost importance that I find a way for Mr Austin Parker to stay with us. I told myself it was because Mother would appreciate me securing the long-term booking, and not just because I was intrigued by him, because my attention snagged on him like a sleeve on a bramble. I wanted to know more about the life of an actor, so far removed from my experiences since I'd shut myself up in the guest house, a bird willingly remaining in an unlocked cage. If he stayed ...

I chewed the corner of my cheek while I waited for him to consider the room offer.

He nodded, and then to emphasize his point wrote: *I'll take it*.

It was only then, when the delight that he would be staying mingled with a sudden twist of anxiety, that I wondered whether I should have been more interrogative. Sometimes Mother interviewed longer stays to make sure they were compatible with our regulars. Should I have tried to discover more about his financial status? Asked for a deposit? I was struck with a doubt that curdled my insides. This doubt must have been written across my face, because Austin Parker began to scramble through his pockets, searching for something, an earnest and eager expression across his face, and then handed me a small bag of coins. A deposit for the room – a meagre one, given that he appeared to be someone with wealth enough to pay for the entirety of his stay upfront, but it was something at least.

'In that case, I believe we have an arrangement, Mr Parker.' A glow of pride burned in my chest. My mother would be pleased; I was certain of it. Without any help from her or Lucille, I'd managed to secure a valuable, long-term guest.

'I'll take you through to our library while I prepare your room.' I gestured for him to follow me to the largest room on the ground floor. Despite its size, the library was cosy, heated by an open fireplace, the coals of which glowed. It was also insulated by floor-to-ceiling shelves filled with books, old and new, a mixture designed to appeal to a great spectrum of readers. Indeed, our guests would often make trades, leaving behind something they'd finished reading in exchange for something they wished to take. One guest had recently left *A Study in Scarlet* on the shelves, and having read it in a single evening, I was desperately hoping that when they returned, they'd bring a further adventure featuring the consulting detective.

The library held five comfortable armchairs, and the finishing touch in the room was a taxidermy owl, who watched over proceedings, wings spread. After my tasks were complete, this room was where I tended to unwind of an evening, alone with a book, increasingly finding that I longed for somebody who might read alongside me, somebody who would chuckle or thoughtfully murmur if I shared a line aloud with them. I let myself wonder if Austin was the person I'd been waiting for. Mother was always too busy and Lucille said she didn't have the attention for literature. And, usually, I found it difficult to start conversations with our guests beyond what was required for my service role, always second-guessing myself.

When I guided him into the library, we found it empty. Although it was a public space in the guest house, I was suddenly anxious about the propriety of the situation – the two of us, alone together, late in the evening. I felt as though I shouldn't linger, or else risk my reputation. Of course, I had found myself alone with male guests before, but this felt different.

'You can borrow any book you choose,' I told him. He shook his head and from a deep pocket in that fancy coat of his retrieved a rolled-up script, the pages fastened with a clip. He sank into the green velvet chair in the corner of the room furthest from the fire and flicked open the script. He had such expressive facial features, a ready crinkle forming at the bridge of his nose, eyebrows that leaped. He grinned in an apologetic way, showing me the title of the play.

A Tale of Three Hauntings.

'Of course. More ghosts,' I said, sighing at him, though teasingly. Even then, I already had the sense that I was going to be drawn into a dance with Austin Parker, a push and pull, a give and take, where all the other dancers in the ballroom were phantoms.

He scribbled away in his notebook and then held it for me to see.

It is based on a true story.

I raised an eyebrow. He looked at me intently, and I couldn't help but feel as though he actually saw me, not simply noticed me as though I only existed to ensure he had a pleasant stay. I couldn't deny that I wanted to know more about the tale inside the script, about why it was so important to him that he carried it on his person. But of more pressing importance was the preparation of his room. The sky was already under a heavy blanket of night and he might wish to retire soon, to begin his period of recovery with a good night's sleep.

'You'll find plenty of spectres in this town if that's what truly occupies your mind,' I said as I moved to leave. His eyes were bright, his expression keen. The warmth of his smile emboldened me. 'And I'm sure I would love to know more about that playscript.'

I did not wait to see his response. Exiting into the corridor, my heart thudded, unused to such boldness erupting from within me. I fetched a fresh set of sheets and my rags for dusting, and headed straight to the room on the first floor where Mr Parker would be staying. I hoped he would be impressed by the view across the River Esk, which cut through the town, the harbour opening up into the sea, and of the East Cliff on the opposite side, where the ruins of the abbey cut a spectacular silhouette against the evening sky. I could never grow tired of that view. I always thought the abbey ruins seemed as though they were not fully of our world, like a half-conjured creation.

All the time I was preparing his room – stripping the sheets, remaking the bed, dusting the surfaces, checking that nothing had been left behind by the previous guests – I replayed the things I'd said to Mr Austin Parker over and over like a phonograph. I knew that people thought me awkward and strange because of the way I had become someone who always stayed inside. And yet, despite his fascination with ghosts, *perhaps because of it*, Austin Parker had dashed a fracture into my heavily built defences and wedged himself in my mind the way he had wedged himself in the entrance to the Honest Opal.

When I returned downstairs, he was perusing the bookshelves, his hands clasped behind his back. I let myself look at him for just a heartbeat, before speaking. 'Your room is ready, Mr Parker,' I said, and gestured for him to follow me.

He wrote a quick missive.

Call me Austin. Given I shall be staying a while, I think we ought to drop the formality.

I supposed he was meeting me in my own forthrightness, then! But I rather liked it, and enjoyed conspiratorially murmuring back, 'Well, then you can call me Alice.' Alice, not Miss Everglass, as all the other guests referred to me. Alice, the name that was usually reserved for Mother and Lucille. Suddenly, a new bashfulness reared its head in me, and I felt myself withdrawing behind the mask of professionalism.

'I'll show you to your room,' I said, guiding him through the guest house. At the room's open door, he strode in confidently, but stopped abruptly at the window. He went very still, transfixed by the view, the moon hanging like a pearl at the throat of the sky. When he turned to me, he sighed, and touched his own throat. It seemed that, despite the brightness and levity he conducted himself with, a deep grief had accompanied him on this journey. His voice was gone, so completely gone. I could only imagine what that would mean for him as an actor.

'Sleep well,' I said, and quickly placed the key on the bedside table and backed out of the room, closing the door behind me. The actor was here to stay, and with his arrival I had the sense of the ground shifting beneath my feet. He had written that he'd come to rest and regain his voice. But he was carrying a playscript about hauntings in his pocket and probing about ghost stories. What was it that inspired his interest in the supernatural, and how intensely would he pursue it?

The secret that I kept caged inside me fluttered like my heart, as though it knew how much Austin would love to discover it.

And when I think back on that night now, I am conflicted.

The events of the Otherworld have changed me so completely that I do not recognize that version of myself any more. Mostly, I think of the door to the guest house. It clatters and rebounds in my mind, and sometimes I have nightmares in which I am trying to keep it closed, pressing against the stained-glass panels, heart pounding, breath chasing, while on the other side a shadow shifts and twists.

Sometimes, I know that the shadow is me. An echo of me. The me from before, and she's trying to get back in. She wants to fasten me into a box, along with everything that happened, and fling that box over the edge of the pier so that she can step back into her old life once more.

I certainly wouldn't want to be that version of myself again. And yet, I've learned the true meaning of regret, and it's a definition my heart wishes it could unlearn. Maybe this is what it means to grow up. That we become something so different that our past becomes only a haunting.

3

After I had left Austin, I went to check on Lucille, unsettled at the way she'd taken herself away for the entire evening. Lucille choosing solitude as a remedy for soothing herself was as unnatural as a cat going for a swim.

I was pulled towards the bedroom we had split in half exactly. No heart-soaring view for us at the back of the house. Our room held a walnut-coloured wardrobe with two doors (mine the lopsided one falling off its hinges), a single bed on each side of the room (mine the one with the creaky floorboard next to it), and a bedside table between them, which provided us with one drawer each (Lucille had long ago claimed the top one). In her drawer my sister kept the diary she wrote in every night before bed. I'd often been tempted to look at it, to learn about the inner workings of her mind, given that she seemed so impossibly different to me. I imagined that perhaps inside the pages I would find the recipe for her confidence so that I might brew up a batch for myself.

I'd once gone so far as to take the little emerald-silk-covered book out of the drawer and turn it over in my hands, with my heart thudding and a twisting guilt in the pit of my stomach. I felt certain that if I opened it she would know somehow, or that the second I turned the first page, she would appear at the door. So I had placed it back and sworn to myself I would never look.

Now, I knocked softly at the door. No response. I pressed my ear to the wood and wilted at the faint sound of Lucille's muffled sobs. As I hovered awkwardly, my eye alighted on the framed artworks that lined the rest of the corridor, all of them Lucille's watercolour paintings, inspired by Whitby. She was a wonderful and gifted artist, imbuing the familiar sights with their own moods; in Lucille's renderings, the abbey sulked against a sky struck with lightning, the pier daydreamed about the waves crashing in the distance, the tremendous whalebone arch on the West Cliff seemed lost in rememberings. My favourite piece of hers was not displayed on our walls, though – the one of a train leaving Whitby station, steam billowing. I'd always thought it was so hopeful. She'd gifted that one to her sweetheart, Theodore Truman.

'Lucille?' My voice was as gentle as I could make it. Still no answer.

I knew why she was crying, of course. Lucille and Theodore had been promenading and exchanging tokens of affection for so long that she had believed an engagement was on the cards, and soon. But the news had arrived that afternoon that Theodore was engaged to another, and the wedding was arranged with so much haste that the whole town was aflame with gossip. He was due to be married in just ten days' time. The news had reached us swiftly, and my sister's heart was broken.

Opening the door and poking my head in, I saw Lucille lying prone on her bed, face buried into the pillow. Her usually perfectly pinned hair was loose, cascading in ringlets around her shoulders. Pity swept through me, as well as anger. I'd witnessed my sister's delight in Theodore. She had loved him truly. Now the force of that feeling was matched only by the anguish she was wading through. His betrayal was unforgivable.

'Lucille, it's going to be all right.' I wished I had stronger words, words that would lift her out of the sorrow. I knew as I spoke that she needed more than platitudes, but I had little else to offer.

Lucille's head snapped up to look at me, and she pulled herself to sitting. Her eyes were puffy, the lids painful-looking and swollen. When she spoke, her voice was as sour as lemon juice. 'Don't pretend you have any understanding of this feeling, Alice. What do you know of love? You've never so much as made eye contact with a young man, let alone –' She broke off, her pain mixing with horror as if she were only just realizing the way her words slashed at me.

I winced. It was true that I did not know anything of love, but it wasn't that I didn't want to. My reclusiveness was a source of deep insecurity for me, and usually Lucille was my fiercest defender. She was the only person I had confided in about the horrors I saw, and even though she did not see them, I felt that she believed me. She had certainly kept my secret, and never made me feel as though there were something wrong with me. Although *I* felt that there were – felt it on a daily basis. If anyone questioned why I hated to leave the Honest Opal, Lucille would shut the conversation down. And although my sister always had some emotion tearing through her, she had never, ever directed her anger at me so cruelly before. And so I refused to take the jibe to heart. This outburst could only be a product of the pain. Lucille was emotional, explosive at times, but she wasn't cruel. She was like a wounded dog snapping at the person trying to heal her.

'You're right. I'll leave you alone,' I said.

Her face flooded with regret. 'I'm sorry. I didn't mean to . . . I don't . . . I don't know where that came from. How ghastly of me. Alice, I'm sorry.' She reached out for me. 'Please stay with me. Forgive me.'

Forgiveness came easily, my love for my sister winning. I sank next to her on the bed and rubbed her back. Beneath my hand, her shoulders dropped, and the tension started loosening out of her.

'Oh no, you mustn't apologize. You're quite right. I have no personal experience of this particular agony, and I must say I find myself feeling very thankful about that fact at the moment.' I fell quickly into our easy jesting, hoping to bring a smile to her face. 'You are not making love look appealing. Your eyes look like they've been stung by bees! Is this meant to be something I should wish for? I suppose I could create the same look by plunging my face into a beehive.' It had the desired effect; my sister laughed a little.

'Forget my eyes – it feels as though my *heart* has been stung by bees.' She sighed. 'I feel so foolish. It's as if . . . as if I imagined it all.' Her eyes filled with tears again.

'Well, if you've imagined it, we all have. It's clear to anyone how Theodore feels about you. There's not a person in this town who could deny it.'

Lucille nodded. She knew it to be true, even though she was so bruised by what had happened, by what was going to happen. 'But if that's true, how . . . how could he marry somebody else? I feel sick at the thought. Ten days from now, he will be wed. And not to me. To a *stranger*. No one's even heard of this girl.'

It certainly didn't seem like something that Theodore would do willingly. I struggled to believe that he had been untrue to her.

'I think it must all be down to his father,' I said. It felt likely that the match had been made by the senior Mr Truman, with a financial motive in mind. The tailor was known around town for his grand aspirations for his family. The rush must be all his.

'You do?' She peered at me from underneath dark, wet lashes.

'I find it impossible to believe that he would betray you of his own volition.' And yet that must have been little comfort really. The outcome was the same. Theodore was to be married to someone else. Everything that had existed between him and Lucille, the years of affection and care, the fondness and the hopes for the future, it was all to be resigned to the realm of memory.

She took a deep breath and wiped her sore eyes. 'So then what am I supposed to do?'

'You're asking the wrong person,' I said. If she didn't know what the next steps were, then I didn't have a hope. 'I don't know that there is anything to be done about it. Have you spoken with him?'

Lucille snorted. 'Of course I haven't spoken with him. What am I to do, show up at the shop and throw myself at his feet, beg him to reconsider? Absolutely not. Whether or not he entered into this arrangement willingly, he let me find it out the same way as everyone else. He might have at least written so that I heard it from him first.' She took a deep, shuddering breath and then spoke quietly. 'Everyone will be laughing at me.'

'Nobody is laughing at you,' I said gently, but I knew I couldn't erase the humiliation she felt. My words were empty. They might not be laughing at her, but I could only imagine the way Lucille would have been whispered about when people read the announcement, when they read a name other than hers entwined with Theodore's. It was the sort of drama that gossips in the town devoured and regurgitated, and would continue to for years.

'I can't bear it,' Lucille said. 'I feel as if I've been knocked off the pier into the freezing water.' She grimaced.

'Well, then you'd better swim to the edge and I'll throw down a rope for you. We'll be all right. It's always been you and me.' When she smiled, I thought that it was working. I thought that I was cheering her up. But as I write this account now, the memory echoing in my mind, all I can see is the way the smile didn't quite reach her eyes, the unformed words on her lips. She was already lying to me. 'You haven't cried like this since Mother went to visit Aunt Sybil in London. Do you remember?'

Our Aunt Sybil was estranged from us, but she had taken ill when I was thirteen, and Mother had travelled by train to visit her. Mother had never left us before. Despite the way Lucille often seemed aggravated by absolutely everything that our mother did, the pair of them always bickering, she had been beside herself while Mother was gone, missing her so desperately that it seemed her tears would never stop, would fill up the bedroom and flow out of the window. The incident had become family legend, and Mother liked to use it as proof that Lucille must truly care for her despite their fierce rows.

Lucille stilled, and would not meet my gaze. 'I remember,' she said.

I leant my head against Lucille's, our temples touching as though our thoughts could pass between our skulls. I wished so deeply that in that moment she could see herself the way I saw her – brilliant, daring, effervescent. Why is it that the things we adore about the people we care for are so often invisible to them? Lucille had once told me that she thought she felt everything too deeply, too intensely, and yet I was certain it was this same deep feeling that made her so empathetic to others, the same intensity that made her such an incredible artist.

'I know you will survive this,' I said. That was the one thing I was utterly certain of – that there would be so much more to her life than a failed romance.

If I had known that it was the last evening before everything changed, I would have clung desperately to life as I knew it. If I had known the secret she was keeping from me, I would have had a hundred questions.

But now, there is only one. What can we build from the ashes of the life we used to have?

She brushed her hair back from her face and tied it up with a red ribbon, breathing in sharply. Her dress was covered in damp splatters from her tears, and she clutched at a sleeve to wipe her eyes. 'I'm all right,' she said. 'I'll come downstairs now to help.'

'You missed the most exciting development,' I said, and I told her about the arrival of Austin, swerving mention of how handsome he was, highlighting instead how interesting it was to meet an actor, how his voice had disappeared, the way he spoke through notes, and his curiosity about the ghosts of Whitby. I might not trust him, but I couldn't deny that I was fascinated by him.

'What did you tell him?' Lucille's eyes narrowed when I mentioned the talk of ghosts.

'Nothing.' My stomach swooped. It was the same feeling I'd had when Mother caught me using the master key to try to unlock the cupboard door in the basement dining room, which I'd never seen inside of before and which was always locked. The key hadn't worked, and Mother had scolded me. Even though I hated that churning feeling of being in trouble, it didn't stop me trying the key again another time; the mystery of what might be hidden behind that door compelled me so.

'It wouldn't do for you to become too comfortable with that particular topic of conversation,' Lucille warned.

'I didn't say anything.' My cheeks flushed with embarrassment. Lucille had clearly sensed the way that Austin intrigued me. I had got carried away talking about him.

'Well, you mustn't.' Lucille was firm. 'Ghost is the wrong word anyhow. That's what you've always insisted.'

She was right. It wouldn't be right to call the things that I see 'ghosts'. I've spent a long time thinking about what we mean by that word. And mostly I think that ghost stories are born from a fear of death, people searching in desperation for a sign that when we die, it is not the end. There's a thread of humanity in each tale. But the things that I see? The horrors that move in the shadows?

They are not ghosts, although they do make me feel haunted. They are not human – never have been, never will be. I am certain about that, even though so much about the horrors and their many forms remains shrouded in mystery.

Many people in our town are superstitious, but their tales about an aunt or an acquaintance who once *saw a ghost* were always so much more human than the haunting encounters I'd unwillingly gathered throughout my life, centred as they were around a person who met a tragic end, their essence remaining. I was certain that if I ever shared the reality of my own experiences with any of these people who claimed to believe in the supernatural, they would not be well received, and I'd be branded as completely insane. Which was why it had taken me some time before I felt brave enough to tell Lucille the truth about what I saw. When I did, we both understood that telling anyone else would only lead to trouble. It was better for me to be believed awkward and a recluse, than to be thought mad.

And so I understood why Lucille was protective when she heard me enthuse about Austin Parker.

I cleared my throat. 'I just ... think he's interesting. That's all I meant.'

'Just be careful,' Lucille warned again. She took a deep breath before continuing. 'You know I'd love nothing more than for somebody just like you to stumble in here. That's what you were hoping, isn't it? That he might ... be like you? See what you see?' She watched me, waiting for my reaction.

'No,' I said, and I bit the corner of my cheek. I knew from experience that by watching my face, asking careful questions, Lucille would land right at what I was trying to bury.

'So, it's more that you think he might be somebody who could believe you?' Lucille pressed.

There it was. She'd uncovered it.

I looked away from her, trying to deflect her gaze. 'It just seemed like he was interested in the supernatural ... in an active way. Perhaps as if he were researching it.'

Lucille looked at me kindly. 'From what you've told me, I think it's more likely that this is just a young man who's read too many ghost stories and fancies he might gather a few of his own to take back to his real life when his voice has recovered.'

I nodded. 'You're probably right.'

She stood and smoothed her hair. 'There,' she said. 'Do I still look terrible?' Her face was blotchy, the skin around her eyes looked sore, but her determined spirit shone through.

'You look strong,' I said, and I meant it.

We went downstairs together, and when I reached the front desk, I noticed a slim pile of papers on the desk that hadn't been there before. A glimpse of the first page sent a little shiver of excitement along the back of my neck. Before Lucille could notice them, I swept the pages up from the desk, my heart thudding with anticipation as I slipped them into my pocket for later, hiding them from Lucille.

For once, I was determined to have something that was just for me.

A TALE OF THREE HAUNTINGS

A play

Act One, Scene One

The library in Oliver's apartment. A desk is covered in books and papers. OLIVER, a university student, is sorting through the papers, exasperated. BENNETT enters with a pot of tea on a tray.

OLIVER: *[Slamming his hand on the desk]*
There are no records of him. Not with any of the names he's given people, at least. I've searched and I've searched. I'm beginning to come to the conclusion that he is merely a figment of people's imagination. Remind me, Bennett, what is on my schedule for today?

BENNETT: *[Placing down the tea tray]*
Yes, sir. You have the visit from Mrs Darkwing and her daughter.

OLIVER:
I'm certain that will be another dead end. They're all dead ends. All I hear is yet another ghost story, and yet another claim that this fellow-of-many-names was the solution to their terror. And all this activity within the last three years. Incredibly prolific fellow. *[Sighs]* What time will they be arriving?

BENNETT:
Around two o'clock, sir. I'll make sure to prepare the little pastries you ordered.

OLIVER:
Thank you, Bennett.
[Pours the tea hastily and spills]
This is what aggravation does to me. My irritation prevents me from being able to complete simple tasks like pour a cup of tea. Would you, Bennett?

BENNETT:
Of course, sir.
[Mops up the spill. Pours a cup of tea and hands it to Oliver]

OLIVER: *[Taking the tea]*
Three things these interviews always turn up
About the man: the first, his name does change
And yet clear features make me sure it is
The same haunted man every single time
With eyes one blue, one brown, the hair a blaze
Of red, a strong and tall and youthful man.
Second, they are all eager to profess
How truthful, how sincere, how genuine,
How free of deceit they all do find him.
And third, the stone worn at his throat that he
Will not be parted from, a smooth gemstone

That seems to be crafted of rainbow fire.
So,
What do you make of it, Bennett?

BENNETT:
Me, sir?

OLIVER:
Yes, you have heard most of it, heard most of the interviews in their unfolding. What do you make of it all?

BENNETT: *[Cautiously]*
I perhaps wonder if he does not wish to be found, unless he is needed.

OLIVER: *[Thoughtfully]*
Hmm? Doesn't want to be found unless he is needed.
[Beat]
Then I must find a way to make him needed here.

4

'What is the meaning of this?' I whispered, pushing the pages of the play across the breakfast table when Austin arrived and sat down. I'd been waiting all morning for him to appear, so that I might ask him to explain himself, agonizing over what I would say while brewing the tea, lining out the cups and saucers, making the toast and laying out the little pots of jam. The guests had all come down to the basement, enjoyed their breakfast, and then left, while I was still waiting for him, watching the clock tick on.

I'd begun to wonder if he was coming to breakfast at all and was beginning to clear away the cold toast when he finally appeared, his dark hair sticking up from the top of his head as though it had a mind of its own.

As soon as he sat down, I thrust down the pages. My stomach was filled with nervous knots. Austin's sleepy eyes snapped wider and glittered at the sight of the pages. His eyes were the sort of blue that brought to mind the wildest of storms. He lifted a finger to ask me to wait, before retrieving his notebook from his pocket.

What did you think?

He looked at me with what seemed like nerves as a muscle twitched in his cheek.

Before Austin Parker arrived, I already had enough trouble sleeping. After reading his playscript, it had taken me hours to relax, my mind ruminating on its meaning. He had utterly unnerved me. 'You come here with talk of ghosts and then you leave this scene for me to read, with these pages making odd references to my home. Is this some kind of trick?'

In my bluster, gesticulating too wildly with my hands, I knocked over the porcelain salt shaker from the centre of the table. The tiny white granules scattered across the table, the shaker landing with a crash on the floor and shattering. Immediately, Austin bent to the floor to take a small pinch of the white grains and fling them over his left shoulder. I'd heard that actors were superstitious types but it was a surprise to see how urgently he moved. He tapped at the spill and pointed at me. Sighing, I repeated his gesture. I certainly didn't need to call any more bad luck into my life. Satisfied, he got to writing to me again while I picked up the broken porcelain. Mother would be disappointed, but probably unsurprised. This was why I tried so hard to keep my feelings so tightly under wraps. If I let them bubble to the surface, things got broken.

You noticed the script is connected to this place?

'Yes, I noticed,' I said, sighing at him. 'What was it ... "How truthful" and all those other synonyms, and the gemstone of "rainbow fire". Very clever. The Honest Opal. That's right, isn't it? It's a veiled reference to this place. But why? Who wrote this?'

He raised his finger for me to wait again. I was struggling to find the patience. I'd had no opportunity to read the pages until Lucille had finally fallen asleep, her muffled weeping eventually falling silent some time after the clock struck midnight. Then her heavy, sleepy breathing and the crackle of my candle were the only sounds to accompany me as I read and the characters' voices came alive in my mind.

I'd been intrigued anyway, and then I'd noticed that the main character, Oliver, had suddenly begun to speak in iambic pentameter, the poetry of it standing out from the realism of the rest of the dialogue. It hadn't taken me long to work out what it was trying to say. A handful of synonyms for 'honest', a fairly clear description of an opal. It was a strange, coded reference to my home. The Honest Opal wasn't famed enough to warrant any kind of mention unless you somehow already knew of it. This realization was accompanied by an uncanny sensation, chills running up and down the back of my neck. It was as if somebody were watching me.

A playscript about a student hunting down a man who resolved hauntings? Odd references to the place I lived, my safe haven? It was enough to throw me into a spiral of fear. Nobody knew about what I could see, apart from Lucille; I was sure of it. So why did the threat of discovery feel woven into the pages?

If I hadn't trusted Austin the night before, I was completely wary around him now.

Austin held up his notebook.

I apologize. I should have prepared better for this conversation.

A regretful smile played across his lips as he casually stirred his tea, the silver clacking against the ivy-patterned cup, setting my teeth on edge even further. Unbelievable! My mind had raced all through the night; I'd planned out *all* the different ways I might tackle this conversation to try to figure out what he meant by giving me these pages. I had agonized over it.

But he had simply dropped this script into my life, caused this deep, unsettled feeling inside me, and not even thought about what he'd say next? I huffed by way of response.

He quickly turned to the next blank page.

In my defence, I didn't know if you would see what I saw when you read it. But it does seem like a clue leading here, doesn't it?

'Perhaps,' I said, unwilling to give him any more just yet.

He eagerly scribbled.

Later on, there's a reference to Whitby. I found that first, and deduced the Honest Opal part later when I was researching the area. When I discovered this place existed, it made perfect sense.

My uneasiness began to shift to a tremble of excitement. If I put aside my worries, the whole affair had a thrilling sense of mystery, nothing like the humdrum routine of life at the guest house I was used to. It was as though I was being swept out of the safety of the harbour and facing the excitement and uncertainty of travel out to sea. What did it all mean?

'So, this playscript is why you're really here? You came because – because you think it told you to?'

Well, and my voice is truly gone, so I imagine a convalescence by the sea would be recommended.

He tapped his throat as I read. I watched his lips forming the shape of his words, but nothing came out, not even a hoarse croak or a low whisper. His clavicle sucked in at the top of his shirt. I could feel his frustration. It was as if the chords of his voice had been cut. I didn't doubt him on that point, but still, I was full of questions. I had the sense that I'd bumped into Austin in the middle of a labyrinth, weaving his way through the twisting and shifting paths, the playscript a string he was following. What I didn't understand was why he'd embarked on the journey in the first place, or exactly what he hoped to gain from it.

'What is it that you think you'll find here?' I asked, but he had no chance to write his response as Mother suddenly appeared at the door. Her eyes sharpened with an aggrieved, puzzled expression when she saw that all of the breakfast things were still laid out. Then she spotted Austin, and smoothed her features out into the smile she reserved for guests.

'Ah, our new arrival,' she said. I'd already had the chance that morning to inform her about him. 'Welcome to the Honest Opal.'

He wrote a quick message in return to her greeting.

This place is just what I was looking for.

'I'm so pleased,' Mother said, but heat prickled my cheeks as she began to tidy up around us, glancing up at the grandfather clock. I followed her gaze, the hands of the clock pointing out just how drastically I'd allowed Austin to derail my morning. By this time, I would usually have had breakfast completely cleared but, instead, I was engaged in a conversation that no doubt looked as intense as it felt. I got the sense that she disapproved of whatever she imagined was passing between Austin and me – something about the way she stiffened when he stood to leave, his cold toast uneaten, and gave her a smile that seemed to me that he was used to charming his way out of difficult situations.

The remainder of the day had a strange shadow draped across it. I was unsettled and restless as I got to work with my daily clean, beginning with the attic room where our family friend Dr Binding was staying. All throughout my chores, I thought about the playscript. Not only did I have to admit that I wanted to read more of the story – *Who was the mysterious man that Oliver was hunting down?* – but I also felt captivated by the layer of cryptic encoding someone had written into the script, and which Austin felt had led him to our door. It was the sense of something unfinished, like opening a jar of marmalade, anticipating the tang, smelling the zesty citrus and being interrupted before I could eat it, leaving my mouth watering and unsatisfied.

Underneath this, there was a low, humming anxiety, too. The arrival of Austin, with his fervent interest in the supernatural, had woken up dormant fears about the secret of what I could see being uncovered.

Nothing about the day felt normal. Nothing about it was.

I reached Austin's room but he didn't come to the door when I knocked. Supposing he must have gone out for the day, I used the master key to let myself in, and stopped short. I couldn't help but raise an eyebrow at the way he had made himself so immediately at home. Scattered across the desk were his personal effects – handkerchiefs hand-stitched with a monogram that made me wonder about his mother, a small chessboard that he had set up with the pieces arranged as though he were in the middle of a game against himself, and a stack of new notebooks. His shirts were draped over the chest of drawers and the chair in the corner, rather than being neatly put away. It was as if Austin had exploded himself across the room, instead of neatly inhabiting it. I got the sense he was someone who was used to other people looking after him.

I wanted to search for more pages of the script, a thought born from the same horrid part of me that wished to read Lucille's diary, rifle through Mother's old bureau, or unlock that door in the basement dining room, but I suppressed it. Doing so would be such a dreadful infraction of my responsibilities as his hostess. But such was the extent to which Austin and his playscript had disturbed my mind that the temptation occupied my thoughts.

The day drew on, and as I served the evening meal, I was preoccupied searching for Austin, who did not appear. 'If you're looking for the actor,' Mother said, in a crisp voice, 'he requested directions to the theatre.'

Of course he had. Regardless of what else was twisting

inside Austin's mind, the theatre called to him. Our discussions would have to wait until he returned. I wasn't sure if I was relieved or disappointed.

It didn't dawn on me that I hadn't seen Lucille all day until evening had long drawn in, the windows turned so dark that they functioned as mirrors, reflecting back the light inside.

I was closing the curtains when I suddenly thought of her, and felt a wrench in my stomach. When was the last time that I had seen her? When I had risen that morning, I'd left her asleep in bed, thinking that she needed the rest. But it was strange that she hadn't appeared since then. I went to the front desk first, where Mother sat, repairing one of Lucille's dresses, which had a torn hem.

'Where's Lucille?'

Mother looked up. Her hair was pinned neatly as always, but a loose curl was beginning to unwind above her ear. She glanced at the clock. It was half past nine. 'I'm not sure. I haven't seen her.'

'Since when?'

Mother frowned, not yet alarmed. 'Oh, I don't know, Alice. She'll be around. I didn't want to crowd her given her recent . . . upset.'

I nodded, knowing that Lucille's 'upset' would only ever be alluded to as such and not discussed any further. There was a gaping chasm between Mother and me, formed of all the words we never spoke to one another. Words that might have been. Words buried deep. Words trapped behind teeth.

'Of course,' I said, forcing a smile on to my face. I left Mother at the desk and headed up to the bedroom I shared with Lucille.

I opened our door and froze. The window was wide open, the net curtains fluttering. I shivered and rushed to close it. It was not like Lucille to take an interest in airing our room. On top of which, her bed was made perfectly, all smoothed down, but I knew that my sister usually threw her bed together in a hurry, leaving crinkles in the corner. Everything else was as it always was. Lucille was not there, but all her things were. The blue flowery nightdress on top of her pillow, the ribbons she used to tie back her hair, her little tin of watercolours. I opened our wardrobe, and on Lucille's side were all her clothes. Nothing missing.

I'm not sure exactly at what moment I understood that something was very wrong. It crept in slowly, until it was an icy grip around my heart. I *knew* that she was gone, even though there was no reason I should be so certain. It was just a feeling, but it was deep in my bones.

I performed a full search through the house, checking the basement dining room, the kitchen and the library, winding up back at our bedroom once more. I shook my head. I was getting carried away with myself. There was nothing I could point to that confirmed the suspicions of the awful nagging inside me, nothing immediate to suggest that my fears were based in reality.

And yet. Where *was* she?

Mother had long ago given up trying to control my

sister, but being out at well past nine o'clock at night was beyond even Lucille's flexible sense of propriety for a young woman. If she'd gone into the town, surely she would be back by now. I spun round as though I might find her hiding behind the curtains, ready to jump out and scare me. We used to play those games when we were younger, before I turned too frightened, too sensitive, and Lucille grew too worried about upsetting me to play like that any more.

My mind continued to race. If she had run away, wouldn't she have taken something, anything, with her? And yet, what was the alternative? That she had vanished into thin air?

My fingers tingled. I knew there was one way to uncover my sister's truest thoughts. I hovered by the bedside table and then, in a rush, opened her drawer.

Her diary was gone.

I felt as though I'd been turned to stone. The missing diary was enough for me to know for certain that something was absolutely wrong. Lucille *always* kept that diary safely tucked in that drawer. Its absence was the strongest evidence I had to back up what my gut already knew to be true.

My sister was gone.

I backed out of the room, my vision turning black at the edges as if a creeping darkness was closing in on me from all sides. I reached for the wall to steady myself. How could she be gone? Just ... gone. My thoughts turned to goblins and ice queens and creatures of stories and fairy tales that vanished people away ... and then, inevitably, to the real horrors that I knew lurked among the shadows.

I knew then that I would do whatever it took to find her.

But I could never have imagined what the search would cost me.

5

Lucille once told me that she did not have any memories before me. She was two years old when I was born, and Mother loved to regale us with stories of her with chubby cheeks, golden curls and grabby palms, peering into my basket and gazing at me lovingly, being gentle for the first time in her life as she stroked my hair. The way Mother tells it, she cooed 'My baby' that day and every day after, until I grew large enough to insist I was a big girl.

Every one of my memories is filled with her.

As we grew older, Lucille would say that when we were orphaned (a rather ghoulish and upsetting notion to my mind, but one that she insisted was only a fact that we had to accept, an inevitability), we would need to be determined about ensuring we stayed knitted together. She insisted I promise that we would never be apart, that even when we grew up and married, we would always remain close to each other. It was not a difficult promise to make. I never wanted to lead a life where my sister was not right by my side.

It isn't that we never argued – of course, there were moments where she infuriated me so much I could have screamed, and times where I aggravated her until she did scream – but we always made peace by the time the sun was setting.

What I mean by all of this is that there is a certain weight the word 'sister' has always had for me. It's a simple descriptor on the surface, stating that Lucille and I were born to the same parents. But the word has always meant more to me than that.

Lucille *became* a sister, but I have always been one, from the moment I was born.

And as I grew up, I began to realize that it was also a choice, a deep commitment we had sworn to each other and would keep swearing to each other, every day of our lives.

So I knew Lucille would never have just left on a whim. She would never have abandoned me, not unless there was a truly urgent, desperate reason. And so with her disappearance, it was up to me not to abandon her.

I thought that if I went straight to Mother she would descend into panic, and that would be little help in discovering where Lucille had gone and why. Instead, I wiped the tears that had sprung to my eyes and blew out my breath in a long, steady stream before visiting each room to ask our guests when they had last seen Lucille. It was a task I was ill-suited for: interrupting and intruding, engaging people in conversation without raising alarm. Lucille would have done it all so much better.

The guests in the first two rooms proved unhelpful. Neither the young couple on their honeymoon nor the dour, unimaginative writer had seen Lucille that day and were mildly bemused by my enquiry. After our tense encounter at breakfast, and uncertain whether he had returned from the theatre, I decided to leave Austin Parker until last, climbing the stairs to the apartment in the attic next.

Dr Binding, a widower, was occupying the attic apartment. He was a medical practitioner with a round, firm belly and white hair trimmed so short it looked like the fluffy wool of a lamb. I had known him all my life; he had been a friend of my grandparents long before Aunt Sybil and Mother had even been born. Dr Binding and his wife were almost like extended family, and they used to visit us several times a year with their sweet little dapple dachshund, Silver, whose coat matched his name. Each September, as far back as I could remember, they would celebrate Mrs Binding's birthday at the guest house, and when Dr Binding wrote to request their September week, he would always ask us to provide a bouquet of flowers, to be waiting in the apartment upon their arrival.

And then we did not see them for a year. We presumed, correctly, that something terrible had happened. Eventually, a letter arrived. Dr Binding requested the same apartment, in the usual week in September, as always, but meals for one instead of two. There was no request for flowers.

When he arrived, even Silver seemed different somehow, moving more slowly. We let Dr Binding know that he would receive a cheaper rate if he wanted to take a smaller room, but he was resolute. His visit was to be the same as always, although, of course, it would never be the same again. Every year since then, he had decided to increase the length of his autumnal visit so that it began to encapsulate the whole of the season.

I climbed the steps and knocked on the door, rehearsing in my head what I needed to say. Dr Binding opened the door and the creases in his face deepened with concern as he looked at me.

'Good evening, Dr Binding. I'm sorry to bother you, but ... my sister, Lucille,' I began, just about managing to contain the panic in my voice, or so I hoped. 'I wondered ... have you seen her today?'

He looked hesitant to respond, his mouth quirking. He knew something.

'Yes,' he replied, drawing out the word slowly. He had kindly eyes and a softly spoken manner. I imagined many an anxious patient responded well to his approachable demeanour. 'I did see her earlier, on the landing at the bottom of this flight of stairs, when I was on my way to take my morning walk.'

It sounded rehearsed. As if he had expected somebody might question him about her.

'What time was that, if you don't mind me asking?' I knew I had the air of a detective in my questioning, but it felt crucial that I gather the specifics. Dr Binding might have been the last person to see Lucille before she left.

'Let me see. I would hazard a guess at it being around ten?'

'Ten,' I echoed. When Mother and I were clearing up the breakfast things, and I was quietly fretting about my interaction with Austin, Lucille was on the landing with Dr

Binding. It was a thread to begin to pull on. 'Did you speak to her? What did she say?'

'Oh, just some morning greetings. She's always so polite.'

I gave a tight smile. To guests, she was. She saved her explosions for me and Mother.

'And did you notice anything . . . unusual about her?'

He cleared his throat. 'I wouldn't say so, no. I did hear about the business with her young man, of course. That must have been a dreadful upset for her. I suppose she seemed a little distracted, but no more than one might expect given the circumstances.'

I did not believe him. There was something about the way his eyes flickered up as he spoke, as though he was searching his mind for the lines he'd prepared. I had no doubt that Dr Binding knew something more about Lucille than he was telling me. I stared at him, as though I might be able to see right through his skin, his skull, and get to the thoughts inside.

'Tell me,' I said, my voice breaking despite my attempts to sound measured and strong. It was not the proper way to speak to a gentleman, never mind one who was a guest under our roof, and yet I could not help myself. My fear for my sister had shoved my usual reservation to one side and snatched up the reins. 'Please. Tell me what you know about Lucille.' I choked on her name.

Dr Binding looked anguished. 'I'm afraid I have nothing that I *can* tell you.' He lifted his hands up, their emptiness demonstrating his lack of information. 'Miss Everglass, my dear, whatever has brought on this interrogation? Has something happened?'

'She . . . she's gone.' It was starting to sink in. 'It's so late now and I've looked everywhere. Lucille's not here.'

'I see.' His features sagged with an expression filled with unease, or perhaps resignation. *You knew*, I thought. *You knew I was going to say that.*

And that was the moment I realized there would be nobody I could trust in the search for my sister. Only myself, and even that was something I was going to have to learn.

6

My mind raced away from me. I was caught between realities, tangled in the possibilities of what might have happened. A young woman goes missing and you are left with stark, frightening options: either she had left of her own volition, without taking a bag, without a word to me, her sister and closest confidant, or something terrible had happened. My throat suddenly felt as though it were closing up.

'Do you have any idea where she might be?' I asked, feeling the sting of tears in my eyes.

He did not respond, merely pressing his lips into a thin line.

'Please.' I grabbed his arm, my fingers turned into desperate claws. I couldn't believe Dr Binding would have done anything to harm Lucille, but he knew more than he was telling me. I had no way to prove it, nothing but an unsettled twisting in my stomach. Confusion simmered through me. In all the years Dr Binding had visited the Honest Opal, he had never given me reason to mistrust him. A memory surfaced of him taking care of another guest who fell suddenly sick during their stay with us, paying for medicine from the apothecary out of his own pocket and never asking for it back. He had an upstanding reputation and, the way I understood it, was loyal to our guest house not only due to his wife's love of our seaside town of Whitby, but also because of the friendship he'd once held with my grandparents. I did not believe that he could have caused any harm to anyone, let alone my sister.

And yet I could not shake the sense that he was the last person in the guest house that had seen Lucille, that surely it had to mean something, that he must have a clue that would lead me to her.

'Did she say anything to you? Did you know that she was going to leave? Or ... do you think someone ...' I couldn't finish the sentence.

'I don't know. I'm terribly sorry, but I do not know where your sister is.' He patted my hand, and closed his fingers around mine, gently prising them free from his jacket. 'Might we continue this conversation downstairs? I'm sure that you are terribly concerned for your sister, but I am becoming deeply concerned about you. It will do her no good if you become hysterical.'

Hysterical? A harsh laugh that was more like the yowl of a cat escaped my throat. Of course I was becoming hysterical! How could I be sensible when my sister was missing? I spun on my heel and turned away from him, embarrassed now on top of everything else. I began to rush down the stairs as he called after me.

'Miss Everglass, do take care on the stairs!'

My cheeks flushed hot, my body filled with the urge to flee, as if I might be able to simply run away from this nightmare I had discovered myself in. I went down the stairs at a pace so fierce that on the second flight my foot slipped from beneath me and I landed on my backside, biting my tongue as I hit the steps, bashing my elbow, the pain reverberating up my spine, blood filling my mouth. Thud, thud, thud I went, crashing down the stairs. The tears were unstoppable now as I landed in a pitiful heap on the landing, the back of my head whipping back with a crack.

To add to my misery, a confused-looking Austin, clearly arrived back from the theatre, flung himself out of his bedroom. My face was hot with humiliation, and every part of me ached. Upon seeing me sprawled upon the ground, he rushed to my side. He offered me his hand, his eyes a question – *May I help you?* – and I nodded. Then his hand was in mine, the other on my waist, helping me to my feet as my heart leaped into my throat, beating so fast it felt out of control. I'd never been held that way before, not by anyone.

I heard Mother hurrying up from reception, and Dr Binding following me down from the attic apartment.

'Oh, Alice!' Mother exclaimed as she came round the corner of the stairs. 'However did you manage that?'

I winced, running my fingertips over my arm, feeling the tenderness where the bruises would be later on, the dark blooms forming beneath my skin like storm clouds. I flinched away from Austin's support as the embarrassment crawled all over me.

'I . . . I . . .' My tongue felt heavy and thick, the taste of iron filling my mouth. 'I tripped.'

'Fetch the girl a chair, won't you, Emily?' Dr Binding said authoritatively to Mother. 'Let me take a look at her.'

Dr Binding took the rest of the stairs carefully, his hand tight on the bannister. Mother did as she was told and returned with a chair for me to sink into while Dr Binding bent down to inspect me, placing his hands on my cheeks as he checked my eyes, asking me to look up and down and to each side. My gaze landed on Lucille's painting of the one-hundred and ninety-nine steps at nightfall, all dreamy purples and cosmic blues, and my chest felt as if it were being constricted. The old doctor was brisk and efficient. He was as careful with me as if I were a porcelain figure, and sympathetic, too, asking where it was that I felt the pain. My arm, my ankle, my head and, although I did not say it, my pride. He checked for a break or a sprain and then gently examined the sore lump that was rising on the back of my head.

Mother's face had turned a very pale grey colour. This happened to her sometimes, usually if Lucille or I were unwell. It was as though, at the slightest sniffle, her mind took her to our gravesides. Austin was hovering near his door, a concerned expression across his face. I got the sense he didn't want to leave until he was certain that I had not come to harm. Was that because we had unfinished business, our earlier conversation unresolved? Or was he simply being polite?

At last Dr Binding gave me a reassuring smile. 'Likely to be a bit tender for a few days, but I don't think there's anything to be concerned about,' he said, turning to Mother and placing a hand on her shoulder, which forced her to finally quit her pacing of the landing. 'Do you hear me, Emily? Nothing to be concerned about. Nothing broken.'

'Oh, thank goodness,' Mother said, coming to hover by my side. Her hands were trembling. It struck me again how she looked so much older than the years she had lived.

'Get this girl a cup of tea. That's my prescription.' When Mother had gone, he turned back to me and lowered his voice. 'That was a nasty fall. Watch out for any sickness, or dizziness, and don't hesitate to knock for me if you're worried.'

'Thank you,' I murmured. Austin looked visibly relieved, and, with a tentative wave goodnight, disappeared back inside his bedroom, closing the door with a soft click.

'You must be careful, Alice!' Mother chided, returning with a cup of tea. Even though she was now beginning to calm, I knew that I had to tell her. The dread swelled in my stomach until it felt as though it would block up my throat. Her panic over my fall was ebbing in the face of Dr Binding's reassurances, but I had something much worse for her to worry about.

'Mother,' I said, and then pressed my lips together, apprehensive. She fixed me with her eyes, green as a glass bottle thrown out to sea. It seemed as if she knew that what I was about to say would throw everything into chaos, that it was, finally, something worthy of her panic, after living with her constant anticipation of the worst. She'd been nervy, irritable and intense like that as long as I could remember – and if she had been different before Father died, it was while she was pregnant with me, so I could never know. But I was convinced that the two things were irrevocably linked. Life had served my mother with tragedy, and since then she'd simply been in waiting, an actress in the wings anticipating the moment where the lights would come up on a new scene and she would step on to the stage and play the part she'd rehearsed. As if all the years with Lucille and I were just the interval between dramatic scenes of grief.

I cleared my throat. 'The reason I was rushing ... It's Lucille. She's gone.'

Mother's nostrils flared as she breathed in sharply. 'Gone? What do you mean?'

'I can't find her.' My voice wavered, the magnitude of it settling in. My sister – my funny, brave, passionate, bold, determined sister – was gone. 'She's gone. Missing.'

'That can't be right. She must be out in the town,' Mother said, her voice firm, but somehow also wavering. 'You're mistaken.'

I shook my head. 'It's night-time, Mother. Why on earth would she be out so late? Her diary is gone, too.'

Mother flinched as if I'd slapped her across the face. She looked to Dr Binding, as though he could reassure her the way he had about my fall.

'Now then,' he said in that soothing voice, the one that could have tamed a lion. 'I'm sure there's a reasonable explanation and Lucille is safe and well.'

Mother shot him a glare, and with definitive action made a beeline to the bedroom Lucille and I shared. She tore the door open as if she were ripping into a long-awaited letter. Dr Binding and I watched her absorb the neatness of the bed, the empty drawer I'd left open. I thought she might scream, or cry, but instead she was eerily stoic. I sank on to the edge of my bed, the soreness in my head throbbing as I tried, desperately, not to imagine all of the worst-case scenarios that might have befallen my sister. The answers, I was sure of it, had been recorded in that little jewel-green book of hers, which meant if somebody was responsible for her disappearance they'd known her well enough to remove the evidence; or if she'd gone of her own accord, she'd taken it with her, leaving me no clues and no way to track her down, because that was what she wanted.

Whichever scenario was the truth, I felt utterly upended, tipped into a maze with no route out. I was lost. And the one person who would give me a sense of direction was the one I couldn't find.

After settling Mother and I in the library, Dr Binding arranged a search party out of the male guests. Austin gave me a concerned look as he pulled on his coat.

'I'll see if I can rouse Detective Sunday,' Dr Binding said, and he gave each man an area to search.

'I ought to come too,' Mother said.

'I'm not sure that's wise,' the writer said, but Mother cut in before anyone could try to persuade her to stay in the house.

'If she still had a father, you wouldn't be preventing him from joining the search.' Mother simultaneously raised a fierce eyebrow and a hand. 'I can assure you, I'm more than capable.'

'Are you sure you're well enough?' I asked her, unable to keep the concern out of my voice. Her illness was a strange, capricious thing. Some days she would appear perfectly well and then it would grip her so tightly that she was breathless and sickened and weak.

'I am fine,' she said through gritted teeth, shooting me a glare that told me not to interfere.

'A search like this is no place for a lady, madam, certainly not at this hour, and particularly if you have been unwell recently,' the newlywed added. 'And you may need to consider what we might find . . .'

I winced. He was suggesting they might find a body. My sister's body. This man and his wife were visiting from London, where there had been a spate of awful murders in recent history. They were no doubt on his mind, but surely there was no need to suggest anything so grisly had befallen Lucille.

Not yet.

It was a scenario I hadn't even visited in my worst nightmares.

'You underestimate me,' Mother said, her own jaw tensing.

The writer cleared his throat. 'Mrs Everglass, if I may. You may not be aware of this, as I believe the police have been trying to keep it hushed up to avoid inducing panic.

But on the train on the way here, a fellow passenger let slip to me that there has been an unfortunate episode in the town of late. A body found, looking as though it had had its throat ripped out. The victim was a young visiting sailor. The whole thing seems to have got the authorities rather concerned.' He looked sheepish. 'I was writing about it.'

I frowned. How ghoulish of him, to take such worrying events and try to whip a story out of them. But surely this couldn't be connected in any way to Lucille?

Dr Binding caught Mother's eye, and when he spoke it was with a warm depth of sincerity and respect that made me feel guilty for my doubts about his honesty. 'Emily, dear, in the years we have known each other, which is rather a long time now I might remind you, you have never left me in doubt of your strength and ability,' he said. 'Not once. And only a fool would ever question your dedication to your children. If you want to join us on this search, then you must, otherwise I fear you would never forgive me from preventing you from trying to find your daughter. But I agree with the gentleman's sentiments. There is nothing to suggest anything untoward has befallen Lucille yet. But that does not mean that we will like what we discover.'

Mother's eyes glistened with emotion, but instead of allowing her tears to fall, she hardened her features and nodded sharply. It seemed there was a deep well of strength in her that I had not been aware of, given how prone to panic I had always noted her to be. But on those occasions, nothing was truly at stake. Now, when it mattered, it was as if an unearthly calm had settled over her.

The search party busied themselves in preparation to leave, Dr Binding buttoning himself into his heavy woollen coat and Mother digging in the cupboard under the stairs, emerging with lamps they could carry to carve out pathways of light to aid their search for my sister.

I stood by the fireplace for a moment, its heat not reaching the chill inside me. Then I got to work, banking the coals to protect their smoulder for the morning.

Lucille wouldn't think twice about marching out of that door into the night if it were me who had disappeared. And yet every time I envisioned trying to do it, every part of me tensed up with fear.

I listened to the bustling of the search party getting ready to leave, and tried to summon the nerve to step outside the door with them.

But the memories of the horrors intruded into my mind as I stood by the dead ashes of the fire. For my sister, could I bring myself to be courageous enough to venture out of the guest house? I heard the opening of the door, Mother and Dr Binding and Austin and the other guests ready to begin their search.

I sprinted out into the hallway.

'Wait,' I said, a wobble of indecision in my voice, even as I tried to be brave. 'I'm coming too.'

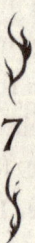

7

The first time I saw one, I was thirteen years old. That year had begun to slide towards its conclusion, and it was the sort of afternoon where, by the time the hour strikes four, the evening is encroaching early, barging its elbows in, shoving out daytime.

That morning we'd left the Honest Opal, heading away from the row of terraced houses on top of the West Cliff, which gazed over at the spectacular abbey ruins and the church on the East Cliff. We'd taken the steep winding pathway down into the town and crossed the drawbridge over the river to the shops on the other side. But we'd been out much longer than we'd intended. Hurrying back across the drawbridge in the direction of home, Mother muttered under her breath at how we had taken too long, and how had it got so late, and how the guests were going to be waiting for their dinner. We passed a public house, a broken glass shattered on the ground. I took care to avoid it as Mother and Lucille carried on.

Then my eye caught something shifting in the shadows

of an alleyway. And once I had looked, I couldn't tear my gaze away, my mouth hollowed out in shock.

'Alice, what on earth are you doing?' Mother snapped. 'We're already late. Stop gawping and get a move on.'

Lucille let out a great sigh of annoyance. They were both too far ahead to see what I saw.

Looking at it gave me a twisting sensation in my stomach, as though my body were contorting to accept the unfathomable sight, a terrifying unreality.

Teeth where teeth shouldn't be, teeth that erupted, teeth that looked painful. Long and sharp and far too many of them.

There was a place where the wall itself seemed ripped, seemed to lead somewhere ... This monstrous thing was tearing its way into our world, a horror that shouldn't have been there.

I didn't want to find out its intentions.

'Come on,' Mother urged, still not stopping, and I dragged my eyes from the horror and followed her home, shivering all the way.

What I had seen was strange and impossible, but I knew that it was not a figment of my imagination. And so that made *me* strange and impossible. Instinctively, I knew that it was not something to talk about.

That was the first night I woke screaming. Lucille was there, stroking my face and comforting me.

'You had a nightmare,' she said. 'What was it about?'

'Nothing,' I said. I couldn't bring myself to speak any of it out loud.

She climbed into my bed and held me as I fell back to sleep. In the morning, she gasped at the sight of me, and screamed for our mother.

My hair had transformed from the rich, golden-red locks I'd had since birth to a shock of pure white.

I stared at the reflection in the looking glass, finding myself different and unfamiliar. The change in me was almost as frightening as the monstrous creature I'd seen.

When Mother saw me, she looked faintly horrified. 'Oh, Alice,' she murmured, touching my hair.

'It must have been the nightmare,' I said, but I knew it was because of what I had seen tearing out of the shadows. I knew it was the terror that had done it to me.

Mother nodded. 'The nightmare,' she said, but she didn't look wholly convinced.

Night after night I woke up shrieking. Mother was sympathetic and worried, but also conscious that my screams would distress the guests, and so she arranged with a new apothecary on the east side for a sleeping remedy, which she carefully prepared for me before bed. I kept my mouth tightly shut about what inspired the screaming fits in the night, saying that I couldn't remember. I would take the botanical-tasting drink before bed, Mother would press her hand against my forehead, and I would feel soothed. After a while, the nightmares became less frequent: once a week, once a month. I was still on edge whenever I left home, jittery and flinching, but I pushed through my discomfort, pulling a mask of normality over my expressions, trying desperately to seem as though nothing had changed.

But I had changed; I knew it. Inside, I felt irrevocably altered.

The next time we passed the alleyway where I had seen the horror, I couldn't help but look again. At first I was relieved. It was empty; no terrifying ghoul to be seen. But then I saw there was a new seam where the rip had been, a lumpy scar in the flesh of the world. It looked like it had been mended, but all I could wonder was on which side of that seam the monster now resided.

For years, I didn't tell a soul.

I had other strange encounters, too. Something moving in the shadows beneath the boards of the pier, a dark shifting silhouette against the underside of the wall where people were crabbing, a scratching noise at the window of the tailor shop run by Theodore Truman's father. But it was that first monstrous creature that was seared into my mind most vividly. It was the teeth. The way it had too many teeth.

The walls of the Honest Opal gave me a feeling of safety I couldn't find anywhere else. And so I left our guest house less and less, as little as I could get away with. Lucille couldn't understand why I would choose to cut myself off from life, but I was just surviving the only way I knew how.

As Mother had begun to grow sick, Lucille had started insisting on me joining her to run errands in the town. It wasn't fair the burden fell all to her, she said, and I could admit she wasn't wrong. And so, once a week, I left the guest house with her. I dreaded it each time.

Then, one day, about six months before Austin arrived, Lucille and I were paying a visit to the apothecary to collect my sleeping tincture. Arms linked, we crossed the drawbridge while gulls called out to each other above our heads, their large, white bodies circling the air like predators. On the other side we headed up and then left down the cobbled street that took us past the Old Town Hall, where a bustling trade took place between the columns of the undercroft, the patrons squawking like the gulls overhead.

The shops on either side nestled together, growing closer as the road narrowed. I kept my eyes diverted as we passed the ginnel leading to Arguments Yard, newly wary of shadows and narrow passageways. It had once been a spot where Lucille and I would joke, finding the most ridiculous thing to begin a quarrel over, just for fun. But I didn't feel like laughing at it any more and kept walking, head down.

The apothecary was near the bottom of the one-hundred and ninety-nine steps, part of a cluster of shops, their doorways open like hungry mouths. The apothecary himself was charming and his wife was exceedingly kind, and they had ingratiated themselves expertly in the town when they'd arrived a few years earlier, as though they'd practised somewhere else before; they had proven themselves to be excellent neighbours and swiftly became respected members of the community.

Inside, the apothecary was a small room with a stone floor so worn it was almost slippery, and a wide counter lining two sides; behind that, one wall was made up of wooden cupboard fronts and another was covered in tiny drawers with glass knobs, topped with shelves lined with bottles of potions that required the apothecary to use a little stepladder to reach them. I knew the drawers that the apothecary would open for my remedy, using little metal scoops to collect the dried herbs and flowers and powder in a glass bottle we brought with us. He stood behind the counter, his blonde hair and moustache elegantly groomed, which was usual, and a piece of silk wrapped around his head covering his left eye, which was not. I wondered what he had done to it. He welcomed us in with a smile, and I placed the bottle on the counter.

'Just the sleeping remedy today?' he asked.

'Yes, thank you,' Lucille said.

Then I saw it. A looming spectre, leaking out of one of the cupboards, the door hanging off its hinges. A horror, though a new kind. It was shapeless, a horrid oozing, like a slick shadow, but even so, I could see that it had some kind of an eye that was slipping down what I supposed was meant to resemble a face. It fixed on me with a hungry curiosity, as though it knew I could see it.

I turned to Lucille and gripped her hard by the wrist. She looked at me, puzzled, and then followed my gaze to the broken cupboard front. Clearly she could see nothing, but her concern for me still showed. Frowning, her demeanour stiffened, and she gave me a tight smile. Her free hand came to rest on top of mine, which was white-knuckled and still clutched at her wrist, leaving little marks from my nails. She prised my hand off her so she could bring out the little coin purse we took on errands with us. As she placed the coins on the counter with a clatter, I couldn't look away from the horror seeping from the cupboard.

I sensed that it only meant harm, that it was not supposed to be in our world, that it had found a pathway through, that it was waiting greedily to consume. It had a need to devour.

We were in danger.

My blood suddenly felt hot, pounding through my veins. A fiery strength roared through me, taking over. I was struck by an impulse so unlike me that I hardly knew what I did next. I snatched the remedy bottle from the counter and I threw it as hard as I could at the creature in the cupboard. As the bottle smashed into glass splinters, and Lucille shrieked, I flinched, my hands shaking and hot, burning with a building intensity I had never felt before.

The apothecary leaped back, his uncovered eye darting from the cupboard to the shards on the ground and then back to me, fear and confusion clouding his face. Lucille's mouth gaped. I must have looked as though I had lost my mind, but I hardly cared. The horror, the oozing, frightening horror, just seemed to expand at my efforts to harm it, seemed to breathe and seethe. My mind was swimming as Lucille made apologies to the shocked apothecary, her voice high and tight as she firmly wrapped her arm around my waist, pulling me back towards the door.

Emerging from the shadows of the shop into the bright sunlight outside, my breath changed almost immediately to deep rasps, and I fled. I ran and ran until I got back to the Honest Opal, flinging myself up the stairs past our stunned mother and slamming the bedroom door shut behind me.

The entire encounter seemed impossible once I'd returned to the safety of the guest house, like a dream concocted by a feverish brain. How could what I had seen be real? Perhaps I truly was losing my mind; perhaps it was a sickness that moved through me.

When Lucille finally returned, the rest of the errands complete and a new bottle of my remedy tucked under her arm, she entered our bedroom and spoke to me with the directness of a judge passing sentence. 'Something has happened to you.'

I shook my head. 'It's nothing. I think I'm just tired.'

She snorted in response. 'Nonsense. You've been tired before and never behaved in that way. What on earth came over you in there?'

'I told you, nothing. Maybe some kind of fever starting.'

She sat down next to me on the bed and pressed her hand to my forehead, frowning. 'You don't feel hot.'

'Really? It felt as though a fire was ripping through me.' This was true. It had felt as though my blood was boiling, my insides melting.

Lucille bit her lip with concern. 'I'd better talk to Mother. She knows something's wrong. Maybe she'll write to Dr Binding and ask if he'll travel to see you?' The physician in town was expensive, which was why she'd sought help from the apothecary first, it being a more affordable alternative. But if it were urgent, serious, then we knew Dr Binding would come to our aid.

'No,' I choked out. 'It will pass.' I did not want to be investigated. I did not truly want to know if the things I had seen were a product of an illness ravaging my body and eating my sanity, or whether they were real, horrifying entities. I was not sure which of the two options were worse. I just wanted to hide.

After, I had this strange feeling whenever I thought about what had happened – a weirdly heavy responsibility, as if I should return to the shop, as if I had unfinished business there.

But there was no chance of me returning. The fear was too great.

And then, a few weeks later, there was a fire and the wife of the apothecary was arrested for murder. She'd started the blaze in their shop, locked all the doors and windows and tried to fight off anyone who made efforts to extinguish it. She swore that the burned body of her husband that they eventually recovered was already dead before she set the fire, that she wasn't responsible. He'd been decimated by some supernatural being, and the fire was to purge the monster.

They said that she was insane, of course.

But I knew. Knew what I had seen, knew that what she said was true. And couldn't help but wonder if I could have somehow stopped what happened to them.

It was after the apothecary's wife was taken away that I decided to tell Lucille. I couldn't bear the burden of it by myself any longer. When I did, she believed me instantly. We both understood that telling anyone else would only lead to trouble. It was better for me to be believed difficult than to be thought mad or dangerous. After all, it wasn't just a good ghost story that I had to tell. It was more visceral, more terrifying... something altogether more sinister. And from then on, Lucille stopped insisting on me joining her to run errands in the town, understanding my fear and tolerating it. So months passed, and I became a recluse.

All this is to say that it took a lot for me to ask to go on the search party for Lucille.

The group now turned to look at me, all shaking their heads as they spoke at once, all except Austin, whose eyes still managed to convey the same message. All concerned variations on the theme of *No*.

'Absolutely not,' Mother asserted, blocking the doorway.
'I don't think that's a good idea,' said the newlywed.
'You hit your head on the stairs,' Dr Binding reminded me.
And I didn't fight them.

Maybe if I had, if I had been strong and insisted that I go, like Mother, they would have let me. But I didn't. I wasn't strong. The truth was that even though I wanted to be brave enough to search for my sister, in the end my fear prevailed.

So Mother pulled the door shut behind her, leaving me alone in the hallway. I paced up and down, trying to ignore the shame that prickled inside me. Because the first thing I'd felt, when they refused me, was relief. Relief that I didn't have to venture into the dark.

I headed up the stairs to my bedroom, exhausted and drained. My head throbbed, and when I rubbed my hand over the place I'd hit it, I could feel a sensitive lump protruding. I knew I couldn't sleep, wouldn't be able to rest until we had some clue of what had happened to Lucille. And so it was almost a relief when, pushing the bedroom door open, I was confronted by more pages of Austin's script, the corners creased where they had been shoved beneath my door, a distraction demanding my attention.

Act One, Scene Two

The morning room in Oliver's apartment. There is a pile of books on every surface and next to the sofa. OLIVER is pacing back and forth behind the sofa when BENNETT enters, accompanied by MRS DARKWING and her daughter, ABIGAIL.

BENNETT:
Mrs Darkwing and Miss Abigail Darkwing, sir.

OLIVER:
Welcome, welcome. Thank you both for coming.

MRS DARKWING:
Of course. Your letter was ... insistent. How could we have refused such an invitation?

OLIVER:
Ah, I apologize. You must forgive my enthusiasm.

MRS DARKWING:
Yes, well ... For all that enthusiasm, I'm afraid I'm not sure that we will be of much use for your research, but we can certainly tell you our story.

ABIGAIL:
Mother is an excellent storyteller. But you ought to have waited until the winter solstice to invite us, and light the candles for the proper tradition of it.

OLIVER:
Ah, indeed! Though perhaps it is better to have the summer sun to illuminate the details of the tale?

ABIGAIL:
There was not much illumination for us at the time. Just fear, all the time.

MRS DARKWING:
Abigail is right.

[Sighs] It began after my husband broke his ankle, and was forced to spend a month at home on leave from his job at the bank. He became insatiably curious about the boarded-up basement below the servants' quarters, and made the foolish decision to hire a labourer to break into it. There was nothing much down there to be seen, just a staircase into darkness and dirt. My husband was disappointed. I think he had notions of discovering treasure or some historic find. *[Pause]* But I'm certain that's what started it all. The meddling awoke ... something.

The very morning after we first opened up the basement, we woke to find all the knives from the kitchen had been taken out and arranged, pointing to the entrance that had been boarded up. We put them all back, but it happened again a few nights later. On another morning, the bathtub had been filled with raw meat from the kitchen.

ABIGAIL:
The mirror was the worst one. Our beautiful hallway mirror was shattered and the pieces left outside the bedroom doors. I sliced my feet to ribbons.

OLIVER:
Good heavens!

MRS DARKWING:
You would think there would be noise, with a mirror being smashed to bits like that, but nobody heard a thing.

It went on like this for some time, with the staff gossiping, of course, and pointing fingers at each other – although each one of them denied it, and I had always run a household where the staff had been treated well, so it never rang true to me that it might have been one of them. But I went so far as to start leaving little traps. You know, folding a small piece of paper and wedging it at the top of the doors so I could see if they had been opened. And would you know, the doors were always just the way I had left them. Impossible. And yet . . .

OLIVER:
You didn't consider a trickster in your household might have noticed you doing it and just reset the trap?

MRS DARKWING:
Of course I considered it! I am not a fool, nor prone to hysterics.

ABIGAIL:
She isn't, for all she loves a good story.

MRS DARKWING:
[Sarcastically] Thank you, Abigail.

Well, we all became quite beside ourselves, as I'm sure you can imagine. Fearful. On edge. Trouble sleeping. And after a while, sleep deprivation starts to make you feel quite strange, quite unwell.

OLIVER:
I understand. And so that's when you began your search for someone who could help?

MRS DARKWING:
Exactly so. There are many charlatans in this field, as I'm sure you are aware. No doubt your research has exposed many ... illusionists ... who claim to be able to communicate with the other side, while simply relying on tricks and nonsense.

OLIVER:
I have indeed. Though some of them can be incredibly convincing.

MRS DARKWING:
At any rate, most of these supposed mediums were rather too preoccupied with the notion of loved ones that might be lingering. I did not need to engage their services. I knew that what we were experiencing was the result of something altogether more ... sinister.

OLIVER:
And so how did you find him?

MRS DARKWING:
[Far-away tone] The man with the gem at his throat.

OLIVER:
[Eager] Yes, that's him. Though he goes by different names, I believe.

MRS DARKWING:
Yes. He's the one who found us in the end.

OLIVER:
[Muttering] That's always the way.

MRS DARKWING:
He was certain he could help us. And he was beyond reproach in his conduct. And he did help us. Although, I . . . I'm not sure entirely how he did it.

OLIVER:
And the . . . presence. The haunting? What happened to it?

MRS DARKWING:
Afterwards, I felt instantly that the darkness had been vanquished. But I . . . I'm sorry. Talking about this all again makes me feel a little strange. I think I need to take some air.
[She stands, leaves the room]

ABIGAIL:
I apologize. It seems the circumstances of the event still have some kind of hold over my mother. Have any other interviewees had the same issue when they talk about their encounter?

OLIVER:
Yes.

ABIGAIL:
I see. And has anybody mentioned the women to you?

OLIVER: *[Leans forward, interested. This is different after many interviews]*
The women? No, they haven't. Who are they?

ABIGAIL:
Two women – sisters, I believe – were in attendance with the man. I feel certain I am not supposed to know about them. In fact, I believe that Mother did not even see them. The man asked us all to vacate to another area of the house while he worked. But I was hiding. I saw them. It wasn't the man with the gem at his throat who banished the presence in our house. It was the women.

8

The pages of the playscript were a welcome diversion as I tried not to think about my sister, about where she might be, cold and alone, if she were still alive. And I found that the pages absorbed me into the story, consuming my own. When Abigail revealed that it was the women at the centre of ending the haunting, a shiver trickled down my spine. This story was already taking twists and turns that unsettled me as much as they intrigued me.

But then I heard the searchers return, and raced downstairs ... only to see that Lucille was not among them. They had not found her.

I'm sorry. I put the pages beneath your door before I knew that your sister was missing. I would never be so insensitive intentionally. You will of course have other things on your mind, and I am sorry to have troubled you with further dark matters. Should you need anything, you must only ask. A.

The note was waiting for me when I awoke the next morning. He must have slipped it beneath my door in the night. My heart beat slightly faster at the thought of him seeking me out in the dark. But his kind words didn't alleviate my distress at waking up to Lucille still gone. I crumpled up the short missive and threw it across the room, where the soft drop of its landing did not satisfy the part of me that wanted to rage, wanted to scream, wanted to throw something much heavier, much louder. Lucille would have done, if it were the other way around. She would have raged until I was brought home safely.

It had been a restless night for me. My head was tender where I had fallen, and I couldn't lie comfortably on my bruised back. I began to drag my clothes on, trying not to look at the empty bed across from me.

The police constable who arrived that morning before breakfast was a young man by the name of Hodge, and it quickly became apparent he was utterly out of his depth. Clearly, we had been sent someone of low seniority, which boded ill for how seriously the police were taking the search for Lucille. Mother led him into the library, the owl looming over proceedings as usual. Incredibly tall, Constable Hodge walked in with his shoulders stooped, ducking to avoid the light fitting, cheeks flushing red. He wore a pained expression and I couldn't tell if that was because he had to drop into the seat of the armchair, too low for him by far, or because he was simply so uncomfortable at having to deal with our miserable situation.

Hodge cleared his throat. 'I've been sent to talk to you about your daughter. You suspect she is missing. Is that right?' At least *he* seemed to be taking Lucille's disappearance seriously, producing a notebook to jot everything down.

'That's right,' Mother said. Her face had a sheen of exertion to it – the stress was taking its toll on her already. 'She hasn't been seen since yesterday morning.'

'And that's out of character?' Hodge asked.

Mother spluttered with indignation. 'Of course it's out of character! You think I let my daughters go out gallivanting of a night-time?'

Hodge flushed bright red so intensely that it flooded his entire face and neck, even to the tops of his ears. 'No, no, I apologize. I'm simply trying to understand what might have happened, the series of events. Is there anywhere she might go unaccompanied?'

'She sometimes runs errands for me during the day. We are a small household, you see. We don't have staff. But she didn't have any errands yesterday.'

'None of us saw her leave,' I added. It felt urgent I make him understand that something was very, very wrong. 'And when I went to look for her, I found our bedroom window was open and her diary was gone.'

In the silence, the gas lamp spluttered and hissed. Hodge bit his lip and his forehead creased with the effort of writing and thinking. 'I see. And what do you think has happened?'

'Isn't the answer to that question why *you're* here?' I asked, desperation making me forget myself. Mother shot me a glare of reproach, but Hodge didn't seem to notice, merely nodding in acknowledgement.

'Indeed, it is. But I would like to know if you have any theories. You're her family. You're the ones who know her best, and what her movements might be. And I have been ... encouraged not to get too excited with my own theories.' He looked downcast, and I wondered quite what exciting theories of his had been dismissed.

'That makes sense, thank you,' Mother said, forcing a smile at Hodge while her eyes simultaneously flashed me another warning.

But Lucille wouldn't hold her tongue if it were me who had disappeared into thin air.

'You ask me what I think happened, but if I knew, I would be doing something about it,' I said, my voice biting, sounding so much more like my sister. 'Here's what I do know: my sister would never simply leave without telling me where she was going and why. And her missing diary is a clue. Lucille is so protective of that little book. That she, or someone else, has taken it is a sign that something is terribly wrong here, but getting to the bottom of what's happened to her is *your* job.'

Mother gripped my shoulder. 'Alice, stop. Constable Hodge is doing his very best to help.' She gave a pointed glance at him, a challenge. 'Aren't you?'

'Of course,' Hodge said soothingly, though his Adam's apple leaped nervously about in his throat. 'I wonder, though, if there isn't a simple explanation that we might have missed. Is there a friend she might have gone to visit? Could she have taken ill, and word simply hasn't reached you yet?'

Frustration flooded Mother's face. In theory it was a perfectly reasonable suggestion, but I knew that Lucille wouldn't visit friends or family without telling us first. And we would have heard from any friend by now, surely.

Mother dutifully started to list friends of Lucille's while Hodge noted them down. It felt like some kind of action, at least. But I was thinking that the only person Lucille truly cared for in town was Theodore. My chest tightened at the thought of him. Did he even know Lucille was missing yet?

'And finally . . . I am sorry to ask, but . . . can you think of anyone who might have a wish to harm Lucille?' Hodge asked, his face twisting uncomfortably.

'No.' Mother shook her head firmly. 'She is a well-liked girl.' I nodded. This at least was undeniably true. Lucille may not have had a wide circle of friends, but she was known in the town for her charm.

Then, as the clock began to chime the hour, Mother turned to me. 'Breakfast,' she whispered, a worried note in her voice.

I nodded. 'I'll take care of it. Goodbye, Constable Hodge.'

I quickly made my way to the dining room, relieved to escape the conversation, sure that if I had stayed any longer it was only a matter of time until I had another angry outburst.

When I arrived, murmuring apologies, all the guests were already in attendance, except Austin. None of them seemed to mind that I hadn't served breakfast yet. The writer sent me a small, sympathetic smile, but I was wondering if he had plans to wrap this tale up in his writing. The young honeymooners had a shine to their eyes, as though the situation were a wedding gift, no doubt thinking of the way they would tell all this to their acquaintances over steaming tea in fancy cups when they returned to their lives. *The girl just disappeared and they couldn't find her. Isn't it dreadful?*

Regardless of our guests' relaxed attitudes towards the lateness of breakfast, the proper thing to do was to make it, to ensure that they were cared for. But as I set about stoking the fire in the kitchen, awakening the smouldering coals, my thoughts turned to Mrs Darkwing and her daughter Abigail from the playscript. I was not frightened by the account of the haunting told in the pages; how could I be after what I had experienced first hand? And yet I could imagine, in the darkness of a theatre, the way the dialogue might cause a creeping sensation at the back of your neck, an unease that would follow you back home, linger in your mind and stop you from sleeping.

It seemed that in the story, the supernatural entity that tormented the family had been banished. Not by the man that Oliver had been seeking in the first place, the one who the playwright seemed to be hinting was connected to our guest house somehow, but by two women who really held the power. Which made the man ... what, simply someone stealing the acclaim that belonged to them? Or a defender, absorbing the risks associated with building a reputation for such work? Whichever way it turned out, for the Darkwings at least there had been peace afterwards. What I wouldn't give for such peace to settle upon my mind.

I wondered, too, what Austin had meant by thrusting the pages of the script beneath my door. I understood that he believed the story within the pages had some connection to our guest house. And I couldn't deny that I had been intrigued by the way its name appeared to be buried in the text, like a secret code. But what I couldn't figure out was what was motivating Austin. It was clearly occupying his mind alongside his convalescence, but now he was entangling me in it. What did he actually *want*?

I began heating a pan of water, the simple normality of the action incongruent with the way life had shifted. My hands felt as though they were not my own, plopping one, two, three, four smooth eggs into the simmering water. It would be easy to pretend that Lucille was just upstairs, preparing herself for the day, tying her hair with the ribbons she loved so much. I closed my eyes and listened to the water bubble. It was almost soothing, until I suddenly started with the sense of being watched, eyes snapping wide open as I spun.

Austin was standing in the entrance to the kitchen. The smile he gave me was half-hearted, and it didn't reach his eyes.

'Good morning,' I said. 'Although I don't know how it can be called that in the circumstances.' He nodded, and rummaged for his notebook and wrote to me.

Words feel tiny and insignificant in the face of a situation such as this.

'They do,' I murmured in reply.

The struggle to find any at all feels rather insurmountable.

'That's all right,' I said. Perhaps he wanted me to share more about how I felt; in the short time we had known each other, I had got the impression that if his voice were functioning, he would have no qualms about spilling his emotions, every chaotic and messy one. I was not prepared to do that. Not yet, at least. 'Thank you for joining the search for Lucille. Did you meet her before . . .?'

He shook his head and sighed a heavy sigh, as though he were weighed down with the awfulness of the situation. He ran a hand through his tousled hair.

'Well, thank you. I wish I could be useful myself but I . . .' I steeled myself for what I was about to say. He would notice eventually. Better to be upfront about it. Even if this is the moment where he decides I'm too strange and begins to distance himself. 'I don't really ever leave the guest house if I can help it.' My face became hot with embarrassment and so I turned my back on him, busying myself slicing the bread ready for the toasting fork. Austin began to scribble again, furiously. He placed his notebook on the table next to me, where the slices of bread were waiting.

We all have our idiosyncrasies. I, for one, have never done very well in silence.

I gave a small smile. I had guessed correctly, then. 'Oh. That must make your current situation rather unbearable for you.'

He grimaced and raised his eyes to the ceiling as if there were answers written upon it. We were both trapped and lost, just in different ways.

I wanted you to know that I understand what you're

going through. I lost someone, too. My grandfather vanished. About six months ago.

I flinched in surprise as I read. 'Then you know the not knowing is the worst part,' I said, taking an almost involuntary step closer to him. He kept his eyes fixed on mine and something alive flickered between us, an understanding that warmed me. I couldn't hold his gaze for a moment longer. 'I read the pages you left me.' Turning away from him again, I grabbed the toasting fork and sat on the little stool next to the fire, beginning to work my way through the stack of bread, one slice at a time.

What did you think about the tale of the Darkwings?

'I think they told a very chilling little horror story. Obviously I was struck by what Abigail said about the two women.'

Before I could read his reply, Mother appeared in the doorway to the kitchen, one arched eyebrow telling me everything I needed to know about how she disapproved of our covert conversing. Austin backed out of the kitchen immediately. As soon as he had gone, I wished he would come back. There was so much more I wanted to ask him.

'Breakfast is almost ready,' I said. I moved to scoop the eggs out, soft-boiled perfectly. I took them out to serve with the toast, slathered with butter and sliced into soldiers for dipping. Dr Binding was busy assigning areas of the town to the party who had searched last night; I was touched that they had clearly agreed to continue their hunt. I hovered, listening to their plans, avoiding eye contact with Austin, while a horrible feeling of being utterly useless crept over my skin.

After they left, I wanted to scream with the agony of it all.

But I couldn't. I just couldn't bring myself to release how I really felt. It seemed too ... messy. So instead I haunted the basement rooms, cleaning the plates, sweeping up toast crumbs. Without my sister, I felt more invisible than ever.

Her having *vanished*, as though she'd been spirited away by fairies, was an unfamiliar sort of awfulness. If we didn't find her, the question of it all would haunt me for the rest of my days. Like I'd said to Austin, the not knowing.

My head filled with a pulsing pain and a persistent echo:

Where are you?

Where are you?

Where in this haunted world *are* you?

9

They did not find Lucille that day either, despite having had the benefit of the daylight. By the time that evening fell, Hodge looked distressed by the whole performance, as if it were a reflection on him that there had been no quick resolution to the mystery of Lucille's disappearance. I brought him a cup of tea to where he was sitting in the library, a hand running over his temples.

'I really thought we'd find her visiting a friend,' he said, shaking his head. 'I thought she must have gone to see somebody and then been struck down with a fever or something.'

It had been a sensible theory, but I was unsurprised his visits to those people's houses had turned up nothing.

'I wonder ... did you try Theodore Truman's home?' I paused before speaking again. It somehow felt like a betrayal of Lucille's privacy, even though the whole town had known. 'My ... my sister was in love with him,' I said tentatively.

Hodge looked me straight in the eye. 'He wasn't at home today,' he said carefully. 'His parents hadn't seen him when

I called, but they did mention that he's getting married soon and had a lot of business to attend to, so I didn't think too much of it. But I assume, therefore, that he isn't getting married to your sister, despite her feelings for him?'

'No,' I confessed. 'But he is in love with her, too. The wedding has been rushed through by his father. It was a shock to all of us when we heard.'

'Ah,' Hodge said. 'And you think this is all connected?'

I had possibly said too much, but I wanted to know that I had done everything I could to try to help Hodge's investigation. 'I just know that my sister was heartbroken.'

'And this Theodore. What is he like?'

'Kind and sensitive, I always thought. I certainly can't believe that he would ever have hurt my sister,' I said firmly. 'I just wonder if he might know something that could help.'

'Indeed. And what do you know of the future bride?'

I was beginning to feel as though I were being interrogated.

'I've never heard of her,' I said. 'But I'm assuming the match is tactical from the perspective of Theodore's father.'

'Maybe she discovered the way Theodore and Lucille felt about each other.' Hodge's eyes were alive now, flashing with inspiration. 'Maybe she didn't want to be in competition for her groom's affections.'

It sounded to me like melodrama, but that didn't mean it wasn't possible. At least Hodge was beginning to explore options other than the idea of Lucille being at a friend's house.

He drained his tea in one gulp, and then handed the cup back to me. 'Thank you for telling me this, Miss Everglass. I'm not giving up on your sister,' he said. 'I'll be back.'

I stayed in the library, grabbing a notebook to try to arrange my thoughts by laying them out on paper. The possibilities took on a bleakness when I saw them written down:

Drowned. Murdered. Fallen from a cliff.

I began to panic that I might have written them into existence, and ripped out the page, balling it up and throwing it on the fire.

Then I felt something light hit my arm and bounce off. Spinning on my heel, raising a hand to the place where I'd been ever so softly struck, I saw Austin Parker in the doorway. By my foot, there was a rumpled piece of paper, similar to the one I'd just cast into the flames. Keeping my eyes on him, I bent to pick it up and unfolded it.

Words not flowing?

I crushed the teasing words in my palm. There was a mildly amused grin on his lips.

'Just organizing my thoughts,' I said. 'Sometimes they feel too unwieldy if I leave them loose in here.' I touched the side of my head. Austin nodded as if he understood and then tapped the chair opposite me, raising his eyebrows questioningly. He could say so much without words, his expressive face so open.

'Yes, I don't mind,' I said, sinking back down on my chair. 'As you can tell, I was finished.'

He dropped down on to the seat opposite, fixing me with his gaze. I felt myself flush a little at the attention. I still didn't quite trust him, but I did find him intriguing. He was so unlike anyone I'd met before, although I acknowledged that I had done a fantastic job of sealing myself off from opportunities to meet people – an unfortunate side effect of hiding away from the horrors.

'Tell me how you came to be an actor,' I said, keen for distraction and diversion from the darkness of my worry about Lucille, when there was nothing more to be done until the morning anyhow.

Austin looked up to the ceiling and released a slow breath. A long story then. And sure enough, his pencil got to scribbling. His tongue stuck out slightly as he concentrated, pausing now and then to find the right word, tapping his pencil on the arm of the chair.

It started when my grandfather took me to see my very first performance in a theatre. I was the only one of my siblings who was interested (there are seven of us, the eldest a sister, followed by five boys, of which I am the youngest, and then my little sister). He took me to see Macbeth. *And it was terrifying and incredible all at once. There really is nothing like the theatre – the audience crowding into the atrium, the darkening of the lights and how everyone becomes silent, the anticipation . . . And then the lighting of the stage and the unfolding of the story, right in front of your eyes, and it's as if everyone in the room is holding their breath at the same moment. But to become an actor myself felt like an impossible dream. My parents do not like the theatre at all. They'd much rather I trained in accountancy like my father.*

When I looked up from his written words, he shrugged with a little smile. A little '*Oh well*', but I could see a flash of pain somewhere behind his eyes. It was easier to spot in the silence, in a way I might have missed if he were speaking.

'I'm so sorry about your grandfather,' I said.

I miss him terribly. I know he's probably dead, but that's hard to accept without a definite answer.

'No doubt he would be proud of you.'

I like to think so. It was only after he disappeared that I made the decision to pursue my dream.

'What is it that made you want to be an actor, instead of just in the audience?'

Six siblings. I wanted people to look at me for once.

I was surprised by his candour. His honesty was refreshing and only intrigued me more.

'You wanted to be the centre of attention?' I asked softly, curious.

He held both of his hands up in an admission of guilt. Then he stood up and grabbed three satsumas from the bowl we kept for guests and began juggling them, transforming into a convincing clown. He gave quite an impressive display, even passing one of the satsumas underneath his lifted leg, getting down to his knees and back up again without losing control of the fruit. I found myself truly warming to him, his silliness removing some of the glamour that surrounded him. A bubble of laughter popped out of me. He wrapped up his act, returning the satsumas to their bowl, a satisfied grin spreading across his mouth.

I gave him a small round of applause and he bowed deeply. 'You have quite the talent!'

I prefer the serious acting, though. I like to tell a story that will tug at your heartstrings. A laugh is good fun, but if I can make you brim with tears? Even better. The only time I ever saw my grandfather cry was during King Lear.

'How did you get into actually performing, then?' I asked.

With much difficulty. My family has connections with lords and ladies, not actors and directors.

Ah. He really was from money, then. I had suspected as much. He added to his page.

So I made friends.

I wanted to probe more, but his responses to this line of questioning had grown short and to the point, written and held up for me without a smile. I got the impression that it was not a story he wanted to dwell on; he had already shown me that he was more than happy to tell a good tale if he wanted to. So I asked him the other question that was burning in me. 'Do you not get frightened on stage, with all those people looking at you?'

Absolutely, I do. But then ... I step out on to the stage regardless, and afterwards I feel invincible.

He was remarkable to me. The idea that he could be frightened and not let it stop him from pursuing his dream. It was different from Lucille, who had always been just fearless. Austin did experience fear ... but he refused to let it get in his way. Interesting. I'd never considered that was possible before.

I've tried to pinpoint the moment that Austin started to change me, the moment I was going to become different because I knew him ... and I think it's this. This moment was the start.

The search continued. We didn't see Hodge, which I trusted to mean there were no developments. The newlyweds left, and I cleaned their room, and I thought about my sister much of the time. During the daytimes, I felt like a spectre of myself, going through the motions of the guest-house's maintenance. It was only in the evenings, when Austin and I met in the warm, firelit glow of the library, that I felt any peace at all. He'd stopped writing to me about ghosts and instead always did his best to divert my mind. We played chess and found ourselves evenly matched. I read aloud to him from the book I was reading and his little written interjections always made me laugh. He helped me to feel a little less lonely. And eventually, I got brave enough to ask him to let me read more of the playscript, and he handed me a single sheet, a monologue.

I turned it over in my hands, the shortness of it surprising me.

Before I had chance to read it, there was a knock at the door.

It was a detective by the name of Sunday. Constable Hodge's superior, finally deigning to pay us a visit. Detective Sunday's face mirrored that of a cliff's – worn over time, displaying a permanent exhaustion with the world beyond anything sleep could smooth over. His pessimism draped over the conversation, and it became clear to me very quickly that he was not going to find my sister. Without troubling to perform any sort of investigation of his own, he sat Mother and I in the dining room to debrief us on his conclusion from Hodge's work. I poured out tea for all of us and curled my hands around my cup.

'Unfortunately, with cases such as this, there often is not a satisfactory resolution,' he said, his expression grim. I got the impression that the empathy had been leeched out from him over the years. 'If she has gone of her own choice, then she doesn't want to be found.'

'And is that what you think?' Mother asked. 'That she just ... left? Ran away?' I bristled at the notion. What happened to Hodge's theories? Was he not going to explore them any further? I tried to make eye contact with Sunday, but he hung his head.

'Well, it's been a week now since Hodge started looking into this case. And in the absence of a body, it's something we have to consider. Though I should warn you that not finding a body doesn't necessarily mean she's alive,' Sunday said, causing more awful scenarios to push their way through the soil of my mind like worms. 'We might assume an accident, being where we are by the cliffs, the sea. Or ... would you say that Lucille was in distress, prone to dark moods?'

My mouth hung open in horror at the suggestion that Lucille might have orchestrated her own demise. Surely not.

And yet, in the last conversation I'd had with her, she had been so utterly devastated ... No. No, I couldn't believe it of her.

'It's upsetting to think about, I know,' Detective Sunday said. 'I am sorry that I'm not able to offer you more closure at this time. But at the moment we have nothing else to go on. I'm sorry if young Hodge got rather excitable about the whole thing, but really we have to consider the most likely explanation. We'll keep our notes and if you think of anything further...'

A bored look was beginning to cross Sunday's features as he delivered this speech. He had somewhere else he'd rather be. He had decided against investigating any further and this conversation was his way of telling us he already considered Lucille a lost cause – dead or disappeared on purpose. I hated him. But I would not beg him to look harder, to try again, to not give up. If I wanted to know what had happened to Lucille, I was going to have to discover it by myself. Anger swirled inside me, and my hands were trembling. My cup fell to the ground, splitting into two pieces and splashing hot tea over Sunday's smart black shoes. He yelped and Mother began apologizing profusely, mopping the ground with her apron, scrambling to pick up the pieces of the cup.

Detective Sunday made his excuses and left with haste after that. And once he was gone, Mother immediately got to work mending the cup, her hands shaking. Whenever she was upset, she always worked herself into a frenzy of repairs, darning or gluing or fixing, and I could tell that this response to the cup was her way of trying to gain control over one small part of the situation.

While Mother feverishly tried to unbreak what I had broken, a mask of concentration on her face, I could only watch, feeling useless. Lucille deserved better than a terrible, jaded detective and a sister who loved her but was weak and terrified of even stepping outside her front door.

Mother put down the cup. You'd always be able to see where it had been broken, no matter how she mended it.

'She'll come home to us,' Mother said into the silence.

I frowned. She had always been the one to warn us of danger, of all the things in the world that could hurt us, and tried to keep us as close to home as possible. Now she was telling me that it was all going to resolve itself?

And then I realized. In that moment, I was just another thing to fix. She would say whatever she needed to, to try to make me feel better, to try to mend me.

'How can you be so sure?' I asked. She came over to me and tucked a loose strand of hair behind my ear. But I flinched away from her touch. 'Mother, don't try to protect me. Do you think she's dead? Really?'

Mother shook her head, and I was relieved to find that I believed her. 'No. I don't think she's dead.' She touched her hand to her chest. 'If she were gone, I'd know it.'

I closed my eyes, trying to work out if I could feel Lucille in my chest. But all I could find there was anxiety, a tightening sensation that felt like a clenched fist. 'I just want to feel as if I did everything I could,' I said. 'If she's in trouble or hurt or . . . That's what she'd do for me.'

'Well, we're not going to give up,' Mother said. 'But you know Lucille. If she doesn't want us to find her then we won't be able to.' The steely determination I had witnessed that first night of Lucille's disappearance had faded, replaced by something like defeat.

So Mother had also come around to the thought that Lucille had disappeared of her own volition. But I just couldn't make that make sense. What reason would she have for worrying us so much? Lucille had always wanted to look after me. I couldn't believe that she'd ever intentionally throw me into the panic I'd been in since discovering she was gone. And I had imagined that Mother would become more frantic the longer Lucille was gone, not less. Her reaction left me feeling as though I was missing something, some key bit of information that everyone else had. Or perhaps I was just tired, and worried sick.

When I returned to my room, the absence of Lucille presented itself all over again. I clenched my fist as I thought about Detective Sunday.

Surely nobody would be as tireless in the search for Lucille as me. But I had been letting my fear of the horrors out there stop me, keeping me trapped inside and worrying, instead of actually *searching*. I would excavate this town as though I were combing the seaside for ammonites. I would be relentless and steadfast.

And I would need to venture outside.

For her, I would do it. When the day broke, I would do it.

Act One, Scene Three

The library in Oliver's apartment. He paces back and forth.

OLIVER:

This could be it. This could be the real thing. The man with the opal at his throat will be here any moment, and this is my opportunity to uncover his ways of working. I do believe this is the closest I have ever been.

My heart, it bounces in my chest. This research is the work of my life, and it has been so littered with frauds. But this man ... There is something in the stories about him. Shrouded in mystery, recollections fogged over, and yet a candle flickers in each tale, like a guide for those who need it. How does he do it?

Abigail said that it was two women who banished the evil spirit that so distressed her household. This man steps out for them. And now he comes to me from the place where the whalebones arch.

I must hold tight to the fiction that I have spun, that I have shared along the web of my acquaintances. It is the fiction that has drawn him out, the fiction that has wriggled and caught his attention so that he has arranged to come to me.

And so here comes my opportunity to interrogate him.

My hopes are pinned.

An aching.

I have allowed myself to begin to truly believe this time.

That I will be led to the veil between our world and the Otherworld.

10

I woke and with bleary eyes rolled over to wish Lucille a good morning. Then I saw the empty bed, and was taunted again as I remembered that she was gone. I kept having to remember, over and over.

As the fog of sleep receded, I climbed out of bed, the old floorboard squeaking beneath my feet. The new scene that Austin had given me lay on top of the bedside table. I read it once more. Oliver's soliloquy had got under my skin. *Where the whalebones arch* was obviously the reference to Whitby that had brought Austin here.

There was something about Austin and the story in the pages of the script that were woven together, and both of them fascinated me. And the mention of an 'Otherworld' – whatever that may be – sent a shiver rippling down my spine. It made me think of the horrors, the way they leaked out from ... somewhere else.

But those thoughts would have to wait.

Ten days had passed since that last conversation I'd had with Lucille. It was Theodore Truman's wedding day, and I needed to talk to him. I needed to know if Lucille had spoken to him before she disappeared. I believed that Theodore loved my sister, but any conversation they might have had that day would surely have been distressing for both of them. I would stay true to my resolution that I would step out of the guest house and begin my own investigations.

Searching my side of the wardrobe for something that wouldn't look too out of place among the wedding guests, I settled for a dress that buttoned at the front. Lucille and I always used to help each other with the ones that fastened at the back – with no maid, we'd learned to dress ourselves. Under the dress, I wore my best pair of sensible black lace-up boots. Just in case I needed to run, though I tried to tell myself I was being overly cautious.

I sought out Mother. She was in the dining room, repairing the upholstery on one of the chairs.

'I'm going to walk into town,' I said, making an effort to sound light.

'Into town? Why?' I wasn't sure if her surprise was concern about keeping me close or shock at the fact that I was leaving the house by choice.

'I need to take some air. I'll be right back.'

She clutched at the high neck of her dress, pulling it away from her skin as though it were suffocating her. 'It has felt rather airless in here this morning.'

'Are you turning unwell again?' I asked, suddenly concerned. I wanted to tell her that she could rely on me, that I would not stop until I brought Lucille home. But if she knew my intentions, she might not let me out of her sight.

'No, no,' she said with a smile I didn't believe. 'Just ... be careful.'

Be careful. Now that was a refrain I'd heard her say so many times that she might as well have embroidered it on all my clothes. *Be careful.* I'd been so very careful for so very long, and all it had done was make me lonely.

I made it to the front door and focused on steeling myself, heart in my throat.

Where I'd failed the first night of Lucille's disappearance, I would not fail again.

I took a deep, deep breath ... and stepped through the door for the first time in months.

I gasped as daylight fell across my face, the fresh air filled my lungs, and the sound of the calling gulls and the crashing waves hit my ears. It was a striking kind of wonderful. For so long, I'd denied myself this out of fear. And even now, it was only fear that had pushed me out of the safety of the guest house, the fear that I might be the only one who could find out what had happened to my sister.

But maybe I had learned something from Austin.

My plan was to go straight to the tailoring shop, in the hopes that Theodore hadn't set off for the church yet. For his sake as well as Lucille's, it troubled me that he was about to embark on a marriage to somebody that was not her. The pair of them being together had always seemed a certainty to me. She used to make him laugh so hard it was undignified; he had infinite patience with her temper, and she calmed in his presence. They understood each other.

And yet what was expected of him was prevailing over the direction of his own compass.

Dizzied by the fresh sea air and the brightness of the outdoors, I stumbled in the direction of the arching twenty-foot-tall whalebones, a commemoration of the whaling tradition of our town. Passing through those great bones, I began my descent into the town.

Now the delight of being outside was wearing off, memories of the horrors were resurfacing, and my palms were sweating, my breathing rough. Gritting my teeth, I kept my eyes down to the cobbles. I crossed the bridge over the river and weaved my way through the busy street to the tailoring shop. Only then did I fully lift my gaze up.

The shop was completely shut up for the day, a notice in the window.

They'd already gone to the church.

I marched on, keeping my eyes fixed down again, my jaw aching from clenching it. These were the streets I'd known all my life, and yet it felt at any moment that I might be confronted by a thing of nightmares. There was a prickling sensation at the back of my neck, and as I ran past the end of the shadowy ginnel leading to Arguments Yard, I thought I spotted something in the passageway. It looked like the shifting, breathing bulk of a slumbering spectral beast and I thought I saw the glint of fangs, stained with blood. Or perhaps it was just shadows, a trick of the light.

My breath caught in my chest and I flinched back as if whatever was in there had struck me.

And then I ran.

I dashed past the apothecary shop, burned out and empty, my hands tingling and a hot nausea rolling in my belly. I didn't want to look. Instead, I focused on the view of the one-hundred and ninety-nine steps proudly coiling up in front of me. Worn and winding, the steps built into the side of the East Cliff led up towards the grassy headland that held the church and the old ruins of the abbey behind it. With a burst of energy, I began to climb. It did not take long for my legs to go heavy with the effort, my chest tearing inside with each gasping breath, as though my lungs were serrated.

Halfway up, I could not take another step, having to stop to catch my breath. From here, I could see our guest house on the opposite cliff. Maybe I was only fifteen minutes from home, but in that moment, it felt so very far. Its safety called me back. But I couldn't give up now. Not when I was so close.

I started on the ascent again. My legs burned with every step, my heart beating so hard I could hear it in my ears – until it was drowned out by the happy chatter of the wedding guests clustered in the churchyard coming into earshot. I was astonished that they could all sound so celebratory; some of these people were friends of Mother, their daughters friends of Lucille. They would have had a knock on the door from Hodge, asking whether my sister had taken ill in their homes, and they would have known she was missing. Yet here they all were, full of revelry. And, I realized with a shock, not one of them had sent a letter or paid a visit.

Some friends indeed.

I paused on the steps, waiting for the group to make their way into the church so that I might linger behind them. There would be no way for me to slip past to try to speak to Theodore before the service now. I pictured him at the altar, waiting for his bride. All eyes would be fixed on me if I tried to speak with him before the wedding commenced. No, that would not do at all. I would have to wait until after it was done, after he had become a husband.

When I was certain that the last of the crowd had flowed into the church, I took the final handful of steps to finish my climb. I knew I had to stay close by so I could find my moment to speak with Theodore when the service was over. Wrapping my arms around myself to guard against the cold, I wandered through the gravestones. Each one told me a story, whether it was of an entire family wiped out in one year, or a stone with no name but instead decorated with a protruding skull and crossbones. Alone with my thoughts and fears, I couldn't help but feel unnerved by all the stories I'd heard about hauntings here on this very cliff: the woman in white seen in the abbey ruins; the coach full of spectral sailors pulled by headless horses, apparitions that paid their respects and collected the souls of those lost at sea; and, of course, Dracula.

And yet, there was no sign of my horrors.

While I was wending my way past the gravestones, I heard the bride coming up the stairs, accompanied by a man and a woman – her parents, I guessed. Trying to remain inconspicuous, as if I were just a mourner come to grieve alone, I watched as she adjusted the ivory silk skirt of her gown so that the train flowed out behind her. Her gown had voluminous sleeves that tapered at the wrist and a brocade bodice with a high neckline decorated with pearls. She looked like a princess who had stepped from the pages of an illustrated children's book. Her cheeks were flushed, a slight sheen to her face from the exertion of the climb. Her features were sharper than the roundness I always associated with Lucille, a few dark strands loosening from her pinned-back hair. Her mother carried a wide, thin box. She opened it to reveal a dainty veil, and fixed it into the hair of the bride, bringing it down over her face. The father, whose golden pocket-watch chain glinted in the sunlight, took her arm. The mother placed a tender kiss on her daughter's hand.

The three of them made their way into the church. They had been so engrossed in their own preparations that they hadn't noticed me. I allowed myself to draw a little closer to the church so that I might hear the music start up for the bride's procession towards Theodore.

I waited. And yet, no music began. I lingered in the shadow of the church, uncertain. Proceedings had been held up, that much was clear. But why?

And then, Mr Truman, Theodore's father, burst out of the church, his face a peculiar, rage-fuelled tinge of red, followed by his wife, who was calling out to him, wringing her hands. Something was clearly very wrong.

'That Everglass girl,' Mr Truman spat, as if our family name were a curse, and my stomach turned over.

11

'He's eloped with her,' Theodore's mother wailed. 'We should have known. That young constable had a whole search party scouring the town for her!'

Mr Truman stamped his foot in rage. 'And I can believe our son would be stupid enough to run off with her.'

His wife sighed. 'He loves her. I tried to tell you.'

Mr Truman jabbed at her with a finger to the chest so forcefully it pushed her back, and she cried out. It left me in no doubt of how vicious he might be if they were in private, and my pulse thudded with dread. 'And I have no doubt you told our son to follow his heart, instead of thinking of what was best for him, what was best for this family. This marriage was a business arrangement. Her father is meant to pay for the new shop!'

To my surprise, Mrs Truman's resolve grew steely. 'Don't you dare. You mean he's meant to settle your debts!' she said matter-of-factly, lifting her chin and meeting her husband's angry gaze. 'I said no such thing to Theodore, but if he has gone with her, and if the pair of them return here married, I won't be sad about it.'

Mr Truman growled. 'Then you're both fools. What are we going to do? That girl is waiting in church to marry our son and unless we find him . . .' The panic was rising in his voice, eating up the anger that had been there before.

'We won't find him. You haven't been able to find him for ten days, not that you admitted it to anyone. We should have called it off days ago and spared that poor girl.'

My heart raced. So Theodore had been missing all this time, too. His parents had been covering it up, trying to save face.

'I wanted to think better of our son.' Mr Truman grimaced. 'I thought he just needed some time to get over his nerves and that he would be more honourable than this. But it turns out you've raised someone who runs from his responsibilities.' He grabbed his wife by the wrist now and began to march her back down the stairs into town. 'We'll go through his things and see if there is any clue as to where . . .' Their arguing voices tailed off as they hastened away.

I shook my head in disbelief. Theodore had left his bride alone at the altar. Even his own parents didn't know where he was. They suspected he and Lucille had eloped . . . and that was the best-case scenario, wasn't it? That Lucille and Theodore were together somewhere, safe. It was what I might have wished for her, that he loved her so much he was willing to sacrifice everything to be with her.

So why didn't I feel any relief?

Because, somehow, I knew it wasn't true.

If my sister had been planning to elope, she would never have kept it a secret from me. But then a tiny voice of doubt cleared its throat, and I heard it as clearly as if it had grabbed me by the back of the head to speak right into my ear.

What if you don't know your sister as well as you think?

Before I had a chance to determine my next move, the bride burst out of the church and began tearing away down the one-hundred and ninety-nine steps, ripping the veil from her head and flinging it to the ground, where it was immediately caught by the wind and danced off into the air.

This was my chance. No doubt concerned members of her family would be about to follow in swift pursuit, so if I wanted to speak with her, I had to be fast.

'Excuse me, miss. Are you quite all right?' I called as I chased after her. She had already got round the bend, but the girl turned and glared back at me. Her eyes were filled with hurt and humiliation.

'Do I look quite all right?' She gestured at the cascading train of her gown. Now I could see her face more clearly, I noticed her abundance of freckles. She looked as though somebody had scattered biscuit crumbs across her nose and cheeks.

Someone called from the top of the cliff. 'Isobel? Isobel!'

'Would you stop staring?' Her words shot at me like tiny arrows dipped in poison. I almost lost my nerve. I almost turned away, embarrassed. But I had already chased after her, already engaged her in conversation, and that was the hardest part.

'I'll do better than that. I'll help you.' The words were out of my mouth in a rush. I scooped up her train. 'Where do you want to go?'

'Away,' she said. 'Just . . . away from here. Never mind that –' She batted my hands away from the train and reached to her waist to unfasten the strings that held it there, then stepped away, leaving the train on the steps like a puddle of spilled milk. It was a strikingly confident gesture, and I felt rather in awe of her. For all her humiliation, clearly this girl did not let much stand in her way.

'I know where we can go,' I said. 'Come on.'

And then we ran, flying down the stairs as fast as we could manage without tripping. I tried not to think about the story of the ghost of a person whose head had broken open like an egg upon a stone step just like these ones. I pushed thoughts of leaking brains out of my own, and asked Isobel, 'Do you know the Honest Opal, on the West Cliff?'

'I can't say I do,' she huffed.

'Well, that's home to me. That's where we'll go. I'm certain your family won't come looking for you at a guest house.' I ripped my shawl from my shoulders and wrapped it around hers. It wasn't the most effective disguise – her wedding dress was still a striking eruption of ivory beneath it – but it hid the impressive sleeves, at least. You'd only be able to pick her out of the bustling crowd in town if you had your eyes focused on everyone from the waist down.

But then, just as we had descended, I was halted abruptly as a figure darted out of the shadows by the burned apothecary store. Isobel carried on running, heading in the direction I'd pointed, seemingly unaware of the fact I had come to a startled stop.

No.

My eyes squeezed tightly shut in fear. I didn't want to look, couldn't bear to see the oozing awfulness of the horror I knew was making its way towards us.

And then it was the strangest thing.

Just as before, I was engulfed by the urge to fight, a crackling heat igniting in my chest. It was a type of rage, of burning blood, and it ran wild through my body.

I would not let this thing devour me.

I raised my hands, preparing to lash out, but the figure grabbed me by the wrists, and I let out a scream, visions of my demise playing out behind my eyes.

12

I struggled fiercely, even though blind panic was taking over the rage I'd felt only moments before. But as I thrashed, I felt a thumb running quickly, urgently, over my wrist, my pulse throbbing beneath it. I took a breath. The gesture was too intimate, too gentle, to be a threat.

My eyes finally opened, and met a gaze of stormy blue that I recognized immediately.

'Austin!' I shrieked his name, faint with relief. I had felt, I had thought ... Shaking my head, I yanked my hands from his grip. 'Why are *you* here?'

He pointed at me with his forefinger. *For you*, he mouthed, and my heart skipped a beat.

Me?

It wasn't much of an explanation, but I supposed he must have seen me leaving the guest house from his window. Decided to follow me. Keep watch. It was either chivalrous, or he was following me for reasons I couldn't fathom. But that could wait. I needed to find Isobel.

I grabbed Austin by the shoulders, urgency taking control of my limbs. 'That girl's family are going to come down looking for her,' I said, nudging my head in the direction of the stairs. 'She's run away from the wedding. Misdirect them. Point them the wrong way.'

And before he had the chance to indicate his thoughts on the matter, I was also gone, chasing after Isobel, my eyes sweeping for white fabric like a seagull searching for food. She must have moved quickly indeed, and as I darted in between the crowds going about their business, looking for her, I tripped up and rolled my ankle, the shock and pain making me gasp. But there was not time to stop. I hobbled on, the throb throb throb of my ankle as keen as the sound of my mother's voice ringing in my ears, reminding me to be careful, to watch out, to take care at all times.

I finally caught sight of Isobel when I got to the bridge. The bottom of her skirt was filthy now, and with her hair clawing its way out of its pins, she looked far more like Miss Havisham than the fairy-tale princess of before. She had stopped to catch her breath and was looking around, clearly lost.

'You run fast,' I said when I reached her. 'But we're nearly there. Follow me.'

'What happened to you?' Her eyes were round. 'I thought you were right behind me but then you were gone.'

'I bumped into ... a friend.' As soon as the word was out of my mouth, I was struck by the weight of it. Austin was my friend. 'He – he was simply making sure I was all right.'

I didn't want to waste time chatting, not least because even if Austin had managed to divert whoever was pursuing the fleeing bride, it was surely only a matter of time before they made their way to the bridge, and people would certainly be able to point us out. Isobel followed my lead as I quickly weaved our path to the guest house.

When we arrived back at the Honest Opal, Mother was sitting at her usual place by the desk. She took one look at Isobel and gasped. 'What ... Who is this? What on earth have you done, Alice?'

'This isn't her fault!' Isobel interjected. 'She was trying to help. I just needed a place to run to, to get away from ...'

My mother looked doubtful. 'Running away from your wedding?'

Isobel snorted. 'My groom did that first.' And then she burst into tears.

'Theodore Truman didn't show up to the church today,' I said, imbuing my voice with the seriousness of it all, knowing how Mother would interpret it. But Isobel stiffened next to me.

'How do you know his name? I never told you it,' she said, her voice cold and cautious.

My breath caught. 'Oh, well you know how it is when there's a wedding in a small town like this! Everyone always knows about everything.' I knew I didn't sound convincing, and felt guilty at the lie. But I needed this girl to trust me, and if she knew of our family's connection to Theodore, it felt unlikely she'd be willing to be honest with me.

Isobel's eyes narrowed, the lines on her brow deepening with suspicion as she pressed her lips together in thought.

I busied myself, grabbing her a glass of water poured from the carafe behind the desk and pressing it into her hands.

'Here, have this. You must be thirsty after the exertion.'

She gulped it down in seconds. 'I want to get out of this gown,' she said firmly. 'Do you have a dress I can borrow?'

'Of course,' I said, guiding her towards the stairs. I turned and met Mother's eyes. She was still shaking her head, very slowly, as though she couldn't quite believe what she was seeing.

In my room, I opened up the wardrobe, giving Isobel the choice of everything that Lucille and I owned. I got the impression that our gowns were quite simple compared to the luxury she was used to; everything I'd learned that morning suggested I'd been right and the Trumans had been desperate to secure the match for the wealth of Isobel's family after all. 'I'll give you some privacy,' I said, making my way to leave.

'No, wait.'

I paused.

'I can't get myself out of this,' she said, gesturing at her gown. 'Do you have someone you can send?'

I almost laughed at the idea. 'Just me, I'm afraid. We don't have staff.' I closed the door again.

'Tell me how you really know Theodore,' she said, her voice steel. 'And don't lie to me. I don't believe he's just someone from your town.'

'I've known him since we were young,' I said, hesitant. 'He and my sister have been very close for years.'

'Ah,' Isobel said, understanding immediately. She directed me to the elaborate hook-and-eye fastenings at the nape of her neck. 'Very close. Well, that explains things, at least. I wonder if he ever had any intention of going through with the wedding, or if the whole charade was always just an endeavour in humiliating me?'

My fingers hovered over the fastenings. It was the sort of sisterly gesture that ached. She had been buttoned into this dress dreaming it would be her husband removing it, that she would be married. And instead, her wedding had been a nightmare of embarrassment.

'I don't think that he ever would have intended to humiliate you,' I said gently.

'Well, what does that matter? The outcome is the same.' She sighed and peeled her arms out of the enormous sleeves.

Had she had any sense of Lucille before this? That was what I needed to ascertain.

'Did he ever give you any reason to doubt him before today?' I probed.

Isobel shrugged. 'No, but then I've only met him once. It was all very sudden. He was polite and charming. But the match was arranged between our fathers. There was no proposal, just a letter from his father to mine. Do you know, when I arrived at the church to find he hadn't arrived, I thought perhaps he had taken ill. But then I caught eyes with his mother and I thought – no, she is not surprised enough by this. I bet she knew all along.' She released herself from the bodice, revealing her white corset, and slipped out of the dress, casting it to one side.

So there was no sign that Isobel knew that Theodore was in love with somebody else. And although she was biting and fierce, I couldn't imagine her causing harm to Lucille. And with that, Hodge's theory that this girl was somehow responsible for Lucille's disappearance withered.

'Theodore's mother doesn't know where he's gone, although you're right that she wasn't surprised by him abandoning the wedding,' I said, and admitted overhearing their conversation. 'I'm sorry if this sounds insensitive, but everyone in town knew how my sister and Theodore felt about each other. It wasn't a secret. From what I overheard, his parents haven't seen him for days. I think his father was burying his head in the sand, desperately hoping Theodore would show up out of honour, if nothing else. So they didn't know, not for certain, but they weren't surprised.'

Isobel went silent, as though the information was steeping itself inside her like tea leaves in a pot. She started looking through the gowns that belonged to me and Lucille.

'And where is she now, this sister of yours?' Isobel spat, looking around the room as though Lucille were about to burst out.

I swallowed and it felt jagged in my throat. 'I don't know.'

'So you think she's the reason he left me at the altar? Well, I should like to speak to the woman who has stolen my fiancé,' she said, in a strange sing-song voice that left me wrong-footed, unable to sense if she was genuinely caustic or just flippant, wielding her words as a deflection of her embarrassment. But I couldn't help but think how wrong she was, how Theodore was Lucille's to be stolen if he was anyone's.

'Nobody knows where she is.' My voice trembled slightly and Isobel flinched at it.

She frowned. 'What do you mean?'

'I mean that she vanished, the day after she found out about you and Theodore. She's just ... gone.' I lifted my hands helplessly, as if under better circumstances I might have been able to present my sister in the palm of my hand, like a mouse.

'How convenient that Theodore is also just ... gone.' The implication hung between us. She'd echoed me so sharply I felt sliced by it, stunned into silence. Isobel's eyes began to sheen over with emotion, and she bit her lip. A deep frown burrowed into her forehead and her voice hardened when she next spoke. 'I thought you were being kind, giving me a place to regain my composure. But now I think you must be some awful ghoul, lurking around the churchyard waiting to see my embarrassment in front of half the town. Was this a plan you and your sister concocted, so she could have a good laugh at my expense later? Did you know he wasn't going to turn up?'

'I came to the church in the hopes of speaking to Theodore. I didn't know. Up until what happened at the church, I thought it was just my sister who had disappeared. I thought Theodore might be able to tell me where she'd gone.'

'I think he has told us plenty in his behaviour today, don't you?' Isobel shook her head as though she still couldn't believe the way things had played out.

'Well, the only ulterior motive I could be accused of having in bringing you here was that I wanted to ask you –' I began, but the question died on my lips.

'Ask me what?' she snapped.

I shrank. I didn't know what to do in the face of her anger, and so I picked up the discarded bodice, the silk sensationally smooth beneath my fingertips. When I looked up from folding it neatly, I saw she was still watching me, demanding an answer.

'Well, I wondered if you . . .' I trailed off. How could I explain it to her? What other explanation was there? I had no proof to back up this vague feeling that there was *something else going on*. 'I wondered if you knew what had happened to her, if you were responsible somehow, trying to get her out of the picture before your wedding. But with Theodore gone too, that theory doesn't make any sense, does it?'

'I wouldn't call you much of a sleuth,' Isobel retorted in a tone so sharp it could cut. She removed the skirt and stood in her corset and petticoats. 'No, I don't know where your sister is. Or the man who was supposed to be married to me today. Don't you think the most obvious solution is that they have slipped away together? Eloped?'

'Maybe,' I said, still uncertain.

'But what is to happen to *me* now, do you think?' She pulled out the most modern and expensive gown that we owned, in a peacock-blue fabric, that Lucille had been gifted by Theodore. He had adjusted the sleeves to give it that voluminous appearance that was much coveted, and that Isobel clearly had a fashionable preference for. She slipped into it. This one buttoned at the front, which she managed quite competently by herself.

'I suppose you will go back to your parents,' I said. 'And if you wish to marry then I imagine they will find you a match.'

'Find me a match?' She let out a heavy stream of breath in a big hiss. 'You make it sound easy. I assume, then, that you have not heard about my family? Or about our curse.'

13

'Curse?' I whispered. My heart stuttered in my chest.

'Well, then,' Isobel said bitterly. 'Let me enlighten you. Any man that marries me will be subject to this curse: if he is dishonest, he will be pursued by a spectre that will drag him to its lair in a cave down by the seaside and devour him. What do you think of that?' She crossed her arms and set her face in a challenge to me.

I had no doubt that this story had been met with a whole range of responses across her lifetime, from fear to horror to mockery. But she received none of these from me. Because I believed her. She had a look in her eye that I had seen in myself in the looking glass.

'Your family is cursed? Haunted by this spectre . . .?'

She nodded. 'It makes finding a marriage match challenging, to say the least.'

So that was the reason a girl from such a wealthy family would accept a match to the son of a tailor. It had been nagging at me, and now I understood.

'You've seen this spectre for yourself?'

Suddenly Isobel could not meet my eyes, and I noticed

that her hand trembled. 'No. I haven't. But you can't argue with a well-known piece of local legend.' She laughed bitterly. 'In a hundred years, there is only one man that married into my family who didn't disappear eventually. And about a decade ago, someone stumbled into that cave and found all their bones picked clean. So the story of the spectre has taken root.'

I grimaced at the image that had formed in my mind. All those bones. Even if it were a murderer, not a spectre, who was responsible for the deaths in her family, it sounded as though those men had met a terrible end. 'Who was the husband that survived?'

She smiled, and it was a genuine one. 'My father, of course.' Of course. I'd seen him at the church. She continued, 'He and my mother are a true love match and he has never once taken the risk of being dishonest since the day they took their vows.'

Yet, I thought. Not been dishonest *yet*.

'And do you not wish the same for yourself?' I asked. 'A love match, I mean? Does your father not wish it for you too?'

'My father lives in fear of slipping up. Supposedly the man who married my aunt was taken by the spectre the day after their wedding, and his only dishonesty seemed to be lying in order to keep a gift for his new wife a secret. I have yet to meet any eligible young man who is willing to take the risk.' She lowered her eyes. 'It seems that Theodore's father was willing to take it on his behalf. I don't know if he even knew of the curse. But I begged my father to accept the match when it was offered.'

This surprised me. 'Why do you wish to marry at all, if you think there is a good chance your husband will be doomed to a horrific death? I don't doubt you believe in the curse, in the spectre.'

'Because I hope for children of my own one day,' Isobel said simply, a dreamy look capturing her eye. And then she shook herself, and glared. 'I – I do not know why I am telling you all of this. Have you slipped me something to loosen my tongue? I feel as though I *have* to tell it all to you. What have you done to me?' She suddenly stepped back, as though she were frightened of me.

Stranger still was a feeling that had begun to overpower me. A feeling that it was my duty to help her, although how, I couldn't begin to imagine. I couldn't let myself get diverted into her horror when I was living through one of my own, and yet I had a sense that I needed to spring into action to free her from her curse. The fire inside was rekindling. My hands tingled, my skin felt as though there were something crawling beneath it that might burst out at any moment, that I would cast off my body as though it were only a cocoon and an unrecognizable me would emerge.

If she was frightened of me, then I was just as frightened of myself.

Mother agreed to accompany Isobel back to the church to find her parents, no doubt bracing herself for the whispers about Lucille and Theodore. I didn't have the chance to speak to Mother about the implications of them both disappearing, although I wanted to know whether she felt, like I did, that Lucille would never have eloped without telling us. But what was it that had actually *happened* to the pair of them?

I wrapped up Isobel's bridal gown in brown paper and tied it with string so that she could carry it home with her. 'Just send the dress back when you have the chance,' I murmured, pressing the unwieldy parcel into her hands.

The strange feeling her story had given me seemed to have sunk into my bones and given them a restless energy.

This was a world of hauntings and curses, and Isobel was just as trapped in her situation as I was in mine.

I busied myself sorting through the post that had arrived over the last few days. I'd let it build up more than I usually would, with everything that had been happening. I had thought it would be a simple, mindless task, but I couldn't have been more wrong.

There was a letter for Lucille.

My fingers trembled, the thick, cream envelope trembling too. The pair of us never received letters directly. This was most unusual. And when had this arrived? Before she'd vanished, or afterwards? The address had been penned in a swooping cursive I did not recognize, and I felt sure I would have if I had seen it before. My insides swirled. Who would Lucille have been corresponding with?

The door suddenly opened with a great clatter, making me drop the letter as though I had been caught with my fingers in Mother's purse.

Austin had returned. His eyes were bright, his cheeks pink and a worried frown gathered across his handsome face. He marched right over to the desk as I scrabbled to hide the letter.

'You followed me this morning,' I said. It was not a question. He had made it clear that I was his purpose for lingering at the bottom of the one-hundred and ninety-nine steps. He began his usual scribble in his notebook.

You said you never leave the Honest Opal if you can help it. I thought perhaps you might need somebody to watch out for you. I wasn't planning to interfere.

'I was managing alone,' I said. 'I don't need some kind of knight in shining armour.'

I saw that!

He raised his eyebrows, his expression a blend of impressed and surprised. An involuntary smile flooded my face. When I had thought he was some remnant of the horror that had devoured the apothecary, I had been ready to defend myself. Perhaps I was stronger and braver than I had ever given myself credit for. Austin continued writing.

I apologize if you feel I have underestimated you. I admire your bravery. But you don't have to be alone.

'I'm sorry that I attacked you. I thought you were ... Well, it doesn't matter what I thought. Isobel and I were in a hurry.'

Did you find out anything about your sister?

He looked as if he truly cared, his forehead creased with concern. Even though he'd never met Lucille, it was obvious that the situation had unsettled him, and at that thought, a wave of guilt crashed over me. He was meant to be staying here for rest, for recovery, not chasing after me and my missing sister.

'No. Or at least, not enough,' I murmured. I still felt some hesitation as I began to explain to Austin why I had gone to the church in the first place. But I was starting to find that holding it all inside me was becoming too much, that I needed another person to talk to. He listened intently as I explained everything that had unfolded that morning. 'So, it looks as though she eloped with Theodore but I ... I just don't believe it.'

Austin tapped his pencil against his notebook, occupied with thoughts I wished I could hear. I could tell that his mind was busy, while mine kept circling back around to the letter to Lucille, and the urge to open it, to know who had sent it.

I wish there were more I could do to help.

He looked so sincere that I couldn't help but reach out to him. And the second I'd done it, my fingertips alighting on his hand, the contact between us sparked, made me feel as though everything inside me was turned upside down. I pulled my hand back, suddenly feeling flushed, and attempted to change the conversation with haste. 'I have been thinking about your playscript,' I said. 'It has dominated my thoughts quite unreasonably. Especially considering that my thoughts have rather enough to occupy them at the moment.'

I caught a flash of eagerness in his eyes, the question there.

'I spotted the reference to Whitby, of course.'

He nodded, as if waiting for more, as if there were something he wanted from me. My heart began to beat a little faster. I was flustered by his gaze, so infused with ... It almost looked like hope. But I could not understand why. I was beginning to get frustrated. It was starting to feel very much like a game, one that I didn't understand the rules of.

'Is this all preparation for a performance of the script?' I challenged him. Austin raised a quizzical eyebrow at me, so I elaborated. 'Is this all so that when your voice is healed, you can take the lead in the show, having done your research about our haunted little town? Is Oliver the tragic hero you want to play?'

Austin snorted indignantly, a breathy noise that reminded me of a disgruntled horse at the front of a carriage.

'That's a no, then,' I suggested, and he shot me a withering glance that told me he was disappointed in me for even considering it. He really did have such a remarkably expressive face. I could see how acting had become his livelihood. I wondered what it would be like to see that face lit up on a stage.

You can't perform a play without a finished story.

'The playscript isn't finished?'

Everything you've read is everything I have.

'Oh. Well then, you'll have to enlighten me what this is all about. Because I don't understand it.'

Austin sighed and frowned. He shoved his hands in the pockets of his coat, that beautiful, luxury coat. He seemed to be wrestling with something. But before he could write to me, there was a brisk rap at the door. It was Constable Hodge.

'Do you have a moment, Miss Everglass?' he asked, and I shot a glance at Austin. He nodded and disappeared up the stairs to his room.

'I won't keep you long, Miss Everglass. I wanted to let you know that we believe we have a resolution to your sister's disappearance.'

Hope clashed with fear. He couldn't speak fast enough for me. What did he know? What had he found? I inspected his face for any inkling of whether it was good or bad news. The answer was altogether more disappointing.

'This morning, Theodore Truman did not attend his own wedding and it seems he has been missing for the same length of time as your sister. Given the circumstances, we have reason to believe that she has left town of her own volition with him.' He smiled, as though this was something I would be delighted to hear. Perhaps I would, if I believed it for a second.

'I see,' I said, my tone chilly.

'She might well return, or write to you soon. I'm certainly hoping so.' Hodge seemed to mean it, seemed to care. I was thankful it was him who had come to visit and not the indifferent Detective Sunday.

'I hope you are right as well. Thank you for your time.'

'You're welcome. I'm pleased that it's a positive outcome. At least ... as positive as we might have hoped for. I understand you'll still be worried about her until she comes back.' Hodge attempted to smile at me, but there was an apology behind his eyes. Then he said a solemn farewell, and sloped out of the door.

'A positive outcome,' I muttered under my breath. From Hodge's perspective, I suppose at least there hadn't been a body uncovered – that was probably what he was expecting. Maybe he would be a good investigator one day, or maybe his empathy would burn out, like Detective Sunday's, but either way, he would never be the one who found my sister. He'd accepted a version of events that made a neat story – *She eloped! What a relief!* – and was content not to look any deeper. I couldn't blame him for that.

Truly, I knew myself to be better equipped than he could ever be to perform this investigation.

After all, who knew my sister better than me?

Dear Lucille,

I am of course delighted to hear that you wish to visit, and you will be most welcome. I send this in a hurry in the hopes it reaches you before you travel. Are you certain that you will not tell Alice, and not come here together? I am sure that you are capable of making the journey alone, but I truly believe that this is the work of sisters, and I would urge you to reconsider keeping this from her for much longer.

Your Aunt Sybil

14

After Constable Hodge had left, I read the letter addressed to Lucille. I felt I had to, if I were going to exhaust every avenue. And once I'd read it, I sat for a very long time in silence.

It was signed *Your Aunt Sybil*. Aunt Sybil, who lived in London, who was estranged from Mother. The first I had learned that Aunt Sybil even existed had been when she had taken ill when I was thirteen, when Mother went to visit her ... and returned with red, puffy eyes. She hadn't spoken about her since, and I remained in the dark about the reason for their estrangement. Any time I tried to ask, Mother turned stony-faced, and told me that the less I knew about her sister, the better.

But Lucille had been corresponding with Aunt Sybil.

And she had kept it a secret from me, something I had thought impossible.

Worse than that. By omission, my sister had been lying to me. For how long? I stared at Lucille's empty bed, turning the information over in my mind, examining the letter again for any fresh insights.

So Lucille had gone to Sybil, then, and perhaps taken Theodore with her. But why? And why hadn't she told me?

It was a relief to finally get some answers as to where Lucille was. But it opened up a whole new chasm of questions within me, too.

That evening, after the guest house was all locked up, Austin didn't meet me in the library the way I'd grown accustomed to, and so I sat alone, waiting for him. I couldn't shift the feeling that there was something he was keeping from me.

The following morning at breakfast, I showed him the letter.

'The railway station,' I said.

He looked at me quizzically.

'It's where she must have gone, if she were travelling down to London to see our aunt. Maybe she went there with Theodore. She was hiding this from me, and I still don't understand why she would go without packing a stitch of clothing to take with her, with nothing but her diary. But this is the most solid clue as to her whereabouts that we've yet had. I need to go to the station and ask if anyone remembers seeing her.'

Austin nodded.

'I also ...' I cleared my throat. 'I just have a feeling that ...' I couldn't express it. It was more than just a feeling, but I didn't know how to explain that to Austin. I had an otherworldly certainty that if I could just get to the railway station, I'd find *something* there. My fingers were tingling. It was the same feeling I had experienced talking to Isobel about her curse, the sense that I needed to help her, the same heavy responsibility I'd felt about the apothecary. A strange prescience.

There was something waiting for me at that station.

Austin's pencil scratched in his notebook.

I think that sounds sensible. And I think if you have a gut feeling, you should follow it.

'All right, then,' I said firmly, bolstered by his reinforcement. 'I'm going to the station.' The decision had taken on a sense of inevitability. Whatever intuition dwelled within me, it swelled at the acknowledgement and my fingers began to sting with heat again.

In ghost stories, people always complain of feeling cold. There is a prickle at the back of their neck and a shiver that runs down their spine and their breath steams up like smoke in front of their face. The haunted are turned to ice.

But for me, being haunted has always felt like being burned.

My reticence about leaving the house was an ever-present echo, even after my somewhat successful venture out to the wedding. I'd spent so long hiding within the armour of the Honest Opal, and my feelings of fear about the outside world did not simply evaporate. I was still unsure as to what I'd seen lurking in the alley, and there had never been any rhyme or reason to my encounters with the horrors before. They could be anywhere, emerge at any time. After all, I was following a pathway that was intrinsically bound up in darkness; it was not rational or sensible. And so I was quite outside of my usual self, pushed to the very edge of what I thought I could handle. Not to mention the feeling that some kind of intuition inside me was waking up, like a rousing dragon in a cave.

Of course, I knew that I could just remain inside, cloistered away. I could refuse to search. I could tidy the guest house every day and keep everything neat. I could insist that my life would stay the same.

But life had already changed irrevocably. Lucille was gone. And I think I knew, even then, that life would never be the same again, whatever the outcome of my search.

'I'm going to do it,' I said, but I did not move to open the door right away. I knew it was because I was convincing myself, not simply stating my intent to Austin, who stood to one side. He had insisted on coming with me, and truthfully I was deeply grateful to have his bolstering presence by my side.

My hand hovered over the door handle, and then grasped it. It felt as though there were years in the moments it took me to muster the strength to turn it, open the door wide and then to step out once more, the light of the sun so bright, the air so fresh that the Honest Opal behind me seemed a cage of my own making, dark and stale. I was still hoping that if I could find Lucille and bring her back, it would feel like our nest again, the place where we could settle into safety.

There was purpose in every step we took down the winding cliffside path. Austin walked beside me. And in the companionable silence we shared, I found there was a space for me to speak that felt preciously comfortable. Usually, with anyone but Lucille, I would have shied away from talking; my thoughts were often busy and muddled, and I felt that once they were spoken they took on a terrible, frightening permanence. The pace of conversation with most people did not give me adequate time to form my thoughts properly, and conversations I'd taken part in would often reverberate around inside my skull when I was alone, and even when I knew that I had been perfectly agreeable, my mind would still perform this torturous exercise, examining my every word for error.

But with Austin, there was only his encouraging, open face. And I knew if I needed to think a little longer, he would wait patiently, just as I would wait for the scratch of his pen. If I said the wrong thing, or the right thing but in the wrong way, there would be no judgement from him while I worked out how to express what I truly meant. And when his own words were formed, I trusted that they would offer support.

I'm trying to write about him the way I remember feeling at the time, in the moment, rather than have my memories swayed by everything that unfolded. I found being around him so thrilling. I was charmed by him. There had never been a young man like him in my life, and although our encounters were sometimes fraught with the oddness of our circumstance, my heart was opening to him in tiny increments.

'I have been thinking about the letter. Whatever Lucille has been discussing with Aunt Sybil, it must be something she wanted to protect me from. She wouldn't have kept it from me to be cruel or for her own gain. The only reason she would hide something from me would be to try to keep me safe.'

Austin nodded thoughtfully. We took the route past the bakery, the tempting rows of lemon buns in the window reminding me of arguments with my sister about the correct way to eat them – the answer, of course, being to tear them in half, butter the plain half and then squash the lemon topping into the middle to make it like a sandwich. Lucille used to bring one home for me once a week when she was running errands in the town. A sickly sadness trickled through me at the thought. But having Austin accompany me was sufficiently distracting from the frightened twisting in the pit of my stomach.

We approached the station and, searching for someone I might ask some questions of, I walked us round to the main entrance. The gaping stone arches were draped with shadows, like velvet curtains framing a stage. The sound of a departing train crashed over me, gathering speed, saying goodbye to the town I'd never left in my whole life, as if it were easy.

And there, tangled around the bottom of an iron handrail on the steps up to the station entrance, almost as though it had been left for us to find ... Lucille's red hair ribbon.

It had been trampled on so many times that it was covered in muddy footprints, but I would have known it whatever state it was in. I reached down to pick it up, unwinding it from the handrail. I clenched the crumpled ribbon tightly in my fist.

Austin had carried on investigating while I had picked up the ribbon, so I took quick steps to catch up with him, following him through the entrance to the station. But as I passed through the arch, my skin prickled.

Something inhuman shifted.

And when I peered into a shadowy corner of the vestibule, I saw a great, shimmering tear in the fabric of reality. It was an impossible rip in the wall, the wall that was *stone*, that should not be able to tear like paper. It was like an entrance, leading into an impossible place, one that was made up of darkness. And as I stared at it, the darkness began to shift, as if it could sense me.

Then from the tear, a horror came spilling out.

My mouth stretched into a silent scream, and a fire of panic began to burn inside me. My eyes roved over the shadows as I tried to piece together what I was witnessing.

'Austin!' I cried, and he turned back. 'Do you see it?' I asked, breathless. 'Do you see that . . . thing?'

He shook his head, but I could tell from the wild fear in his eyes that he felt something, even if he couldn't see it. He began clutching at the neck of his shirt, and quickly pulled out a chain I'd not spotted him wearing before.

My eyes returned to the horror, wrestling with itself as if it were trying to *become* something. Terror scrabbled inside me, my stomach jolting as though it were trying to flee my body. It was like the shadows had come alive with the sole purpose of swallowing the light. The shape of a hand formed from the ooze, grasping and reaching towards me. My mouth went dry and, like I'd sensed with the other horrors before, I was certain that this thing only meant harm, only sought to devour and to feast. It was desperate.

It lurched forward, twisted, and the shape of an almost recognizable face began to form, pained and grimacing. I gasped as the sharp jaw, straight nose and brown eyes of Theodore Truman began emerging. But the face was slightly amiss, an odd approximation of how he looked, as if he had been formed out of clay and the sculptor had got it wrong.

The horror that was not Theodore, but wore his face, tried to pull itself out of the shadows, stretching out for me. A hungry mouth opened up, a dark hollow of nothingness. Longing and desperation emanated from the creature as it strained against its limitations, beckoning me closer, a strong pull that I fought to resist.

Hot sparks rushed through my body. My insides were on fire.

It was leeching energy away from me, and fear flooded my mind. It was trying to steal me away, the way it must have stolen Theodore and then tried to wear his likeness.

I looked to Austin and saw him still nearby, clutching on to a gemstone the size of his thumbnail, in a delicate gold setting, fastened to the chain around his neck. He was holding it out in front of him like a miniature shield, his eyes squeezed tightly shut. It was an opal, a fiery, sparkling opal, and it glowed, surrounded Austin with a golden energy that I instinctively knew was protecting him.

But it was not protecting me.

I gritted my teeth and turned towards the horror. It was focused entirely on me, as though it knew Austin was untouchable. I could feel it already trying to steal parts of me away, my sight tunnelling at the edges. It was going to tear me to shreds, I now understood, and a dread gripped me around the throat. What fear had Theodore experienced as the horror stole away his face to wear as its own? I was sure it wasn't possible to survive it.

And yet the heat inside me, the sparks ... They pulled at me, too. They were the key to overpowering the horror, I realized.

But then ...

'Alice?' a fearful voice rang out, resounding like a church bell.

Lucille.

15

I reeled at the sound of Lucille's voice. Through the tear into our world, in the distance beyond the horror, wrapped in darkness, there she was. I could see her, and she was a light in the endless shadows of that other place, that *Otherworld*. Just like in Austin's playscript. A real place.

'Lucille!' I cried out, and then she was reaching towards me, and there were tears pricking at my eyes. But in my moment of distraction, the horror lunged at me again, with a renewed desperation, as if it had latched on to the sound of my voice, the hands emerging from the sludge reaching for me, gripping my wrists and *squeezing*. It hurt, worse than anything I'd ever felt. Those hands were physical and strong. Certainly not a figment of my imagination, as I'd always wondered.

I felt the fire in me immediately rush to my defence. Not just for me, but for Lucille, too. A blaze gathered in my hands so intensely I thought I might be able to release flames from my fingertips. I didn't know how to wield this fire as a weapon, but I tried to focus on allowing the sensation of the burning to move through me. I felt something build, responding to my will. An energy, begging to be used, and so I did. Without thinking, I plunged my hands into the horror in front of me. I was instantly full of a searing heat, as though I had delved them into hot coals rather than darkness.

I gasped.

The horror let out an inhuman shriek, echoing the screech of metal wheels on track.

And then, before I could do anything more, the horror was being sucked back towards the tear, losing its grip on me. The two sides of the tear between the worlds were being pulled together, sealing it shut. I looked at Lucille and her eyes met mine. They were frightened, but determined.

It was *her*. She was closing the entrance to the Otherworld, power streaming from her fingers in a steady glow of light as fine as thread, sewing together the tear as she moved her arms.

The horror was caught, still half tangled in the Otherworld, half in ours, and as the seam closed it severed those grasping hands.

It was gone.

And so was my sister.

The seam was now a healed wound over the stone, a thin, angry line. The horror's hands writhed around on the ground in their death throes, before losing their form, leaving only a grim smear of sludge behind.

'Lucille?' I sobbed. 'Lucille!'

I was flailing wildly, my fingers scraping along the rough stone walls as if I could pull her out, and then Austin was there, his freezing hands on my arms, bringing me to a stop. He was an anchor, although his own breathing was coming furiously too. The danger dissipated, so had the glow.

'She was here,' I said, shaking in disbelief. 'She's in there!' I pressed my fingers into the seam that had been open mere moments ago. The stone grated against my fingertips, rasped beneath my nails. I was trembling all over, my legs weak from the exertion of the encounter with the horror. It was like walking through a nightmare in daylight.

I looked down at my hands, bloody from scraping them on the seam. I had failed Lucille, and she had saved me. 'The horror, it would have killed me if Lucille hadn't closed up the entrance.'

Austin held me still, tried to steady me. The endless blue of his eyes could have drowned me, I was so weak. He shook his head slowly and I understood that he hadn't seen the horror, the tear or Lucille. But he had felt *something*, had reacted in fear.

'Miss, are you all right there?' A station guard dressed in a crisp uniform had appeared, his brow furrowing as he took in the sight of me, wearied and wobbly, and Austin with his hands on me.

'Yes, yes,' I said, trying to muster a smile. 'I just felt a little faint, but I am quite all right now.' I pulled back from Austin and arranged my skirts properly. 'Thank you.'

The guard didn't seem reassured. He glared at Austin, who, of course, said nothing. 'You've just missed the train if you were headed to London,' he said. 'And there's no more today.'

'That's not a problem. We were just taking a walk,' I said, scrambling for an excuse for our odd behaviour. 'I like to come and see the trains. I'm sorry that we missed that one. I like to watch them depart.'

The guard's face broke into a smile then. 'Ah, I am the same! I never tire of it. The sound, the steam, the speed. It is simply marvellous, truly.'

I tried to show enthusiasm, but I felt as though one of his marvellous trains had thundered through me. I tugged at Austin's sleeve, and we said a polite farewell to the guard before stumbling out into the thin daylight that strained through the overcast clouds. My body felt crushed with exhaustion, and I collapsed on to a bench overlooking the bridge, my head in my hands, Lucille's voice and the screech of the horror echoing around my mind.

I ran through the events that had unfolded in the station vestibule, trying to make sense of them. What was it about me that meant I could see these awful creatures that everyone else seemed to be blind to? This one – and I felt certain it was the same type of monstrous being that the apothecary had been a casualty of, remembering his injured eye and the eye in the cupboard – devoured people, stole parts of them. And when they were strong enough, when they had eaten enough, they would wear the faces of their victims in an awful imitation of a person.

And now Theodore Truman was dead. I started to cry, the awfulness of it clobbering me like a physical blow.

Austin sat next to me and placed his hand gently on my back as I sobbed.

What did this mean for Lucille? She was in the Otherworld still, and the entrance was sealed. She was alive, at least, and that should have been a comfort, a guiding light in the maze I was lost in, but it was a torment instead, because the light did not illuminate my path. How long could she survive in there? How could we get her out? She was trapped in a place that I couldn't reach, that she had sealed against me. To protect me, making a sacrifice of herself.

On top of this, the horror she had sealed in with her had somehow found a way to tear its way from the Otherworld into my little town, and I knew that it wasn't the first.

For a long time, I'd known that I could see supernatural entities that others could not. But I had spent *years* trying to avoid dealing with this truth about myself, and now the consequences were spilling out. I had lived in a frozen denial that these devouring creatures had slowly but surely been gaining strength. Theodore was dead, and Lucille was lost, and there was a blaze that lived inside me so powerful that it was frightening, and even with this power in my fingertips, I had been useless. I hadn't managed to destroy the horror. I'd only survived because Lucille had been there to save me. And there was that new knowledge, too. Lucille also had a power. But what was the extent of it, and how long had she had it?

All I wanted to do was run back to the guest house and crawl under my bedsheet and never, ever leave. At the same time I knew that the only way I could bring my sister home safely was to immerse myself ever deeper in these strange happenings.

I squeezed my eyes tightly shut and bunched my hands into fists. I didn't want this. Hadn't I been brave enough already? Shouldn't it be enough that I'd stepped out of the guest house and *tried*? I had done the thing I'd dreaded, and it hadn't won me any prizes or brought my sister home.

I unfurled myself and stared out across the bridge, at everyone going about their business, their lives unchanged.

There was only one other place I could think of that might still have an open tear in the world. As soon as I had thought of it, my legs burned with energy once more and I thought perhaps I could go just a bit further. Springing to my feet, I looked at Austin. 'Follow me, or don't,' I said, grimacing with the determination that was turning me into steel. 'But I know where another one of those entrances is, and I can't stop until I get Lucille back out of there.'

His eyes widened, but he nodded sharply. He gripped the charm around his neck. It had protected him, and it seemed it would continue to protect him from the horrors that were leaking out into our world. I would question it later, but right in that moment, all I felt was a desperate yanking towards my sister, whatever the cost.

I ran, my feet pounding on the ground, my breath harsh in my lungs, causing a sharp pain that made my stomach roll over inside me, threatening to empty itself. Although I knew Austin was right behind me, I was barely aware of him, following my hope and panic.

But when we reached the burned-out shop that had once

been the apothecary, the recklessness that had propelled me forward was stilled. Trepidation rippled through my body. I flexed my fingertips. Inside that shop, there had been a tear to the Otherworld and a horror that had killed the kind and interesting man who had helped me to sleep. His wife had been condemned for his murder. Who knew what we might find inside.

Austin stood next to me, appraising the building. He straightened up as if to fortify himself, and his hand bumped against mine. When I turned to look at him, his eyes met my own and I felt a shared understanding pass between us. This was dangerous work. We wouldn't leave the other behind.

I shuddered, remembering the night of the fire. I'd been able to see the smoke from the guest house, billowing up into the sky. I blew away the memory and focused my thoughts instead on my sister.

Pushing open the door, which had been left unlocked in the wake of the investigations that had followed the fire, I stepped inside, with Austin right behind me. It was a charred husk of a room, utterly unrecognizable from how it had been. I looked to the corner of the room, where I'd seen that awful creature, that single, sagging, misplaced eye that had watched me.

My hopes were instantly crushed. Where I'd expected to see another entrance to the Otherworld, there was just another closed seam. It had the silvery look of an old scar. This entrance had already been sewn up and my chance of passing through it to find my sister had gone.

I slammed my fist down on the scorched remains of the counter in frustration, the pent-up fight in me needing a place to erupt. Pain shot through my hand in response, jarring into my wrist and I blinked back tears.

'I can't do this,' I whispered. 'I'm not fearless enough or strong enough or clever enough to work out what is happening. I'm the wrong sister for this. If it were the other way around, Lucille would know what to do.'

But what good would it do to lament and remain paralysed with fear? Bitterness at the unfairness of the situation would only poison me from the inside out. My life would be long and sorrowful if I gave up now, and yet to carry on would draw on a strength beyond the resources I had. Even the fire that had sparked up inside me, this power I didn't understand, depleted me; it might have saved me, but it left me feeling scorched and raw.

My next steps were so uncertain. The tears dried on my cheeks as I contemplated the routes forward.

Before she'd gone, Lucille had been in contact with Aunt Sybil. If I could find more of their correspondence, then I might begin to understand why they had been in touch, and how it was connected to her disappearance. Could I press Mother further about her relationship with her sister and how it had fragmented? She was always so guarded, but could our shared devastation at the absence of Lucille make a difference? I also felt convinced that Dr Binding knew more than he had told me. I noted him as another person to question when I returned to the guest house.

Austin nudged me, and I wiped my eyes. He lifted up his notebook.

What did you see?

His words were simple, but they took my breath away, etched pencil markings in a notebook with the power to halt me, as if I were a pocket watch and he had taken a hammer to my mechanisms. Was that excitement I saw, flickering behind his eyes? I flushed, feeling so vulnerable and exposed. The moment I'd been dreading was upon me.

He tapped the words to emphasize them and I unfroze, taking a great, shuddering breath. And then, for the first time since I'd confided in Lucille, I spoke about the horrors aloud.

'It was like ... seeping darkness spilling out from the shadows, crawling and alive and ... pieced together almost as if it were trying to become human. As if it were trying to build itself a body ... and it looked like Theodore Truman.' I wrapped my arms around myself as though they could hold in the overspill of anguish that threatened to pour out of me. Keep it all inside, push it all down. 'I've seen one of these horrors before. They steal parts of people for themselves. The first horror I saw was different, but no less monstrous. I was thirteen, and that first time was when my hair turned white. I had nightmares – I still have nightmares. And now I fear ...'

I shuddered. My stomach knotted up. But when I looked at Austin, there was a wild delight about him, a sheen of excitement emanating from him. I couldn't understand it.

'Wait a moment.' I recoiled from him and stared. He blinked, confused at my sudden change in demeanour. 'You were frightened ... but you were prepared.' The words tasted sour in my mouth. I gestured to the charm around his neck. He nodded, a wary look in his eyes, as if I'd cornered him.

'You've experienced this before.'

Austin winced, and I knew I was right.

'Why did you come here?' I demanded. 'Tell me the truth.'

All right. I thought the coded message in the pages of the play would lead me to someone who could see the Otherworld, see its monsters.

Austin had come to the Honest Opal looking for *me*. Not in spite of the awful secret that had forced me into becoming so reclusive, but because of it. But why? To research me, like Oliver in the play? Or because he wanted something from me? Why did it feel as though he were still dancing around the edges of a true confession? What was he holding back?

'I don't understand,' I said. 'Where did the playscript even come from? Who wrote it?'

My grandfather.

Austin wrote quickly, his writing becoming messy.

I'm here because of my voice. I followed the clues to find someone with a connection to the Otherworld, because they're the only way to get it back.

There was something utterly desperate in his eyes. He was proving as enigmatic and as much of a puzzle to solve as the playscript. His grandfather had layered his script with references to my home, leading Austin right to me. But what on earth did the playscript have to do with the affliction of Austin's throat, and why would all that lead him to believe that somebody like me could help him? Certainly, I did not have the ability to restore his voice, if that was what he imagined. The palms of my hands felt as though they were cold and sweating, and a whooshing noise filled my ears, blood rushing. I trembled as I pieced it all together.

'You couldn't see that horror in the station, but you could feel something. Was the feeling the same as when you lost your voice? Did one of those things take it?'

Austin nodded fervently.

Words continued to rush out of me like a stream. 'And you came here because you wanted to find somebody who can see the supernatural so they can help you get your voice back from the horror that stole it.'

I hoped that you would be here. I found you.

'Oh, you found me,' I snapped. 'But it's nothing like your playscript. I don't go around ridding people of their hauntings. I hide away from the awful things I see. And now something terrible has happened to my sister, something not of this world. One of those horrors has devoured her sweetheart, and Lucille is lost in that other place.'

He pressed his lips together. I held his stare, ignoring the pleading in his eyes. He'd been avoiding the full story, but it all needed to come to light now.

'I need to know everything, Austin. I need to know everything you know about the Otherworld.'

Then he slowly began writing.

It will take me some time to write it all.

'Then I suppose you had better begin.'

With exhaustion dragging at me, I turned from him and marched back to the guest house, the heartache catching in my chest with every step.

16

My bedroom felt suffocating. From being the place I felt most safe, knowing that even when the nightmares struck my sister would be there with me, stroking my hair and reminding me to breathe, it had transformed into a place tangled in unrest and mystery, my questions growing like ivy over our belongings.

This was the room where Lucille had lied to me. Was there a moment I should have spotted that my sister began acting differently, when she began keeping secrets?

Before she had disappeared, I had never realized how my stability was so built upon her presence. When had that begun? When I had first confided in her about the horrors? Or had I always been this way, grown this way since being small, a seedling searching for her light?

There had been a time when I'd had more confidence, when I'd been braver. But that was a long time ago.

Pity Lucille, then, that she only had me to rely on.

And Austin, who had pinned all his hopes on me.

When my thoughts shifted to Austin and the secrets he had kept from me, my face heated up as though I were sat in front of the kitchen fire. I had known from the start not to trust him, and yet I had become entranced by his mystery, and even allowed myself to think that he had begun to care about me. When he had trailed me from the guest house, and again when he had accompanied me to the station, I had thought it was that he was trying to keep me safe. And maybe that was still true, but it was not for my own benefit. It was because he wanted something from me. When had he realized that I was the one he was looking for? I had a sense he had suspected for some time, perhaps even since the first moment we met, and the encounter at the station was a mere confirmation.

He had dripped the pages of the script like water from a leaky tap, not enough to quench my thirst for understanding. The whole time, he was wearing some sort of powerful, protective jewel around his neck (not unlike the one in the playscript, I considered), and waiting, waiting for me to reveal my most vulnerable truth.

And through all of this, in tiny ways, I had let him wind his way around my mind. And, if I was being truly honest, a part of my heart.

I had been foolish and naïve, and I swore I would not be so again.

It was all connected: the playscript, the guest house, Austin's lost voice . . . and me.

Whatever Austin believed me to be, I was not. Just because I could see supernatural entities did not mean I would be able to get his voice back.

I shuddered.

My own body no longer felt as though it belonged to me; I had become something monstrous and frightening. What I had uncovered was a fire that ran through me, uncontrolled and provoked by the horrors. When I thought about the way the blaze had ripped through me, I felt weak.

It was so desperately awful and unfair. I had given up so much of my freedom to hide away from the fact that I was different, that I could see things that others could not. I had suffered the nightmares and sequestered myself from the world. And what was my reward? The loss of my sister, the evolution of my curse, and pursuit from a young man with selfish motives.

I had not asked for any of this, and yet it had all come for me anyway.

The grief arched up inside me, and I was so tired of keeping it all in. That was what I had always done – suppressed my anger or my sorrow or my fear. I'd been a locked box, so concerned with being measured and thinking, always thinking, of Lucille and Mother.

The air in our room was heavy with Lucille's secrets, like an oppressive sky before a storm.

What would it feel like, for once, to rage?

A growl in my throat turned into a visceral roar. It was so freeing, to let the anger out, a wild animal released from a cage.

If only Lucille had told me about her plans, could I have stopped it all from happening? If I had gone with her to the station, would I have been brave enough? Would I have been filled with fire to defend her and Theodore? Could I have saved him? Could I have kept her close?

It was agonizing.

Aunt Sybil had wanted her to tell me. She'd said as much in her letter, the one that Lucille had never had the chance to read.

I truly believe that this is the work of sisters, and I would urge you to reconsider keeping this from her for much longer.

The work of sisters. But my sister had chosen to cut me out. The meaning behind this might be encapsulated in another letter somewhere, but Lucille must have hidden them all. So I ripped through our room like a tempest unleashed, tearing the sheets from Lucille's bed, upturning the mattress and releasing the chaos of my feelings into the desperate hunt for the letters. Turning my frustrations to the chest in between our beds, I emptied out everything and, finding nothing, yanked Lucille's drawer all the way out and flung it to the ground, where it landed with a crash. The wood splintered, skittered across the floor, and a false bottom dislodged.

I was still.

My breathing took a moment to slow, my eyes wide. Crouching to the ground, I sifted through the broken pieces of wood and uncovered what the false bottom had been hiding. Not the letters from Aunt Sybil, but something more surprising.

A key.

Silver. Glinting. Promising.

I picked up the key and cradled it in the palm of my hand for a moment. Something else that Lucille had been hiding from me.

The key was the same size and weight as the keys we had for each of the rooms, which I kept on a ring and used when I was cleaning. The only place in the guest house I didn't have access to was the cupboard door in the basement, the one that Mother had scolded me for trying to open all those years ago.

I was struck with an intense urge to sneak down to open it immediately, and at the same time guilt ricocheted around my conscience. Whatever was in there, Mother did not want me to know about it.

But Lucille had already discovered the secrets locked behind that door, and if I were going to trace her journey into the place where the horrors came from, then I needed to know everything she knew.

Or, at least, that was what I told myself.

Emily, dear sister,

I am so sorry. How can I convey the depth of my regret? Benedict was a wonderful man. I'm so sorry for my part in your loss. I understand that you hate me for it. I was unprepared for the strength of that monster. It was a mistake to tear the entrance. I will bear the responsibility of your grief for my entire life.

Dr Binding wrote to me. He hopes we will reconcile. Does he know what we did?

I love you. Will you let me come and care for you when the baby arrives? Will you please let me come?

All my love,
Sybil

17

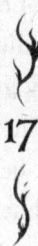

It wasn't a cupboard at all, but a whole hidden room, with a great seam that tore through the wall, though it was mended up. I reached out a hand to touch it. It was raised and uneven, like scar tissue. All my life, this door had been locked.

This was what Mother didn't want me to know.

The Honest Opal had once contained an entrance to the Otherworld.

In the room, there was a wooden box tucked away on a set of shelves that were otherwise empty. There were fingerprints in the dust that covered it. Lucille had been here before me. I opened the box and found a teapot that had been hand-painted with stars, a pair of spectacles and, folded up in the bottom, there was a letter from Sybil to our mother.

I read the short missive, breathless with the sadness of it. I could not imagine Mother's pain to have lost her husband while Lucille was so small, while she was pregnant with me. It was unbearable to even consider.

I thought, perhaps, that the spectacles belonged to Father. One small item of his, the only one left in the house as far as I knew, that Mother couldn't bear to throw away. But what was the meaning of the teapot?

Lucille always said she didn't remember Father, and she was uncharacteristically gentle and restrained on the topic. Mother was tearful whenever she spoke about him, and so we chose not to probe. She'd always told us that he died of an illness, but that had been a lie. Aunt Sybil had torn an entrance to the Otherworld in the basement of our home, and the thing that had escaped had killed my father.

Which meant Mother knew about the Otherworld. She knew about the horrors.

And Lucille had already found this truth, and chosen to keep it a secret from me.

Handling each item with care, I packed the little box back up. I imagined Mother doing the same thing many years ago, her heart broken. Little wonder that she was so protective of Lucille and me, that her anxiety had cast such a long shadow over our lives. Now I had some context for Mother's deep fear of anything happening to either of us. She had faced a violent, unimaginable loss, and her own sister was responsible. Then she'd had to cope with a new baby, and somehow continue to be the perfect hostess for the guests of the Honest Opal, or else risk her livelihood, risk our futures. I ached for her. No wonder she held us so tightly, and was so worn through. There was a guilty sick feeling in my stomach that I had invaded her privacy so fully, but I reminded myself that Lucille had been here first, digging through our past.

I locked up the door to the hidden room once more. What was clear to me was that Aunt Sybil was central to all of this. She was the reason my father was dead, and Lucille had been pursuing contact with her, despite having learned the reason for the estrangement. Sybil had once torn an entrance to the Otherworld in our home, and I had just seen Lucille close one. Perhaps Lucille had been reaching out to Sybil so that she might mentor her in the ways of the dark place.

But if that were the case, then why had Lucille shut me out? That thought had the bitter taste of rejection. Maybe it was because she knew I wasn't strong enough.

Taking a deep breath, I made my way to Mother's room. She'd been feeling weak that day and had gone to rest. When I knocked on the door, she called for me to enter and I found her sitting on a high-backed chair, the one with the seat covering she had hand-stitched. There was a sick, sour scent in the room. Her eyes had a far-off look to them, as though she were lost in thought. I noticed that the pillow on her bed was stained with splotches of blood. I looked away quickly, not wanting her to catch me staring.

I came towards her and stood by her chair, unsure of quite what to say or do.

'Hodge came back yesterday,' I started, and Mother's head snapped up, her expression fearful, as though I were about to land terrible news on her head. 'He said that they're closing the investigation. They believe that Lucille and Theodore have eloped.'

I could tell from the look on her face that Mother did not believe it any more than I had done, even before I had seen the horror that had stolen Theodore's form, and heard Lucille's voice straining through from another world. Since the moment we knew she was gone, our intuitions had told us that the truth was dark and wrong.

'I don't believe it,' I said firmly.

'No,' Mother murmured. 'I think you are right. If they had eloped, she would have told us she was going, or she would have written to us. She would have known we supported them.' It was true that Mother had always been positive about Theodore. She believed that the pair were a good match and no doubt would have been delighted if the romance had progressed in the usual way. Even if it had been an elopement, as long as they had been legitimately wed, Mother would surely have welcomed them back home. My stomach clenched remembering the horror wearing Theodore's face, a face we would never see again. It was a tragedy, and his own parents would never learn the truth of what had happened to their son.

I hesitated. I knew that I needed to press Mother about Aunt Sybil, but the thought of having that conversation made my palms sweat. There was no easy way to go about it. All I could do was ask her directly.

'Did ... did Lucille talk to you about Aunt Sybil before she vanished?'

Her face froze. The only part of her that moved was her chest, rising and falling in a controlled way that I knew was an attempt at soothing herself. In the silence, my mind raced, and I wished I could peer inside Mother's head and see how her own thoughts jostled. It felt like an eternity before she spoke, and when she finally did, her voice was soft.

'Yes.'

I waited for more, but Mother was not forthcoming. She pressed her lips together and fixed me with a stare.

'A letter came for Lucille,' I said. 'From Aunt Sybil.'

'I see,' Mother said. Her hand twitched into a fist, the only sign of the tension that I knew would be wreaking havoc inside her. 'Well, it was some time ago your sister mentioned her. I advised her to stay well away.'

I cleared my throat. 'The letter seems to suggest that Lucille was planning to go to visit her.'

'And you think that's where she's gone?' Mother spoke as though I was merely confirming a conclusion she'd already reached. So this was why she'd been so adamant that Lucille was still alive, why she'd been able to reach a grim sort of acceptance so much faster than I'd been able to understand.

But I didn't know how to reply, because I knew that Lucille hadn't made it to Sybil. She was trapped in the Otherworld. I wanted to talk to Mother openly about everything, but the words dissolved on my tongue before I could even begin to form them. If I began to spill it all out – the Otherworld, the horrors and the fact I had uncovered the greatest tragedy of Mother's life, the one she had hidden for so many years – I knew I risked rupturing carefully sewn wounds.

'I'm not sure exactly where she is,' I said in the end, 'but I think I need to find Sybil.'

'No,' Mother snapped, lifting her hand like a barrier against me. 'Don't you even think about it.'

'If you would just tell me –' I tried again, hoping against hope that she would finally admit the truth to me, so that I could confess my own.

'If your sister has decided to ignore my advice and knock on a door that I insisted she should keep firmly closed, then I have to accept that,' Mother said, her voice shaking. 'But Alice, I am begging you, don't try to follow her.' I started to wonder if Aunt Sybil was somebody to be frightened of. She was powerful enough to tear entrances into the Otherworld. She was responsible for the destruction of my family.

Although my relationship with my mother was not precisely an easy one, it had never been in my nature to challenge her too directly on anything, and now it was harder than ever. I'd always wanted to be amenable, compensating for Lucille's dramatic explosiveness, and now ... Well, I didn't want to cause Mother any more pain.

Mother closed her eyes and took a big, deep breath, letting it out in a noisy stream through pursed lips. When her eyelids batted open, she looked stricken. 'I need you to trust me when I tell you that I have *always* been trying to keep you and your sister safe.'

And I did trust that was all she had wanted. The haunted look on her face had a depth of emotion behind it that I would never have understood without knowing the truth about how my father died. But still, she was impossible, an impenetrable barricade. I could only imagine how that would have incensed Lucille when they'd had their own version of this conversation. But Lucille had not been deterred. Aunt Sybil had drawn her in regardless of Mother's cautions.

And now it was my turn. I backed away from Mother.

'Where are you going, Alice?' she asked.

'Out.'

If Mother wouldn't answer my questions, I'd have to find someone who would.

18

The wind coming in from the sea whipped around me the moment I stepped out of the door. Venturing outside still came with a sensation of dread that threatened to pin me to the walls of the guest house, but the only way out of this nightmare was to press through the fear. Understanding that was one thing I could thank Austin for.

Dr Binding was taking a rest on a bench outside the guest house, looking out towards the abbey. Silver sniffed around on a nearby patch of grass, his coat gleaming in the afternoon light.

I watched Dr Binding for a moment before he spotted me. He had seemed genuine in his fear for Lucille the night she'd gone missing, and had joined the search. But he had been so reticent to speak about her, and I'd suspected from the start that there was something that he wasn't telling me. He'd known our family for so long, since before Mother and Sybil were even born, and the letter suggested he'd tried to help them reconcile. What I didn't know was how much he'd seen of the disintegration of our family. These were the questions I thought Lucille might have had for him too.

'Miss Everglass, my dear!' Dr Binding greeted me. He couldn't hide his shock at seeing me out of the house. 'What are you doing out here?'

'I've spent long enough hiding. And I'm tired of everyone trying to protect me and keeping secrets from me,' I said with a firmness that was new and refreshing to use.

He looked weary then, his usual optimism draining out of him. 'I see. And you've come to press me for answers, I suppose.'

I gave him an apologetic smile. 'I'm afraid you are correct. You spoke to Lucille the morning before she disappeared and I think you might have been the last one to do so.'

He nodded slowly, his gaze heading out over towards the abbey. 'Yes,' Dr Binding confirmed. He whistled to call Silver back from where he had begun to wander a little too far.

'And she spoke to you about Aunt Sybil.' It was a guess, and a bold one. I lifted my chin in a determined sort of way and stared at him until he looked at me.

Dr Binding raised an eyebrow. 'She did.' He reached down to run his hand over Silver's soft, dappled coat. The little dog flopped down on to his belly next to his master, resting his head on Dr Binding's foot.

'And I think she confronted you about how much you really know about our family. So what did you tell her?'

'You are tracing her footsteps quite efficiently.' He hesitated, and I could see the internal debate. 'I pause, not because I want to obfuscate or cause you difficulty in your search for your sister. I pause because I made her a promise.'

'To keep it a secret that she was in touch with Aunt Sybil?'

'That I would try to protect you from the truth.'

I scoffed. 'Why?' And even though I was desperately concerned for her, and missing her so terribly, a familiar irritation lifted its head, woken from slumber. Why did she think she could puppeteer my life like that? Any truths about our family history belonged to both of us equally, and it was not her job to determine my access to it.

'You must understand that, as a doctor, I take the oaths I make to others very seriously. I am not one to break my word.'

'I do understand,' I said, 'but *you* must understand this in return. I will not stop, with or without your assistance.' I stamped my foot, meaning to assert my determination, although it possibly made me appear more like a petulant child.

'I feared you might say that.' Dr Binding ran his fingers over his forehead, ironing out the tension. 'And in that case, if you are going to barrel into it all anyway, then perhaps the best way I can truly protect you is to inform you. It is quite the ethical quandary.'

'I am not investigating this to fulfil some thirst for knowledge. This is about Lucille. About bringing her home, safe from harm.'

Dr Binding nodded slowly. 'You speak as passionately about her as she did about you.'

'About me?' I wrinkled my nose in confusion.

'Yes.' His eyes crinkled at the edges as he looked at me. 'Your sister wasn't searching for knowledge either. She was trying to help you.'

Unease shifted inside me. 'What do you mean?'

Dr Binding lowered his voice and spoke so gently and with such kindness that it took my breath away. 'She wanted you to be free from your hauntings. That was what was driving her. But I am afraid I don't think that can ever be the case.' A lightning strike of shock impaled me. Lucille had told him about the horrors? About the things I could see. Dr Binding, rational, sensible Dr Binding, was aware of my supernatural curse. My mouth hung open a little as I floundered for words.

'She – she told you?' I felt crushed by the betrayal of it. Lucille had shared my secret while guarding her own.

'Perhaps you are concerned that your sister has broken your trust,' he said. 'I must assure you, she only confirmed something that I'm afraid had already become apparent to those who know the signs.'

'The signs?'

Dr Binding continued. 'You and your sister, you have been born to a different sort of life. One that your mother has tried to shield you from, and I'm afraid in her refusal to acknowledge what you both are, she has caused a lot of pain. But she behaves this way because she is fearful for you.'

'I don't understand.'

Dr Binding patted the place on the bench next to him and I sank on to it. We both looked out across the beautiful brokenness of the abbey.

'I have told this out of order,' he said, a touch of self-deprecation in his tone. 'I will start from *my* start ... Although you must understand, this all began over fifty years ago now, when I was a young man. I just ask that you have some patience with me.'

'Go on,' I said, knowing that this was the moment where my understanding of everything was about to shift forever. I was going to learn the truth that had been hidden from me for my entire life.

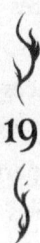

19

'It began at university, when I was just twenty years old,' Dr Binding said. 'That was where I first met Dorian.'

It was not a name I recognized. Dr Binding went on, describing Dorian as a scholar with an insatiable appetite for storytelling that distracted him. He came from a wealthy family and it was expected that Dorian would one day manage his father's properties, keep the accounts and marry well, and yet he was always to be found reading or at the theatre, endlessly absorbing stories.

The two became firm friends, and Dr Binding learned that Dorian had a preoccupation with ghost stories and tales of the supernatural. These notions were a source of fascination to the both of them – the young doctor who was desperate to rationalize it and have it all make sense, and the young scholar who believed so fervently that this was a world filled with magic. And not just any magic, but a sinister magic that lurked in shadows, with vicious teeth.

When Dr Binding began to talk of such magic, my stomach flipped in recognition.

Together, Dr Binding and Dorian attended séances, visited mediums and explored places reported to be haunted or troubled by folkloric entities. Monsters, ghosts, demons. While some of these experiences were unnerving and strange, Dr Binding and Dorian only discovered tricks employed by charlatans to make people part with their money. Hidden wires and knocking on tables and homemade monstrous footprints of ectoplasm – all designed to take advantage of people's wish to believe in something.

Dorian almost gave up hope of uncovering anything real. Dr Binding certainly encouraged him to stop.

But instead, Dorian changed his angle. He began conducting interviews with people who believed they had experienced the supernatural. And through those multitudes of interviews, he eventually heard tales of a man who was the real thing, who could reach to a world beyond our own. Not that he could speak to loved ones who had passed; no, he never claimed that. But if you were troubled by strange or frightening disturbances, if you felt *haunted* by a ghoulish presence, then this man was the one who could banish the darkness for you.

I listened intently to Dr Binding, as though he were telling me a bedtime story, a sinister one, like all the dark fairy tales. And then he said something that made my blood run cold.

'All the encounters said this man wore an opal at his throat, and could be sought out in the town with the whalebones.'

'Here,' I murmured. 'Whitby.'

The man with the opal. Dr Binding's story was echoed in the pages of the script that Austin had been sharing with me, the one that his grandfather had written. I was sure now that the script was a reflection of these memories from Dr Binding's youth. And the opal was the one that Austin wore now. I'd seen it, protecting him from the horror.

'Yes, here,' Dr Binding said. 'Although his location was a rumour, the stories said that if you truly needed him, you only had to put a whisper out into the world and he would find you. Of course, Dorian wanted to speak with this man. Study him. And I'll admit, after reading several of Dorian's interview transcripts mentioning him, I was curious, too. So Dorian put out whispers of a false haunting, and the man with the opal arrived at his door.'

I shivered. Dorian was Oliver from the play. I was sure of it. Their stories seemed to mirror each other precisely. 'A false haunting?'

'Dorian told a tale, although you would be right to call it a lie. He stole elements from a young woman he knew whose family had been helped by the man with the opal when they were terrorized by an unsettling presence. In the end, Dorian married her, but that was much later.'

Whoever this real young woman was, she had become 'Abigail Darkwing', then. I felt sure that the writer of the play – Austin's grandfather, I reminded myself – would have changed her name, too. It was a stark reminder that I hadn't been reading about fictional characters that purely existed for actors to inhabit, to slip inside their skins; they were real people. Austin's grandfather had captured their story in his playscript; well, hadn't Austin warned me from the start that it was based on a true story? I wondered how Austin's grandfather had first come to hear the tale and pondered at how our families' lives seemed so intertwined.

'After that first meeting, the man with the opal promised to return and help, and Dorian invited me to the apartment to see what unfolded. The man with the opal insisted that we were not to be anywhere near the room while he worked, for our own safety. But Dorian and I spied.' He sounded ashamed at the memory of it. 'He was accompanied by two women.'

'Sisters,' I murmured.

'Yes – sisters. One with hair as white as yours, my dear, and back then she wasn't much older than you are now.'

'Oh.' I had thought it was something strange and exceptional about me. But now an understanding was dawning on me about how the playscript connected to me and my family.

Dr Binding continued. 'The sisters were the ones with the power. The man with the opal was married to one of the sisters and he had no powers at all, as it turned out. His act was merely a layer of protection. And so, that was how I met your grandparents.' His eyes turned misty.

There was a lump in my throat. My grandparents had died before I was born. Mother barely talked about them – another grief among many. I'd been reading their story, and had not even known.

Dr Binding looked at me, concerned. 'I'm sorry, Alice. I appreciate this is a great deal of new information to learn about your family, and its history. But you said you wanted answers . . .'

I nodded firmly. 'I did. I do. Please go on, Dr Binding.'

'As you wish. Well, then. The man with the opal, your grandfather Tom, first met the sisters when they banished a ghoul that had plagued the public house where he worked. And he fell in love with and married Julia, the sister who was gifted with healing and the ability to mend, knitting together broken things, including the wounds of her sister and tears in the fabric of the world that let the demons through.'

Like Lucille.

'Her sister, Tessa, had the power to destroy the demons breaking through from the Otherworld, the ones that sought to devour.'

Like me.

A pattern, repeating across time.

My cheeks were wet with tears, and I pushed them away with the palm of my hand.

'I don't want to upset you,' Dr Binding said. Now that I was crying openly, he was growing hesitant again. 'Do you want me to continue?'

'You have to,' I said. 'I need to know it all. I should have known this all along, and then I wouldn't have felt so alone.'

His eyes crinkled as if he understood, as if he regretted his part in my not knowing.

'As I say, your grandfather Tom was a shield for Julia and Tessa. The sisters knew how well their abilities invited sinister intentions and accusations of madness or of being dangerous. At Julia's insistence, Tom wore the opal, imbued with protection, which had been in the sisters' family for generations. And he presented a front to the world that kept the identities of the sisters hidden, but still allowed them to fulfil their important purpose.'

'Destroying the monsters from the Otherworld and closing the entrances to our world,' I said, and as I spoke the words, I felt inside my chest a sense of rightness about it, a sense of destiny and purpose that I'd never felt before. This was what I had been made to do, I realized. It was an oddly comforting feeling, in among the dread and terror of what surely lay ahead.

'Exactly,' Dr Binding confirmed. 'When Dorian and I revealed ourselves from our hiding place, Tom was furious. But Dorian was eager to tell them all that he meant no harm, that he would keep their secrets. Your grandfather already owned the guest house here in Whitby, but Dorian offered to provide them with funding, and he provided them with accommodation in a townhouse for regular visits to London. London, which was rife with hauntings, humming with supernatural activity. In return, he expected to be able to see their work in action, to learn and to understand what was in the Otherworld. As to why he wanted to know what was in there ... Truly, Alice, I don't know. I still don't feel that I understand what was going through his mind. For me, I wondered whether

Julia's extraordinary mending power could be channelled into medicine. We experimented with it, but it seemed her healing was limited to damage caused by the Otherworld, rather than human afflictions.'

Dr Binding shared with me that what formed between them all was like a family of its own. Him, Dorian, my grandfather, my grandmother and her sister. They pushed each other, they championed each other, they raged at each other, they saved each other. They destroyed monsters and they sealed entrances to the Otherworld, and all the time Dorian was gathering information on it all. But then Dorian began to push for more. He began encouraging more dangerous experiments, like trying to create their own entrances to the Otherworld. And when this was accomplished, he wanted them all to go *into* the Otherworld together. He claimed what he needed to know could only be found within its realm. The sisters refused – but he pressed and wheedled.

My grandparents began to retreat from Dorian. Their appetite for the danger of their work had dissipated. What had been a close friendship began to sour. And when my grandmother fell pregnant, the expectant couple cast their adventures aside, returning to the Whitby guest house. And where one sister went, the other went too.

Dorian was left feeling completely rejected and furiously powerless. His access to the supernatural had been rescinded, and whatever plans he had been forming in regards to the Otherworld were extinguished. Instead he wrote papers and spoke in academic circles about some of what he'd seen. It seemed he'd meant to spite my family, hoping if he revealed enough of their secrets then it would force them back into being amenable to him.

It did not work. The sisters were resolute.

By this time my grandparents had two little girls, my mother and Sybil, and my grandmother knew what awaited her daughters when they grew up and came into their powers. Having seen her own mother killed by a demon when she was young, she wanted her girls to experience a happy, normal childhood. And when the day arrived that the girls' powers awakened, they would then be trained.

The plan backfired on Dorian in other ways, too. With no evidence about the sisters and their powers, Dorian became a laughing stock, disgraced and discredited. His approaches to the scientific community were mocked and he was advised to focus on fiction, with patronizing scoffs.

'I felt my loyalties pulled in two directions,' Dr Binding admitted. 'I didn't want to see my oldest friend embarrassed, and yet I understood that your grandparents wanted to protect their girls. There was time enough for them to be exposed to the darkness of the Otherworld. In the end, I was a coward. I simply retreated from the conflict. I put all of them out of my head for years. So many years passed. I got married, embarked on a happy, separate life.' He smiled, before a dark cloud passed over his face again. 'But sometimes I would get a creeping sensation, as though I were being watched. And then I'd remember about the Otherworld, about those lurking things I could not see, and I'd wonder if something was close by. I also followed a fictional serial that Dorian was publishing in a newspaper, and every so often I'd recognize a turn of phrase, or a particular look in a character, and see one of us. I knew, too, that the fierceness in Dorian's heart would not have died, no matter how many years passed.'

Something began to grow clear to me, in a horrid, creeping way. The playscript Austin was so obsessed with, that was so deeply entwined in the history of my family, was surely written by Dorian. Dorian, who had turned to fiction when the scientific community rejected him. Hiding breadcrumbs of his knowledge about my family in his work for years. And when my family had decided to remove themselves from him, the hints in the play leading to the Honest Opal became a threat. One that said: 'I could reveal everything about you in a moment.' It said: 'I could publish your names and where you live.'

Even so, his clues had been more than sufficient to lead Austin right to our door.

And, of course, if it were Dorian who had written the playscript ...

Then that meant he was Austin's grandfather.

Dorian was Austin's grandfather.

The one who had gone missing six months ago, just like Lucille had disappeared now.

And another thought crashed unwelcome into my mind: perhaps Austin had known all of this, all along. He knew, and had been keeping it from me. Just like Lucille.

The question circled my mind like a slowly descending seagull on the pier, ready with its eager eyes and sharp beak.

How could I trust Austin at all?

My hands twisted in my lap. I fixed Dr Binding with a hard stare. 'You are correct: this is an awful lot of information to hear in one sitting. However, I have just one more question for you. If you completely distanced yourself from them all, then how is it that you're here? You have been visiting us for years. What brought you back?'

Dr Binding raised his eyebrows and cleared his throat. 'I received a letter from your grandfather, imploring me to come quickly . . .' He trailed off and cast his gaze back to the abbey. He shook his head. I wondered what horrors were playing out in his mind. The wild look in his eyes reminded me of a spooked horse. 'So I came back. I found that the girls had indeed come into their powers – Sybil to fire and destruction, your mother to light and healing. They were a handful of years younger than you and Lucille are now.' That age aligned roughly with the time I'd first started to see the horrors too.

'As they had grown stronger, as they had learned how to wield their powers and began to fight alongside each other, the sisters of the generation before had been diminished to a shadow of their former selves, skeletal and weak. Julia's healing was powerless in the face of the deterioration. And Tom begged me to do something, anything, to save her, and Tessa too. But the deterioration was irrevocable. And this had all happened before, for too many generations to count. The strength of the sisters transferring on . . .'

I felt sick. 'And now it's happening again. Lucille and I, we're stealing the power away from Mother and Sybil. That's why Mother is so ill.'

Dr Binding bit his lip. 'I think so, yes. Both Julia and Tessa aged in an accelerated fashion, like nothing I'd ever seen before then, like no illness of this world. And then they died. And took your grandfather with them, dead of a broken heart. And until the birth of your sister, your mother and Sybil took up their roles and fought alongside each other.'

I was deeply shaken by all that I had heard, but it had also given me knowledge, clarity and, above all, a sense of purpose. I couldn't stop what was happening to us all, so I had to make sure that this power that was racing through me, begging to be set free, was not wasted. The time had come to *use* it.

20

When I returned inside the Honest Opal, I was simmering with my new knowledge. Mother had always known what we would become, and had done nothing to warn us. Where she and Sybil had been trained as their powers came to life, Mother had chosen to hide the truth, only for my powers to emerge in secret, in isolation.

I already knew that when I confronted her, she would tell me that she had been trying to protect me, but I wasn't sure that I could forgive her for that. Some fundamental connection between us had been frayed – in her denial, in her protection of me, she had done untold damage. All this time, when I had been so frightened, she could have explained to me that this was to be expected. When she saw my hair turn white with fear, heard me screaming in the night, surely she must have known what was happening, and instead of inducting me, she bought me sleeping remedies. When I thought about this fact, the anger shocked me, my blood seeming to heat in my veins, my breathing jagged.

I had felt so alone in my strangeness, in my terror, and all this time, Aunt Sybil had been the same as me. What Lucille could do, the gift she shared with our mother, was something precious, not like the horrible power that flowed out of me. That thought gave me an unpleasant twinge of envy.

They could mend.

But I had been made for destruction.

My mother was going to die because of me. She was very sick, and growing sicker, and she was going to die, sooner than she should have to, because of this power that had betrayed her.

I wondered whether my mother's fear of mortality was part of the reason she had kept our powers secret. Perhaps it had been because she was frightened of the way that her body would be sickened by the loss of her own power. Or because she was frightened for my sister and me, having already lost Father and knowing the dangers of the Otherworld, having already seen her own mother deteriorate and die. One thing was clear to me. Mother had suffered unimaginable loss, and it had informed *everything* after. Seen through that lens, it was hard to hold on to my anger, particularly with the knowledge that my time with her would be so cruelly cut short. My anger dissipated like the ink on a letter left in the rain, the shape of the words running into obscurity.

And now ... at least now I knew what sort of family I had been born into. I was born to see the things I could see, and it had a purpose. This was the information that Lucille had been quietly gathering, too, and this was why Aunt Sybil had implored Lucille to tell me the truth in her letter, because this work was made for both of us. Me to destroy and her to mend. A queasy jealousy rippled through me again.

What was happening to me felt monstrous, while Lucille got the ability that was beautiful, that was healing.

When had she realized that her powers were erupting, too?

Dr Binding told me she had been cagey when he had asked her, that she didn't want to talk about herself, and that her intentions, always, were about me. All she wanted was to keep me safe, and that meant finding out as much as possible about what my being haunted by sightings of the horrors meant.

What was it about me that made Mother and Lucille feel that they had to hide the truth from me to keep me safe? Was I truly so fragile that I might shatter into pieces? Were my loved ones merely trying to respect what they thought I would wish, living in fear and denial, or did they just believe me wholly unsuitable for the destiny that I was being called to?

But I had learned the truth, and I was still standing, fire and brimstone alive inside me. The idea that I was some delicate thing that needed to be guarded and protected made me want to revolt against it.

And now that I had the truth, I had to choose: suppress the destiny I had been thrust into, or follow Lucille and fall headlong into this terrifying new reality.

Before Lucille's disappearance, I would have embraced cowardice. But knowing that she was sealed away in the Otherworld . . . Well, I would do anything to get her back.

When I went to Mother's bedroom at last, to air all the unspoken truths between us, what I found horrified me.

Mother was sprawled across the floor, a dark, stinking substance leaking from her lips, eyes closed, a picture of death.

Alice,

I fear I have gone about this all the wrong way. And yet how do you begin a thing like this? How do you tell someone: I've been searching for you, oh please, I'm begging you, help me, I think you are my only hope?

You surmised it correctly – my voice was stolen by one of those horrors. I could not see it, only sense it. A dread-filling presence that tightened itself around my neck, stealing my voice away. And that's why I came here, searching for you.

You know it was my grandfather who encouraged me in my love of the theatre. Well, he is probably the person I have to thank for who I have become today, for better or worse. Since he went missing, my family do not talk about him. He was already a widower, so my father has taken over his estate fully, as though Grandfather is dead. I suppose he must be, hard as it is to accept. He is the only person I have ever felt understood me.

My grandfather had an obsession throughout his life with telling stories. Haunting fireside tales that would chill your bones. He told me stories about the Otherworld, a place where the supernatural resides, where the impossible is possible, and about places where the Otherworld collides with our world, and its entities push through. He told me stories of creatures that we cannot see, but sense. Creatures that want to devour us. This is what he told me:

The horrors gain strength when things in our world are broken.

A bone. A promise. A heart.

He warned me, firmly, never to give the creatures a chance, never to break something and to mend any such unlucky thing with haste. Now I know why he was so intense. But my grandfather told his tales of the Otherworld in such a way that I could never be certain if it was all a performance, a version of himself that he had crafted because it fit with his eccentric literary reputation ... So I always took them for fiction.

Is it enough to tell you that I broke a promise? That was my mistake.

My grandfather's disappearance made me rethink a lot of things. I decided to pursue my acting dreams. I worked with my father for a short time, assisting him with managing the family wealth. But the theatre was calling to me, and so I decided to try and make my acting dreams a reality. I secured my first role and got lodgings of my own. My father loathed this, just as he had always loathed my grandfather's obsession with the supernatural and how it had been a shadow over our family's reputation. He cut me off financially. My parents have always found me a source of bafflement due to my sincerest refusal to embark on any profession they would determine respectable or useful. Although my grandfather's wealth should relieve my father of any need to work, he prefers to keep his mind busy, prefers to continue to accumulate. He works as an accountant, and he wanted the same for me. After being cut off, I had to stretch out what was left of the allowance I used to receive from him, and my wages from the theatre.

And here I am rambling, perhaps assuming too much that you care about anything more than that which has caused our paths to cross. My apologies, Alice. I confess it is a relief to tell more of my life and the person that I am and why, not just the circumstances that have brought me to your door. I want you to know me – please believe me on that, if nothing else.

When I broke my promise, an entrance to the Otherworld must have torn open in my dressing room at the theatre. Alice, I can't see what you can see. I have no gifts of the supernatural sort. I did not see the demon from the Otherworld that stole my voice. But I felt it. I felt it even before it had the strength to take something from me. The corner of the room had an icy chill about it that stole my breath, and now I think the creature there was sucking in every breath I took, so it could grow stronger.

But I felt certain that the answers would lie in my grandfather's research. As a much younger man, he had studied at university, inherited property, attempted to be a proper gentleman, as was expected of him. But he was obsessed with investigating the supernatural.

I pored over my grandfather's old notes from that time. My father had wanted to throw them out, but I had salvaged them, kept them in my lodgings. Grandfather had kept transcripts of interviews, odd notes as if to nudge his memory, and drafts of his stories, too. You might have read them: they were serialized. Gruesome little tales. I wonder now how many of them were true. He was always fond of embellishment, so it's difficult to tell.

Among these documents was a recent ticket for a jewellers, and when I went to collect the piece it was for, I was given the opal necklace you have seen me wearing. The jeweller was a very good friend of my grandfather's. He said that my grandfather was agitated and distressed when he had brought the necklace in. It was broken, the setting at risk of losing the opal, and my grandfather had requested that it be mended with the utmost urgency.

He gave the necklace to me. It is unnaturally heavy, and did not fit neatly underneath my costume at the theatre, so I kept it tucked in my coat pocket, a way to feel as though my grandfather was near.

I recognized the gemstone from the pages of the script, but I didn't know what it meant.

As I continued to work through my grandfather's documents, I came across a story that chilled me, one that he had never told me. It seemed more like a stream of consciousness, an entry in a private journal, not something he was working up for publication.

And certain details made me believe that this story, at least, was true.

As a boy, my grandfather was climbing trees in a forest near the family's country estate. He fell and broke his arm. And then he felt hot breath on the back of his neck. A seam to the Otherworld must have opened, something monstrous emerging. He couldn't see it, but he could feel it, and knew it wanted to swallow him up.

So he ran.

It was only later he learned that his little sister had followed him out to the forest. That she was nowhere to be found.

A fruitless search for a kidnapper exhausted his devastated parents – this was the part I knew to be true.

He never slept a full night after that. He always wondered what happened to his sister. Was she devoured by the monster? Stolen away? Was it his fault that she was gone? Or was the whole incident entirely in his head? I believe this was how his obsession with the supernatural started. I could tell from the transcripts that much of his investigations were met with disappointment; many people were willing to take his money and made promises that remained unfulfilled. It was the hope that was the most painful, I imagine. The idea that he might be able to find his sister.

But none of this explained the phenomenon in my dressing room at the theatre. As time passed, the disconcerting feeling in the room only grew stronger.

I only had to enter it and my brow would bead with sweat, the cold from the corner making all the hairs along my arms stand upright. My heart would clench inside my chest and I would be struck with the urge to run away . . . even as I was fulfilling my life's dream. Though I spent as little time in there as possible, often choosing to wait in the wings and watch the action on the stage instead, it was impossible not to have to return there for my costume change. Perhaps you remember my saying that I was playing the part of Benvolio. I would change costume for the beginning of Act 3, the scene being the tragedy of the brawl that ends with Mercutio and Tybalt dead, and Romeo banished. And while I changed, I ran my lines.

'I pray thee, good Mercutio, let's retire. The day is hot, the Capels are abroad. And if we meet we shall not 'scape a brawl.'

And I tried to ignore the fact that I felt I could almost catch a glimpse of some evil entity lurking in the corner of the room, a malevolent presence. I continued repeating my lines, muttering them under my breath.

'For now, these hot days, is the mad blood stirring.'

And as if my voice were something that it wanted to eat, I felt the being move closer, being braver.

And then it clenched around my throat.

Two things happened simultaneously. An extreme pain in my throat, a slicing sharpness that hurts to even conjure in my mind. And the pocket of my coat began to glow. I flailed for my coat, thrusting my hand into the pocket and pulling out the gem that had belonged to my grandfather. The moment it was in my hand, the light surged around me and the entity released its grip on me. I felt it shrink away and I slipped the chain around my neck, filled with a sense of well-being and safety. I was consumed by its glow. Protected.

But I didn't have time to think about what I'd just experienced for long. I was due on stage, even as my hands were trembling with fear. There was an audience waiting.

That's how I discovered the damage that had been done. I could not speak a word of my lines. And when I fled from the stage, tears of embarrassment stinging my eyes, and returned to my dressing room,

I heard a voice, my voice, whispering my lines in the corner.

I haven't been back since.

Knowing the real power of the opal made me think there was more to the playscript than I'd gathered on my first read. The playscript is incomplete. Or, at least, if there are more pages, I do not have them. I am working with a limited set of information here. But there was enough for me start believing that I needed to find the sisters within, if I were to hold any chance of being reunited with my voice.

Now you see why I have come to find you. And, Alice – whatever it takes to bring Lucille home safely to you, know this: you have me by your side.

Yours, Austin

21

Scooping Mother up into my arms, I was struck by how light she felt. Before she got sick, she'd always been so strong. The movement of her chest was slight but definite... She was still alive. Her eyes fluttered like moth wings as I laid her on the bed. Delicately, I wiped her mouth, the black substance thick and sticky and emitting a horrid rotting smell.

My heart was in my throat, the shock of seeing her sprawled on the floor tearing through me. I had thought her dead at first glance, and to know she was still alive did not alleviate the horror of having believed her gone, even for only a moment.

I watched her, taking in the hollows under her eyes, the way her lips had thinned, the way her skin hung over her features more loosely now. It was as if she had aged decades in the space of days.

Because of Lucille and me.

We were both using our powers and growing stronger. More than ever, it felt like a curse rather than a gift.

Resting my head against Mother's chest, I listened to the

steady beat of her heart. There was a strength in it still, at least – a determination.

'Hold on,' I told her, as I left with the intention of hunting down Dr Binding. But when I stepped out on to the landing, Austin opened his door at the same time. His hair danced around his temples as though he had been running his fingers through it. He clutched a sheaf of papers, proffered them with a nervous bite of his lip. I could picture him, hunched over the desk in his room, scrawling away. I accepted the letter with a murmured 'Thank you,' and put it straight into my pocket. Then I left him standing there in a sort of hurt confusion. Perhaps he had imagined that I might read it right away, in front of him so that he could watch my reaction.

But I had more immediate concerns.

I rushed to knock on Dr Binding's door, and as I garbled out an explanation of how I had found Mother, his brow furrowed.

'This is not good,' he said, not sparing my feelings. 'This is a drastic acceleration.'

We hurried to the room, Dr Binding bringing along the leather satchel he carried his implements in. He performed an examination of Mother and sighed. 'There is very little I can do,' he said. 'This I know from experience. Unfortunately my medicines will have no effect on her, but I can try to make her comfortable.'

'How ... how long does she have?' I asked, my voice a whimper.

'I could not say.'

I bit my lip. 'It's connected to Lucille and I using our powers, isn't it?'

Dr Binding nodded. 'It's possible. When Sybil and your mother began, they were very sparing with it. They wanted to learn as much as they could from your grandmother and her sister, so they took things a little slower.'

'But that's not fair!' The words exploded out of me. 'How could Lucille and I have known? They were taught! They were guided! They didn't have to figure it all out for themselves, fighting against secrecy!'

Dr Binding looked at me sympathetically, which was almost worse than if he had admonished me for my outburst. 'I know,' he said, in a quiet voice. He looked at Mother. 'But she was so certain that she was keeping you and your sister safe. She would not listen to me, not a jot. She has continued to close entrances and quietly heal you for years, though.'

Close entrances. No doubt it was Mother who had sealed up the alleyway where I'd seen that first horror, and the one in the apothecary, too. But healing me? I wasn't ill. I asked Dr Binding what he meant.

'Your nightmares.'

I pressed my lips together and clenched my eyes shut, trying to fight the tidal wave of sorrow.

'Do you think Sybil is as sick as this?' I asked, my eyes fixing on Mother's fingernails, the edges of which were crusted with blood.

Dr Binding opened up his palms, gesturing that he did not know. 'I said all this to your grandfather, many years ago. These ailments are so beyond my understanding of the human body. It is impossible for me to make predictions or say with any certainty how events will unfold. All I can say is that I fear both of them are borrowing time.'

I nodded, a bitter lump of understanding in the pit of my stomach. Ultimately, I had a choice. Stay with my mother as she sickened, which was what my heart wanted to do. Memories of her caring for me as a child resurfaced – the way she held me in her lap, humming a soothing tune and gently brushing sweat-stuck hair away from my forehead as a fever rampaged through me. There was love in every touch.

The other choice tugged at me, even as I swelled with grief and guilt at the notion of leaving Mother. But she was not the only one who would be sick. This affliction would be affecting Sybil too, I felt sure, and I had no way of knowing how deeply she was succumbing. If she died, then I would have nobody to teach me about the fire inside me. And this fire was the only weapon I had to bring my sister home.

'If she wakes and is in any pain, there is a remedy I can prepare for her,' he said, his eyes crinkling and compassionate. He was used to this. He had probably counselled many daughters through the loss of a parent. I blinked back tears.

When Dr Binding had excused himself, I climbed up on the bed next to Mother, propping myself up with pillows. I would stay with her for the night so that I could watch if she worsened, or be here if she roused of her own accord. If she needed water, I would be here. If her brow began to bead, I would mop it. And if she retched up more of the black sickness, I would be there to clean her.

And as I waited to see if she would rouse, there was something else I had to do.

By lamplight, I read Austin's letter. Here he was opened up on these pages, as though I'd taken a weapon to his head and spilled out the contents. My imagination brought his voice to life, the way his face would look if he were speaking the words to me.

For all my distrust of him, the contents of this letter revealed a vulnerability that I had not expected. Perhaps he had kept these truths from me, but he had not lied to me. Not once. Given the wealth of his family, no wonder he had such a valuable coat; that he had been cut off financially explained why he had not paid for his room in full.

The image of the wealthy young man in fancy tailored suits shrank next to the one of the actor and his passionate, creative storyteller soul.

It was his grandfather who was the one who had encouraged this side of him. It was strange to hear the other side of the story about Dorian. Dr Binding's version of events painted him as a difficult and selfish man who had domineered over his friends and sought to use their gifts to his own ends. But Austin's story revealed more – that Dorian was, in his heart, still a traumatized young boy who had lost his sister in horrifying circumstances. No doubt this experience was at the core of why he had been pressuring my grandparents to go into the Otherworld.

Maybe he hoped to find his lost sister. Putting the pieces together made for a nuanced and conflicting picture. A man who was broken by the Otherworld.

As is often the way, there are many truths.

The end of the letter made my pulse quicken. *You have me by your side.* It was quite the statement, and it dizzied me. The road ahead was haunted with challenge; I knew that, and the notion that I did not have to travel it alone warmed me, an internal glow that promised to light the way.

And yet ...

I wanted to trust Austin, I did. But I couldn't quite allow myself to believe that he intended to stand by my side because he wanted to help me find Lucille. No, the map he was following was the one to get his voice back. I was a route to get what he wanted, and I would be foolish to forget that.

Beside me, Mother's breath was light and peaceful. It would be easy to imagine she was only resting, not being scourged by a curse that was sapping her energy, siphoning it to us. Like Isobel, who bore the weight of her family's curse, and the Otherworld spectre that had attached itself to them, now I bore the curse of mine.

I squeezed my eyes shut and made a resolution.

The ability within me existed for a reason, even as it felt terrifying and uncontrollable. This power was the key to bringing my sister home. Maybe it could be the key to bringing Austin's voice back to him. And beyond that? I imagined myself destroying the demon that stalked the loves of Isobel's family, freeing her from that curse. I knew that if my power could be used for good, then that was what I needed to do.

Eventually, Mother stirred. Her eyes opened and she squeezed my hand.

'Alice,' she murmured, her voice a croak that didn't sound like hers.

'I'm here,' I said. 'You're not well. It's happening. The transfer of magic. And I know about it. All of it. I know what I am, what we are.'

'I should have told you,' she started. Her eyes brimmed with tears. 'I didn't want any of this for you, or your sister.'

'I know,' I said, my face resting against her shoulder.

My chest creaked with the weight of a strange, pre-emptive grief. I had this horrible knowledge that our time together was like sand slipping through a timer. Mother was here, still. She had not left me. But I was going to leave her.

'I saw Lucille.'

Mother's eyes brightened. 'You saw her? But where ... where is she now?'

I took a deep breath. 'I think she's inside the Otherworld.'

Mother let out a horrified sob. 'But how?'

I told Mother about what had happened at the station, how Lucille had sealed the entrance to save me.

'I can't find a way to get her out. I fear she's trapped.'

'Time doesn't move the same in there,' Mother said, grimacing. Then she looked at me with piercing clarity. 'If she went into the Otherworld, only a fraction of the time will have passed for her.'

Another impossible thing to understand. So much had happened, but for Lucille it will have been nowhere near as long. So there was a greater chance than I'd hoped that she would manage to survive the Otherworld.

'These are things I should have told you a long time ago. Sybil and I ... We were trained to use our powers against the Otherworld. We closed entrances, and I would heal her when she fought. I stopped when Lucille was born, but when I was pregnant with you, Sybil came here with a man named Dorian, an old friend of our parents. He wanted to go into the Otherworld.'

Even though I hated the way that he'd torn my family apart, I couldn't blame him for being willing to do whatever it took to find answers about his little sister. I could understand him. I was willing to go to the ends of the earth to bring my own sister back.

Mother's eyes turned cold as she continued. 'Dorian's plans to go into the Otherworld are the reason your father is dead. I thought he was a dangerous man, and I was proved right. But Sybil was so influenced by him ... and I let her convince me. Because I wouldn't travel to London, they came here to rip an entrance, so that they could use my magic for healing. They went into the Otherworld, and something came through. Your father ...' She broke off. I could tell from the pain on her face that the whole thing was playing out in her mind. 'I had always used to face the monsters of the Otherworld with Sybil, but since Lucille had been born, it felt so different. I ran. Your father didn't survive, and Sybil destroyed the monster. And then ... she went right back in after Dorian and left me to cope. It was hours for them. It was *months* for me. Pregnant with you, raising Lucille. Alone. Grieving. Guarding the entrance, terrified that something might come through, but not wanting to seal my sister inside.'

'That's awful,' I said, the words too weak for the horror of what she'd been through. I took her hand in mine.

'It was our fault. We ripped that hole ourselves.'

'How?' I asked.

'We broke Dorian's arm,' she whispered, and I wondered if this was the first time she had spoken about it out loud. My stomach turned. 'When they came back, I sealed the entrance we'd made and then I cast protection around this house too, so it would forever be safe.'

This was the crux of it; Austin's family and mine had collided in a terrible way two generations ago, and the damage was written over everything that had happened since.

The horrors gain strength when things in our world are broken.

A bone. A promise. A heart.

Dorian and the broken arm. Austin and the broken promise. Lucille and Theodore with their broken hearts.

What part of me would the Otherworld break?

'I need to go and find Lucille,' I said.

'I know.' Mother sounded defeated. Her battle to protect me and my sister had been a losing one. 'All this time, I was trying to keep you safe. I suspected your powers were waking up when your nightmares started, when your hair turned white. But you didn't tell me. It seemed like you wanted to ignore it, and I wanted to let you. I always felt so burdened by what we were born into. I so desperately wanted something different for you and Lucille. But I fear that all I've done by trying to protect you is make you doubt how capable you are. When you were younger, you were always so feisty and brave. I know you can do the most incredible things, Alice. I'm sorry if I ever made you doubt that.'

'I'm going to find Lucille and bring her home,' I said. 'It's what she'd do for me.'

'I should come with you,' she said, pushing herself to sit upright with a twist of pain. 'Your sister needs me.' Determination pierced her words. For a moment, I caught a glimpse of who she was when she was at full strength: endlessly protective, so ferocious. There was nothing that would stop her from trying to protect us.

'No, Mother. You're not well enough. I will tell Lucille how badly you wanted to come with me. No, better than that, you can tell her yourself when we return.' I tried to help her to get as comfortable as possible, growing teary.

She put her hands on either side of my face, so that I was looking straight into her eyes. Her hands were trembling with the effort, but her stare was so still that it pinned me in place.

'Remember to have faith in yourself, the way you did before you learned to be frightened.'

'Hold on for us,' I said. It was a selfish thing to say. Maybe I should have told her that we would be all right, that she had done an incredible job trying to keep us safe, but she didn't need to any more. Instead, I begged her to hold on. I wasn't ready to say goodbye.

'I will,' Mother promised.

The quiet peace that had been so hard won by Mother on my behalf, the life that I had once known, was over.

It was time to discover what lay ahead in my new one.

22

Austin was sitting in the library, a book open on his lap, but I could tell from the way he gazed ahead that he was not reading. When I entered the room, he turned his head. Gone was all the charm that he had first arrived with, and something softer remained in its wake – a smile that was more hesitant, eyes that were more searching. He closed his book, and there was something very final about the thud.

I wanted to ask him about his broken promise.

'I read your letter. Thank you for your honesty,' I said, sinking into the chair opposite him.

He nodded in acknowledgement, and I continued. 'But you should know ... I don't think I can help you get your voice back.' A muscle in his jaw twitched. 'I wish I could. But I'm not what you came here looking for. I don't know how to defeat the creatures of the Otherworld. Perhaps I was made to, but I haven't been trained.'

He shook his head, and picked up his pencil.

You are so much more powerful and capable than you realize.

My breath caught. It felt as though nobody had ever believed in me like Austin.

'Perhaps. But that power comes at a cost. My mother is sick. Part of the way this curse works is that as Lucille and I develop these abilities, our mother and Aunt Sybil begin to waste away.'

He wrote for me in his notebook.

I'm sorry.

'There are so many things that feel horrid and unfair about all of this.' I cleared my throat and then I told him my mother's account of when my father had died. He winced, as though it was painful to listen to and shuffled in his seat, his expression conflicted. 'The thing is, I understand how your grandfather must have felt, why he was so driven to find a way to get what he wanted. I would do *anything* to bring Lucille back. I need to go into the Otherworld.'

Austin stared at the fireplace, a philosophical expression on his face, as though he were a statue whose artist had wanted to portray a person thinking.

So what are you going to do?

'I'm going to travel to London to meet my aunt Sybil . . .' I trailed off. Now I'd spoken my intention aloud, my palms were sweating with nerves and I felt rather nauseous. 'She's the only person who can teach me about how my power works. How to use it without it destroying me. And then . . . then I'll go into the Otherworld to find Lucille.'

You mustn't travel alone. I'll come with you.

I paused, looking at his words on the page. He was right

in one thing, of course. I really ought not to travel alone. Who knew what dangers I might face on the journey alone?

And yet, the alternative would surely be frowned upon. A young unmarried couple journeying together unaccompanied.

'It wouldn't be proper,' I said, 'for us to travel together.'

Well, then, we ought to be married.

His face was serious. It was suddenly hard to breathe deeply.

'O-ought we?' For a fleeting moment, I allowed myself to imagine it. A ring on my finger, the firmness of his hand on my waist, the soft press of his lips against mine. My cheeks flushed.

Well, you wear a ring and nobody will be any the wiser. Your reputation would remain intact.

'I see,' I said. Of course the actor would propose a performance. It was easy for him to put on that charming smile and show everyone what they wanted to see. I couldn't deny that there was a slight twinge of disappointment in my gut, although I did realize how ridiculous that was – his profession, the high-class ancestry of the family he'd been cut off by, the deeds of his grandfather – oh, I could think of a hundred reasons why we were an ill-suited match.

And yet, this rational part of me was a dim flicker in comparison to the fiercely intensifying blaze insisting that we were, perhaps, perfect for each other.

I looked at him. Our two uncertain futures seemed to jumble together in the space between us. I had learned to be still and quietly content next to him, comfortable in the silence. There was nobody else like him in my entire life.

'Well, then I accept,' I said, and a tight smile crossed my lips. It already felt like a lie, and my gut clenched. The smile he gave me back was disarming, a flicker of delight at the corners, eyes glittering and reflecting back the sparks of the fire. In that moment, I could almost believe it was real.

I didn't ask yet.

The mischief ran rampant across his features, and I rolled my eyes at him. 'You are ridiculous.'

He got down to one knee and reached for my left hand, cradling it in the heat of his palm. His finger ran over the one on mine that ached with significance.

It was a joke. He was performing.

It felt more real than anything I'd ever experienced.

When he looked up at me, his eyes a question, and his lips moving soundlessly in declaration, I understood why women in literature swooned. There was a dizziness to it all, compounded by the hot flames of the fire sinking into me.

Then he made it silly, turning it into a pantomime of expectation, clutching a hand to his chest, and despite how seriously I wanted to take myself, I laughed.

He grinned and there was an unbridled joy on his face. That had been his intention all along, to break me into laughter. He just loved to entertain, and for my part, I found it was a relief to embrace the silliness of it. The situation we found ourselves in was dark enough, without refusing to find any mirth in it. Perhaps instead of a performance or a lie, I could find something honest in this necessary deception.

A game, the sort children play, where they can be anything and do anything. Could I imagine myself the actor's wife, the honeymooners travelling to London for a taste of adventure?

'That's enough now,' I said, pulling my hand away and playfully swatting him on the arm. 'We have to prepare to travel.'

He nodded, arranging himself back into a picture of propriety. It was so easy for him to switch like that. I envied him the ease with which he seemed to move through moments, without seeming to cling on to the intensity of emotions the way I did. He seemed to me to be the sort of person who, if he was caught in a rainstorm, would still manage to emerge unaffected, miraculously shielded from the downpour.

Before I could go to gather the belongings I wished to take, Austin raised a finger, instructing me with that small gesture to wait, just a moment. He tore a shred of paper from his notebook and twisted it. Then he grabbed my hand once more and wrapped the thin twist around my finger, a ring made from paper.

Even though he bought me a real ring to wear on our journey, I kept the paper one, too. I unwound it, just once, so hungry for all of his words that I just had to see if anything had been captured. Just a shred of something that was on his mind at some point, a note for himself that he had been jotting down.

One day,

But whatever the rest of his thought was, it is lost now, left unfinished.

Just like the rest of our story.

23

A few days later, my first journey by train was far beyond my wildest imaginings. The chug and the hiss and the rattle and the *clack-clack-clack* of the train as we thundered along set me on edge at first, painfully aware that I was moving faster than I had ever moved in my life. I sat opposite Austin and looked out through a great window on to the world whipping past. The green of the moors and the blue of the sky were a captivating blur. Our journey was to take all day.

Austin reclined in his seat, coat slung across his knees, legs stretched into the walkway and feet crossed at the ankles. He was not entranced by the racing landscape, did not jump at every clatter and judder in fear that the carriage might fall apart about our ears the way that I did. He was used to this kind of travel, and his calmness was contagious after a little while; my breathing slowed and my clenched jaw released.

Austin had knocked on my door that morning and evaporated before I had roused myself to open it, so I found a little box that fit in the palm of my hand left there, as if it had appeared all by itself. Inside, there was a simple ring, polished to a shine.

I'd never had a gift like that before, so imbued with meaning. The significance of it sank in as I slipped it on to my finger, the metal cool and unfamiliar against my skin.

I fiddled with it on the train, twirling it round and round my finger. Looking up at Austin, I noticed he had slipped on a matching one. I'd never known a man to wear a ring as well. He noticed me watching him and smiled.

'I always wanted to travel by train,' I said, a wistfulness stirring in my belly. Austin raised a single eyebrow. *Go on*, he seemed to be saying.

It was strange to remember that once I had been a little girl with a sense of adventure. I had read voraciously and widely from the library in the guest house, stories of exploration and mystery, and I had inserted myself into these stories in my own imagination. The places I thought I might go one day had been unlimited back then, the challenges I thought I would overcome unnumbered.

That little girl had been buried beneath the overprotectiveness of the people who loved me, and my own fears.

'When I was younger, I used to dream of being some kind of adventurer,' I admitted to Austin, as we sped further and further away from the only town I had ever known. I brought my voice down low. These words tumbling out of me were meant for him alone. 'Truthfully, I think if you had told me then that I was destined to be some sort of mystery-solving, supernatural-hunting adventurer, I would have been delighted. The fear hadn't set in then. One day, when I was seven, I packed a little bag with sandwiches and left the guest house by myself and went down to the seaside. It was a bright day in the height of summer. I suppose I was lost in an invention of my own imagination. Playing. I dug in the sand, pretending any slightly interesting-looking pebble was holding a secret ammonite.'

Austin smiled at my telling. Perhaps he thought this was just a fond childhood memory. The next part stuck in my throat. I had never told the story before. Not even to Lucille. This was the memory that haunted me, as deeply as the first time I saw one of the horrors.

'And the waves were so inviting, the way they came in and out. I decided to paddle into the sea and let them lap over my toes. And that was fun, so I decided to go a little further and jump over the foamy crashes as they came in. And then ... I decided to go a little further. I ended up with the water right up to my neck and I was still excited, still unafraid. Until I couldn't touch the ground any more, and the rolling of the water was a drag, pulling me further away from the shore. That was when the fear set in. I wasn't strong enough to swim back to shore.'

I had almost drowned.

I lowered my eyes. Even so many years later, thinking about that day made panic rise in my chest. The sharp pain when I inhaled water, spluttering, the tug of each wave, the scream that hollowed out my mouth. None of those images or sounds turned into words. That was the most I'd ever managed to speak about that memory. Not even Mother or Lucille knew I'd even been on the beach that day.

'If it weren't for a man who swam out to get me, I would have died.'

Austin was watching me. He reached across and brushed my knuckles with his fingertips, as soft as gently falling snow.

'I stopped considering myself much of an adventurer after that. My mother was perpetually grieving, my father was gone. And I just thought ... the world is too frightening. It is full of loss. I still read my books, of course. But I stopped imagining myself walking in the steps of the main characters. I stopped dreaming.

'And then I saw that first horror, pouring out of the Otherworld, and the nightmares started. I just felt that I was too sensitive, that being in the world required a toughness that I did not possess.'

Thoughts darkened Austin's eyes, and I could see a vague frustration as his lips twitched. He wanted to speak. The notebook emerged. He hesitated a few times, scribbled out his words with an almost imperceptible shake of his head.

I have seen you be tough.

But your sensitivity is a gift as well.

My heart felt a size too big. I couldn't meet his eyes, felt bashful and tongue-tied in the face of his encouragement.

Tough. Sensitive. Brave. Afraid.

When we have got your sister and my voice back, the next thing we will go in search of is moments that make the world feel less awful.

'"When"?' I said. 'Not "if"?' Oh, to have his confidence that we were going to be successful in all our endeavours.

He underlined it.

<u>When.</u>

'When,' I repeated, nodding my head. I would borrow his assurance and then maybe it would start to feel as if it belonged to me. 'Tell me, what will we find? Tell me one thing that makes the world less awful.'

Chocolate, of course.

I tilted my head at this. He had raised a ghost of a smile on my lips at least. 'And what else do you see in our future?'

We will walk in parks and smell beautiful blooms in springtime. We will go to see a comedy performance and catch sight of the stars as we leave the theatre. And yes, we will eat chocolate, let it melt in our mouths. Accumulating these moments of light is how we'll fight the darkness.

Delight fluttered inside me at the thought. I had robbed myself of so many of these moments. The scenes that Austin conjured for me felt like the peak of a mountain we had yet to climb, misted over by cloud, something I could only just catch a glimpse of. But that glimpse was real enough. The rich taste of chocolate rolled over my tongue. Light to fight the darkness.

He had woven a spell around us. It felt like escape.

As our journey continued, I allowed myself to relax as much as possible, to read the book I'd brought with me, to put the fear and the anticipation of it all in a box, ready to be opened on our arrival.

'When we get to London, we will go straight to my aunt Sybil,' I said. We'd set off early, but with the way the autumn evenings liked to creep, I knew that darkness would begin to wrap around us before we arrived in the city.

What is her address?

I wrote it down for him, memorized from the return address on the letter she'd written to Lucille. It did not mean anything to me, as somebody who knew very little of London.

But when Austin read the address, his eyebrows raised and he looked at me, mouth slightly open.

'What?' A new nervousness swam in my belly like a little fish. 'Is it an awful area? Will we be in danger?'

He shook his head briskly and waved his hand as if to brush away my concerns.

The property is a small townhouse at the edge of the city.

I laughed. 'You must be very knowledgeable about the districts of London to place the house so well from the address alone! So do you think we ought to be quite safe there?'

I should think so. The property belongs to my family.

24

London was an overwhelming cacophony. I thought I had known what to expect, but from the moment we arrived, I felt as though I had been plunged into the sea, having lived all my life in a rock pool. The busy market days in Whitby were nothing compared to the crowds of the city. The sheer number of people we crossed paths with astounded me, and I was struck as I contemplated that each one of these people were going about their own lives, each experiencing any number of hardships and moments of light and heart-swelling loves and world-shattering griefs.

It was almost too much to comprehend, and the constant movement of it all was exhausting to my eyes.

And everything was grey. The stones of the ground, the buildings that clustered together, the smog that hung in the sky, the faces of the people. Lucille would have found it so miserable and uninspiring; I thought of her watercolours and how she always used so much colour to bring her landscapes to life. The vividness of the coast and the moors had evaporated. There seemed to me no colour in London.

Austin offered me his arm and I rested my fingers against his coat, the fabric a soft luxury. The ring on my finger caught my eye; I had not got used to its presence there, and whenever I became aware of it, suddenly it was the only thing I was aware of, the weight of it encircling me.

Without Austin's help, I would have been lost to the city, swallowed up by the noise and the chaos. But he knew this place well, slipped into it with ease. He knew how to weave our way through the multitudes of people, even as I stumbled, clinging on to him like a barnacle on a rock.

As we emerged from the station, a deep unease crept through my bones, the sensation of being watched. My eyes became darting and frantic, responding to the fire that began to burn in my pulse. With each beat of my heart, the heat was rising.

Nearby, there was a threat from the Otherworld. I could feel it. A monster, a demon, a spectre ... Whatever it was that lurked somewhere close, the power inside me was reacting to it. It was alive, waking from slumber, seeking out the danger.

Austin noticed the change in me. Our eyes met. He searched my face, questioning, concerned.

'I'm all right,' I said. Whatever sort of monstrous Otherworld horror was roaming in among the crowd, I wasn't ready to face it. But I was beginning to learn that this was how it would work. The destructive power inside me would always be primed to find the threat of the Otherworld, would always be drawn to vanquish it. That was why I'd had such a strong sense of urgency around wanting to help Isobel, why I'd reacted so strongly to the horror in the apothecary. This was what I was built for.

But if I threw myself into hunting the monster whose presence was calling out to me now, I risked destroying myself in the process. I needed Sybil, and I needed my sister.

'Let's leave this place.'

Austin squeezed my hand and, eventually, the sensation began to dim.

We boarded a horse-bus, a public transport of the likes I had never seen before, with a two-storey carriage. We climbed a winding staircase at the back to perch on a seat so high above the ground that I thought I might fall, bouncing and lurching with the uneven movements of the horses pulling us along. Austin seemed rather used to this mode of transport, too. I imagined his family would have had the wealth for a private carriage, but this certainly matched his convivial nature and was more suited to the actor on a jaunt about town. He smiled broadly at our fellow passengers, and I was certain that before his voice had been stolen away, he would have engaged each of them in conversation and by the end of the journey discovered the name of their childhood dog, a deep, dark secret from their past and the reason why they had latterly argued with their spouse. And, of course, he would have managed to promote his latest show and ensure that the newest acquaintance purchased a ticket. That was just the kind of presence Austin had.

The whole experience was dizzying. It didn't seem that I was truly living these moments; it felt more like playing out scenes from a book in my mind. I pressed my hands into the wooden seat of the bus, tried to grab on to something real, something tangible.

The horse-bus eventually took us to a calmer area towards the edge of the city. When we left the bus, Austin pointed me in the direction of a quieter street. It was lined with trees and crisp, rusted leaves that had fallen at their feet.

Austin had recognized the name of the property from his family accounts. Shade's View. With the disappearance of his grandfather Dorian, the management of the family wealth, including the various properties they owned, had transferred into the hands of Austin's father. This was the work Austin had been enlisted to assist with. No doubt his father had been hoping that Austin would be content in the monotony of managing his future inheritance.

Austin said that Shade's View was run at a loss, one they could afford to absorb, but a loss nonetheless. Whoever occupied it did not pay rent, and it had been quietly assumed that it housed a mistress, perhaps an illegitimate child.

Now, Austin and I knew better.

I shared with him what Dr Binding had told me about the days of the friendship between our families, that at one point, Dorian had provided a townhouse as London accommodation for my grandfather, his wife and her sister, a base for their investigations with him. They must have been staying at Shade's View. Until they refused his request to enter the Otherworld and their feud began, that is. And now, it was where Sybil resided, having fled to London after the incident that killed my father.

This was also where Mother must have come when I was thirteen, the visit that would have coincided with my powers waking, with the start of her and, I assumed, Sybil's illness.

And while Mother had retired from their work together, Sybil's presence in this house suggested that Dorian had continued to fund her destruction of the Otherworld monsters. Either in gratitude at her giving him the opportunity to try to find his sister . . . or because he hoped for revenge to be wrought on the Otherworld that had stolen the little girl away.

The houses were hushed like guests clustered at a funeral. Shade's View itself was a tall, well-kept townhouse. With a candle-white front door, and gleaming windows, it was unobtrusive and certainly no more noticeable than the others. My palms began to sweat at the idea of coming face to face with Sybil. Truly, I had no idea what I was going to find. I did not have the luxury of the correspondence that Lucille had engaged in. Sybil might be angry at our imposition – we had of course arrived unannounced. She might be terribly unwell, like Mother, or worse, she might already be dead in her bed. Hot bile rose in the back of my throat. Turning to Austin, I gulped the burning sensation away.

'We're really here,' I said, shaking my head.

He gave me an encouraging smile. A bubble of nervous laughter escaped my lips.

'I never . . . I never thought I'd do something like this.'

An expression I couldn't read crossed Austin's features. He moved his hand – the one with the ring – and touched it to mine, so that the rings made a little clink. His unconventional choice to wear a ring gave him a way to let me know that he was on my side, without words, without pen and paper.

'Stick together,' I said, turning the words into a slight question. He nodded sharply and did it again. *Clink.*

25

The knocker on the door to Shade's View was a ghoulish thing, the sinister face of a beastly creature biting on to the hanging brass circle, with bulging eyes that seemed to follow me. I gripped hold of it and knocked three times, sharp raps that would not be missed. And then I waited. Austin had told me that they funded a skeleton staff for the house, so it wasn't a surprise when the door was answered by a housekeeper, an exhausted-looking woman, mid-thirties, perhaps, whose scraped-back hair was haphazardly escaping its confines.

'Lucille Everglass?' the housekeeper asked, her tired eyes brightening. My heart gave a jolt at the name. Of course, they had been expecting her. 'I'm the housekeeper, Mrs Spencer. Miss Grey will be so delighted to see you; she's been waiting.'

I shook my head. 'No, I am not Lucille. I'm her sister, Alice.'

A confused expression crossed the housekeeper's face, but she covered it quickly. I wondered how close of a confidant she was to Sybil. I saw her eyes searching behind me for my sister, but they landed on Austin instead with a suspicious squint.

'And this is Mr Austin Parker. My ... well ...' I floundered, gesturing towards him and he raised his hand in greeting. I saw the housekeeper's eyes flick from his hand to my hand, spotting the matching rings. I couldn't bring myself to utter the lie *husband*, and I hoped that she would make the necessary assumptions that would keep my reputation intact, travelling here with him as I had, otherwise unaccompanied. But I needn't have overly worried myself with that; the housekeeper had other concerns. She had flinched at his name.

'Parker?'

I nodded swiftly. 'Yes, that's right.'

'Begging your pardon, we aren't due an inspection,' she said, her voice hesitant. 'The house is ... Well, that is to say that I've been doing my best – but Miss Grey has not been well, you see, and ...'

Austin raised his hands in a gesture of surrender, and I stepped in to speak.

'We're not here to inspect anything,' I said. 'Mr Parker is simply accompanying me. Are we able to see my aunt?'

'Well, then. You had better come in,' she said swiftly, welcoming us through the door into a narrow entrance hall.

For all her worry about the condition of the house, the parquet floor of the hall was immaculate and shining. As Mrs Spencer led us through into the drawing room, an eager fire dancing in the fireplace, I could tell that she took great pride in keeping everything in order; there was not a speck of dust on the lampshades or the sideboard and its contents, which included a sizeable collection of unusual teapots, each one hand-painted with a different illustration. Upon one, I recognized the abbey from home. The teapot I'd uncovered in the small basement room must have belonged to Sybil, once upon a time, or else she had gifted it to my mother.

'Do take a seat while I see whether Miss Grey is able to join you here.' She gestured at the settee and I gratefully sank down on to it. Austin sat down to the right of me.

As the housekeeper left, we glanced at each other, a nervous flicker passing between us.

After a wait that seemed to stretch for the longest time, I heard the creak of steps coming back towards us. Mrs Spencer reappeared, an apologetic expression across her features.

'I'm sorry, but I'm afraid Miss Grey is not well enough to see visitors this evening,' she said, and my heart sank in disappointment. 'However, she has told me that you are very welcome to stay tonight, and she will endeavour to speak with you in the morning.'

My eye twitched. We'd travelled so far, so much further than I'd ever gone, and it had taken so long that my legs and hips were stiff with it, all to be told that we had to wait even longer. It was also not a good sign that Sybil was too unwell to see us. There was so much that I wanted to learn from her, and I needed her to be well enough to impart that knowledge. And yet I knew that the stronger I grew (and Lucille, in that faraway place, whose power would also be shifting and developing, so long as she avoided harm), the weaker that Sybil, and Mother too, would be, the closer to death.

Some lingering anxiety quivered inside me. We did not truly know what we were dealing with when it came to Sybil Grey, and everything I'd learned so far had etched a fear of her into my skin, which prickled at the thought of us being under the same roof overnight, even though I had no other plan. Perhaps it was silly to be frightened of her, when I knew she was so incapacitated, and yet ... I also knew her to be powerful, a destroyer of demons and shadows and monsters, with a fire inside her that she could channel. Who knew what else she was capable of, what magic seethed in her, what damage she could work even when she was ill.

All of these tangled thoughts remained unspoken while Austin got out his notebook and began writing. Mrs Spencer frowned with confusion.

'Mr Parker has temporarily lost his voice and so is unable to speak,' I said hurriedly. 'He communicates by writing for the moment.'

Mrs Spencer waited patiently. Austin lifted up the notebook.

Thank you, Mrs Spencer. We'd be very happy to stay. I do hope Miss Grey has a peaceful night and feels much better come the morning. We are very eager to meet with her at the earliest opportunity.

Mrs Spencer seemed satisfied at this. 'Oh,' she added, conspiratorially. 'I ought to mention that Miss Grey has given me permission to allow you to access the archive. That's why you've come, isn't it?'

The archive? I'd never heard of such a thing. I could only assume that this was connected to Lucille's planned visit here.

'My aunt doesn't want to meet with us first?' I frowned.

'The archive is well protected,' Mrs Spencer said, and I got the sense she meant *magically*. 'Will you have a cup of tea and some supper first?'

We both nodded eagerly at this, parched from the journey. My stomach was beginning to gnaw at itself. I was fairly certain that we weren't about to be poisoned by the housekeeper, though the thought did rear its head. Suffice it to say, the distrust I felt at that time was difficult to shift.

Mrs Spencer took one of the teapots from the collection, hand-painted with a charming grey stripey cat, where the handle was the tail, and gave a wry smile as she noticed me watching her. 'Miss Grey is exceptionally fond of tea. She paints these pots herself. Or, rather, she used to before she grew unwell.'

My chest tightened, twisting with sadness. The teapot I'd uncovered in that basement room, I now felt certain, had been painted as a gift to my parents. Sybil was artistic. Learning that about her made me think of Lucille. An alternative form, but the heart of it was the same – a love of creation. There were threads tying us to each other, even if Mother and Sybil had tried to unfasten them.

When Mrs Spencer returned with the hot teapot, she brought with her two bowls of porridge, topped with cinnamon and raisins. It was just the way that Mother had made it for me and Lucille when we were young. The smell transported me back to the Honest Opal and Mother's comforting arms wrapped around me as I gulped down the warming porridge, the raisins little bursts of sweetness, milk dribbling down my chin. A yawning empty feeling that was more than hunger went through me. Homesickness. It was the furthest I had ever been from home. And my mother... my mother who was sick, who was dying.

And yet we had come for a reason, and I could not give up on Lucille.

'I'll make up a room for you both,' Mrs Spencer said, leaving us to our supper. It took a moment for her meaning to sink in, and when it did I almost spat out my porridge. I turned to Austin. 'A room,' I whispered. I raised a single finger. '*For you both*. One room!' My alarm must have been evident. My eyes felt as though they had gone out on stalks and my breath was suddenly rapid.

It wasn't right. It wasn't proper. We were not really married, and if anyone knew, if anyone found out... Shame at the very idea of it bloomed in my cheeks. A bedroom was a place for a married man and woman. Not... whatever Austin and I were becoming to each other.

I should have thought about this. I chided myself as he quickly wrote his response, my palms sweating. How could I have been so stupid? I knew from running the guest house that even married couples sometimes took separate rooms when travelling, and I had incorrectly presumed that was just what would happen. But if we questioned it now, we'd surely be asked why, and what could we say? We would be exposed as liars and frauds.

Austin tapped me on the shoulder and showed me his notebook.

Alice, I would hate for you to think that you're not completely enchanting to me, but I hope you know I would never do anything to compromise your reputation.

My imagination filled in what he was alluding to and I flushed. The thought sent a thrill through me, one that was surprising, and also undeniably captivating. In among the reassurance of his respect for me, was that also an intimation that he was developing the same feelings that I was? I found I could not tear my gaze away from his lips, my misbehaving mind conjuring a reverie of them landing on mine, his hands running over my skin.

Was I allowed to want that?

Surely such thoughts were too shocking.

He looked at me earnestly, though with something else written across his face, and I thought for a terrible moment that he might be able to see what was playing out in my mind.

'My reputation! I fear that is already in ruins either way!' I said, keeping my voice to a hush. 'Whether we keep up the pretence and share the room tonight, knowing what people at home will think if they ever find out, or we tell the truth about our charade and ask for separate rooms, and I'm exposed as a liar to Mrs Spencer and my aunt! Oh my reputation is destroyed whatever we choose.'

He leant back, a smile dancing across his lips.

You're panicking.

'Yes! I am!' It came out as a squeak.

If I asked him to leave, to find somewhere else to stay, he would do it. I did not know how far away we were from the place he called home; in fact, I did not know which place he would call home at all. I wanted to know where he rested, where he was most comfortable, where there was no act. He'd given up the lodgings where he'd laid his head when he was working in the theatre. Would he go back to the ancestral home where his parents lived? He had not told me about it, but I was picturing a grand manor house, perhaps further out to the country. Probably not his first choice, given the way he'd written about his father. Maybe he would find a way to get access to the London apartment that had belonged to his grandfather, the one that was the setting for all those scenes in the script.

But I didn't want him to leave. I wanted him by my side to discover what the archive held, to meet Sybil in the morning. I finally believed that I didn't have to carry the weight of Lucille's disappearance by myself, and I wanted him with me. We could get his voice back. We could bring Lucille home. Together.

When he next lifted his notebook for me, his words were neatly and carefully formed, with none of the scribbled haste that I'd grown accustomed to. Another smile, this one altogether mischievous.

Well, if any of your fears come to pass, I suppose I shall simply have to marry you for real.

26

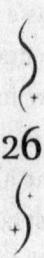

The archive was housed in a room at the very top of the house, an attic space that had been repurposed for this use. The moment I stepped inside, I felt a cosy sense of safety I'd thought was utterly unique to the Honest Opal. This room had been *protected*. In spite of that protection, the room was deeply scarred. There was evidence of tears in the fabric of our world that had been stitched back together, lumpy seams like the ones I'd seen in the station, the apothecary, at home. Sealed and healed now, but once a place where monsters could break through. One on that wall and that wall, and in the floor, and in that eave. I knelt down next to the one on the floor and ran my hands over it, tentative, as though my touch could break it open again.

This was a place where the Otherworld had collided with ours, over and over again.

There was a bookshelf filled with huge, weighty tomes with cracked spines and various bookmarks sprouting from the tops of them. But for all they had once been well referenced, now they were covered in a thick layer of dust. A huge map of the country had been painted on one of the walls and ominous black circles had been marked on at various locations, some of them crossed out with a pale blue slash. Markings of hauntings, I supposed. Most of them centred in London, but some as far north as Newcastle. Whitby, of course, had its fair share.

Mrs Spencer had opened the door for us and let us wander in, giving a wry smile at our amazement at what we were seeing. 'Miss Grey said to take as much time in here as you need this evening. Keep your questions for the morning.' Then with a little nod, she excused herself and left us to examine the space.

Austin and I looked at each other, eyes wide with disbelief. Whatever I'd been imagining we'd find at Shade's View, it wasn't this. Truly, this made the whole endeavour feel very real.

Austin was trailing his fingers along the spines of the books. He pulled one down and opened it up, the pages falling to a striking hand-drawn illustration of an almost-human creature with a great gasping mouth, lined with serrated teeth and sharp, dagger-like incisors, and long, long fingers with nails that could be weapons. I had not seen anything quite like this before.

'What is that you're reading?' I asked, faintly horrified.

Austin handed the book to me deferentially. I read through the notes, the description of this monster and the way it had drained several victims of their blood ... and I found myself wondering whether the writers who wrote supposed fiction about such horrible things had ever come across these nightmares for real.

When I turned the pages, I did so slowly at first, trying to take it all in, and then began to flick faster and faster. There was so much to look at, so much I needed to know. Austin moved beside me and hovered, peering at the pages as I skimmed through them. His breath was a warm summer breeze on my shoulder.

The book was a sort of almanac, a marriage between a journal and an encyclopaedia.

'It's like a – a guide of what to expect with each horror,' I said. The first pages began with a detailed inventory of the contents of the book, written in a looping handwriting that coiled across the page like wriggling snakes. The writer – Sybil, I was sure, the elegant handwriting a match for the letter to Lucille I'd intercepted – had carefully numbered each page in the bottom corner. There were lengthy, descriptive passages interspersed with illustrations of the sort of creatures that lurk in nightmares. There was something rather like the bristling beast with the bloody maw I was now sure I'd seen in the ginnel in Whitby. And in another notebook the many monstrous teeth that belonged to the first horror I'd ever seen. It was a shock to see it again even after so many years. If I kept looking, perhaps I'd find a spectre like the one that had attached itself to Isobel's family, devouring the dishonest, and something like the horror from the station.

So much painstaking work had gone into making these records. Sybil had documented all the awful things she'd faced from the Otherworld, with all sorts of useful details, including the location of their emergence, any witnesses, a self-created scale of physicality, from terrifying but harmless auditory hauntings to flesh-and-blood monsters with the power to rip a person limb from limb. And each of these was accompanied by excited declarations: DEFEATED!!! DESTROYED!!! CLOSED!!! SEALED!!!

'It seems almost as though... she enjoys it,' I murmured, a little shocked. And I couldn't deny that somewhere behind my own ribcage there was a thrill of excitement. Here was proof that these powers could be used for good.

And that's when I noticed the accompanying dates.

'Sybil wrote this journal when she was still working with my mother,' I murmured, running my finger over the date on a page describing an encounter with a horde of tiny, vicious faeries. 'Look. Twenty-five years ago. Before Mother was married.'

Austin nodded thoughtfully and went to pull down another book. He blew the dust off the cover and opened it up. More of the same, an almanac of the horrific.

'Who needs ghost stories?' I said, and Austin gave me a wry smile. The entries in Sybil's books, with her haunting gift for illustration, were worse than anything a writer could dream up.

What frightened me the most was knowing that somewhere, in one of those many books, I would come across what had happened that terrible day at the Honest Opal, the day my father was killed.

I promised myself then that if I found that entry, I would not read it. I thought that if I did, I could not bear it. My imagination was bad enough without needing the details, without sharp words that could wound me.

But I did know that, eventually, I would have to work my way through as much of the archive as possible. It was like having a glimpse into the rest of my life.

I opened another almanac, spotted the dates creeping forward through time, and put it back on the shelf. I preferred to go backward instead. Backward we went, right back to Sybil's first journal. I was scouring through the contents pages, flicking through the images, looking for something that matched what we'd seen at the station.

But there were still more and more books to search, and once I had gone back far enough, we discovered another handwriting style. This one was all writing, no illustrations.

'This must be from the generation before,' I said. 'My grandmother, or her sister.'

Austin determinedly pulled down another journal from the highest shelf, a section we had yet to tackle. A different handwriting style once more. These books represented generations of my family and the monsters they'd slain. It would take months and months to work through every book.

I rubbed at my tired eyes, feeling exhausted and exasperated, but also a strange sense of wonder. The archive was the most incredible resource. It was an academic log of decades, and it was also a nest for a hunter, a place for the planning of destruction.

We continued to browse through the pages in a companionable quiet without the need to share what we were thinking. Austin was idly flicking through one of Sybil's earlier journals and I noticed him stifle a yawn, his eyes growing misty. But then suddenly something caught his attention and he straightened up, scrabbling around for his own notebook.

Does your power ever feel alive?

I frowned. 'Alive? In what way?'

He showed me a journal entry that Sybil had written. It seemed to suggest that her power, the power we shared, was like a creature that inhabited her. The thought made me flinch. It was unbelievable enough to imagine that there was fire that raged inside me, that could destroy. But to imagine that it was alive, living inside me? That was even more horrific somehow.

Read it, Austin wrote, and held out the entry to me quite forcefully.

I sighed. I had spent an evening examining accounts of frightful creatures beyond my wildest imagination, but really, it was myself that I needed – no, *wanted* – to study, to place beneath a microscope and understand.

What I was becoming, what I could really do ... and what lived beneath my skin.

It's alive, the power from the Otherworld. That's the part I never understood until I felt it. In all the stories I was told when I was younger, I could never have imagined that the power would feel so sentient.

When Emily and I were little, we were always told that one of us would learn to heal and the other would learn to destroy, and I tried to imagine what that would feel like. In reality, it is like ... a burning that could be endless, that could consume me if I let it. When we are training, it flickers awake, and when I stand before a threat from the Otherworld, it rushes uncontrollably. It has its own whims, its own plans. It lives inside me with a heartbeat all of its own. Isn't that terrifying? To feel so out of control. To feel so vulnerable.

But what I'm beginning to understand is that I can *communicate with it. If I ask it to help me search, it leads the way. If I ask it to defend me, it's there at my fingertips in moments. I'm starting to feel as though I might be able to work together with this force within me.*

After all, we both want the same thing. Not just to survive, but to FLOURISH.

27

My breath escaped me in a great wave. Reading the words Sybil had written all those years ago was like having her wrap her arms around me and tell me that I wasn't alone. I could feel her sense of fear and awe at her growing power, but there was something else I'd never had. An excitement. A thrill. A confidence in her ability to learn how to tame it, to use it.

Perhaps ... perhaps that was an option for me, too. My body began to tingle at the thought of my own potential.

I was blinking astounded tears away when Mrs Spencer knocked quietly at the door to the archive. She had a weary look about her, drooping like a plucked flower. 'I am sorry to disturb, but the hour is late, and I am about to turn in for the night. Before I do, would you like some more refreshments? More tea, perhaps?' she asked

'No, thank you,' I said, shaking my head. A yawn escaped with the end of my sentence. Although the fearful illustrations in Sybil's books would no doubt haunt my sleep, I knew that I needed to think about trying to rest. 'I think ... I am also ready to turn in.'

The housekeeper visibly relaxed, her relief palpable. She must have been wanting to end her own day for some time, to get some sleep before beginning her endless list of tasks all over again the next morning.

'Very good. If you follow me, I will show you to your room. I took the liberty of taking your cases there already.'

We followed her down the stairs as she led us to a bedroom that made me stop again with awe. Everything about the room, from the autumnal pattern of the wallpaper to the hardwood floor adorned with a soft, rectangular rug, felt so opulent compared to what I'd left behind at the Honest Opal. The bed, immaculately made, had a giant wooden frame, with bed hangings in a rich, jewel-green fabric, decorated with embroidered leaves in shades of red and orange and brown. Just a taste of the life that Austin had surely lived.

It was easy to see how Sybil might have become drawn in by a life like this, when Dorian had approached her. And when it all went wrong, when they opened a door in the Honest Opal and a monster tore through my family, Sybil had chosen to stay here. She must have grown accustomed to it. More than that, reading her journals, it was clear that she relished her life, savoured the destruction she wrought, and the defeat of the horrors. Destruction that *saved* people.

'Thank you, Mrs Spencer. Please do call on us first thing in the morning when my aunt is ready to speak with us.'

The housekeeper nodded, and then left us alone.

Alone.

The click of the door behind her was thunderous. Austin and I were completely alone in a bedroom together. An anxious thrill thrummed through me, and the tiredness I'd felt before dissolved. For all the expectations of propriety that had been drummed into me, that I knew were expected of me from my mother, from society, from everyone ... right at this moment, fear of potential consequences seemed illogical. I trusted him. He had said he would not do anything to compromise me, and I believed that to be true.

It was myself I didn't trust. I was captivated by him, entranced by the way his face wore his feelings. And when his gaze met mine, I blushed.

When had it happened? There must have been a precise moment where the way I felt about him had tipped.

When we had first met, he was simply a dashing actor, and yes, I had noticed that he was handsome, had been intrigued by him. But I had known to be cautious, not to trust him.

That had changed.

He was mesmerizing to me. I had lost myself in longing.

I wondered how much, if any, of my feelings were written across my face, as Austin quickly dropped his gaze and began his usual scribble.

I will sleep on the floor.

Austin busied himself, grabbing one of the large and very comfortable-looking pillows from the bed, as well as a crocheted blanket that had been laid decoratively at the foot of it. He arranged this in a little pile on the floor away from the foot of the bed, like a nest, and gestured to it with his hands.

Ta-da! His proud little expression made me smile. Seeing this, he reached for his notebook once more. My heart stuttered at his words.

I told you: you don't need to be worried. If your reputation is ever drawn into question, I'll simply have to marry you.

'Only then?' I said, caught up in the moment. But as soon as the words were out of my mouth, I was overcome by a strange out-of-body sensation. The boldness shocked me, as though it had come from someone else using my voice, and yet I knew that the intention behind the words was true, as true as anything I'd ever spoken aloud. I wanted to know how he felt about me in return.

He raised an eyebrow and a slight smile played across his lips as he wrote.

I see! You get one glimpse of a property I might inherit one day if I make peace with my father, and now you have designs!

As I read the words, my mouth dropped open, all the delight of the moment gone. How could he suggest that? Did he think that I'd taken one look at this fancy room, so much more costly than anything even close to an approximation of the Honest Opal, and decided to make overtures with my mind on his future fortune? The notion was mortifying.

I spluttered. 'I meant . . . I thought . . .' I was at a loss for words, shrivelling up with embarrassment. I could barely look at the next thing he hastily scrawled.

A joke, Alice. Forgive me.

'I spoke in jest as well,' I bluffed, the spell that had momentarily hung over us broken. Austin took up his pencil again, but was more thoughtful this time.

I would never want to upset you. I am sorry. I've never met anyone quite like you before, Alice. You are remarkable.

Words clustered in my throat, but none of them were ready to emerge. *Remarkable.* Nobody had ever called me remarkable before.

I won't let any harm come to you for my sake – and that includes your reputation.

'Is that a promise?' I asked.

His eyes suddenly darkened, a frown clouding his face like a thunderstorm. I got the impression he was no longer in the room with me, but had gone someplace else in his mind. And then I remembered his letter. It was a broken promise that had opened up the door to the Otherworld in his dressing room, a broken promise that had led to the theft of his voice, a broken promise that he had been unable, or unwilling, to tell me the nature of.

I had thrown his mind to a dark place. My regret was instant. The questions I longed to ask pulsed between us with a heartbeat of their own. What was that fateful promise, and who did he make it to?

'I'm sorry. Forget I said anything,' I murmured. He flinched at the sound of my voice, torn back from wherever he had gone in his mind. I wasn't even sure that he'd heard what I said. He looked back at the nest he'd made on the floor, no longer grinning at me endearingly. The message was clear: time for bed, and an end to conversation.

I attempted a smile. 'Well, thank you for being so respectful, for sleeping on the floor. Goodnight, Austin.'

He nodded, and I turned away, heart hammering.

Mrs Spencer had brought up our bags, and I rummaged through mine for my nightdress. Then I clambered up on to the bed and pulled the curtains around, creating a closed-off hideaway. Wriggling out of my dress and undergarments and into my nightgown on top of the mattress was a challenge, and when I was done, I could hear Austin shuffling beyond the curtains, no doubt also preparing for bed.

I'd done some damage to whatever it was that had been growing between us, like a great, clumsy idiot accidentally stamping on a newly sprouted seedling. Regret clambered all over me, my face all hot with the embarrassment of it, and I tossed and turned when I should have been having the most comfortable night's sleep of my life.

The trouble was, I thought, not that I had spoken, but that I had not committed to what I wanted to say. I had hedged around it, turned it into jest, tried to draw him out by *almost* telling him how I felt. What I had not done was tell him honestly: when this is over, I still want you by my side. Perhaps forever.

I did fall asleep eventually. And when I did, it was listening to the sound of his breathing, just on the other side of the curtain.

28

When I woke the next morning, I scrambled to my knees and pulled the bed curtains aside, just a little, so I could safely peer out without exposing myself.

But Austin's nest was empty, the pillow still crushed from the weight of his head, the blankets a crumpled pile. He had kept his word and his distance.

It was only my own failure to express what he'd grown to mean to me that had left me feeling as though I had got it all wrong.

After getting myself dressed, I made my way quickly downstairs. Whatever happened today, it was going to be momentous, and I wanted Austin's company as soon as I could have it.

I found him sat at the table in the dining room on the ground floor, sipping tea. When I walked into the room, he looked at me as though he were wary. I took the chair opposite him and cleared my throat as though doing so could clear our awkwardness, too.

'Last night,' I said, in a quiet voice so as not to be

overheard if Mrs Spencer arrived, 'I – I fear I came across as awfully clumsy.'

He started to write something.

'Wait,' I said, raising my hand. His pencil stopped mid-curve, his hand hovering at the page. He fixed his gaze on me, and I steeled myself to be brave and, more importantly, clear. 'I do not think I could have come this far without you. Without the things you shared with me, without you here by my side. I know that the circumstances that have brought us together are cruel and frightening, and the worst of it is not over yet. But I want you to know that I'll try anything I can to get your voice back. And when we have found Lucille, and all this is over . . . I – I want you to stay with me on this path.'

There was a slight sheen to his eyes. I held my breath as he picked up his pencil.

I am not going anywhere, Alice.

I didn't want him to make promises to me, promises it might hurt him to make, promises that he might not be able to keep. Those words were enough. I just needed him to know, before we jumped from the cliff edge, that I was with him. And I was truly beginning to trust, finally, that he felt the same way about me.

The truths that we had uncovered had knotted us together.

I held my hand out to him in a fist, the shining metal of the band he had given me glinting on my finger. He recognized the gesture immediately and, with a grin, clinked his ring against mine. A steady golden warmth trickled from my hand through the rest of me. If we were together, I felt certain that there was nothing in this world or the Otherworld that could stop us from taking back the things we had lost.

Mrs Spencer came into the room with toast. 'Miss Grey is just stirring,' she said. 'I'll help her to dress and then bring her down to meet with you. She is very eager.'

She encouraged us to wait in the dining room and then disappeared upstairs. As we waited, I fidgeted in my seat. Aunt Sybil, finally. I had no idea what to expect of her, besides, of course, that she would appear much older than her years, that the betrayal of her magic would be ravaging her body, like Mother's was. Austin placed a steadying hand on my knee, which was jittering up and down, his mouth twitching with a smile as though he found me endearing.

I heard her before I saw her. The slow, creaking progress of her descent down the steep staircase. As the door opened, my anticipation was a hummingbird at the base of my throat.

Aunt Sybil was oddly familiar. It was uncanny, and gave me the sensation of missing a step on a staircase. Her nose was a gentle slope, slightly upturned at the end, just like mine. Her cheekbones were high and reminded me of Mother, but her eyes were different, a chestnut brown. Her hair was the same shocking white as my own.

Though I knew she was still in her mid-forties, she had the appearance of somebody significantly older. She was tentative and stiff in her steps; her skin was greyed with illness and folded with wrinkles, eyes watery. Mrs Spencer helped her get comfortable in a red velvet-upholstered chair in the corner of the room, away from the dining table.

'Alice,' Sybil said, her voice rich and strong despite her frailty. 'It is rather a surprise to see you here – though, I admit, a wonderful one. And in the company of Mr Parker, too. I see congratulations are in order.' She nodded her head with her eyes firmly fixed on my wedding band.

I flushed instantly. 'We ... That is ...' I stumbled, but Austin was already rapidly writing, and the message he lifted up to Sybil was, to me at least, the perfect response.

We discovered that we are very much aligned in what we believe.

'Ah ha,' Sybil said, understanding his inference. 'Very good. And very wise on your part, Alice, to secure a match before travelling here.' She raised an eyebrow, and I wondered if she realized that it was all a performance. Then she winked at me and I was certain she knew, but didn't have any objection to the fact and wouldn't expose our charade. I was learning what an untraditional sort of woman Aunt Sybil was, although she would continue to surprise me.

'I feel very fortunate to have met Mr Parker,' I said with a smile that was genuine.

'Now tell me what brings you,' Sybil said briskly. 'And where is your sister?'

I glanced at Mrs Spencer, uncertain whether to launch straight into the untrammelled truth of why I'd come, of my experience with the horrors and the Otherworld, and to ask my aunt to tell me everything she could about the gift, the curse, that we shared. Yes, she had shown us to the archive, but how much did Mrs Spencer *truly* know about the supernatural?

Aunt Sybil clocked my reticence. 'You needn't be shy in front of Mrs Spencer. Do you imagine she has watched me decay rapidly in front of her eyes without an understanding of who and what I am? Mrs Spencer knows everything about me, and she is a trusted confidant.' Sybil patted Mrs Spencer's hand. 'I will say, though, this is the sort of conversation that requires a strong pot of tea.' Mrs Spencer sprang into action at this cue, no doubt dashing to select one of the teapots from the sideboard in the reception room.

'We've come because we need your help. Lucille is lost in the Otherworld,' I said.

Sybil let out a curse word under her breath. I tried to contain my shock at hearing her speak that way. I told her everything, about Lucille's disappearance and what happened at the station, ending with Lucille sealing herself inside the Otherworld to save me from the horror that was bursting through. At my word 'horror', Sybil barked out a laugh. 'That's a very apt name for them. All sorts of horrors come through from the Otherworld. But then, if you've looked in the archive, you might well know about the demons I've faced.'

I nodded. 'I saw some of your drawings. They were terrifying.'

She waved a dismissive hand. 'I never manage to capture them just right.' She let out a sigh. 'Well, if there was something coming through, then your sister has made a wise choice to seal the entrance off. Time isn't the same in there anyhow, if that reassures you. From Lucille's perspective not as much time will have passed since she saw you. Now, tell me, what have you seen?'

It *was* reassuring to know that time was passing slower for Lucille, but it didn't make me any less afraid of what she might be facing. 'It was a sort of . . . formless monster. It had stolen parts of a person to try to create a body for itself. I saw another one of them a few months ago.'

'Ah,' Sybil said, nodding knowledgeably. 'Mimics. I've crossed paths with that kind before. Terribly aggressive things. Some of the Otherworld monsters want to feed on our fear, or feed on our presence. Some of them attach themselves to us, like a curse. And some of them, as it sounds like you've discovered, simply want to completely consume us. But *all* of them are drawn to us because they are made from a place of darkness, and we are filled with light.'

I shuddered, thinking of Theodore, the sorrow at his horrible end rising fresh.

'You say you've crossed paths with mimics before,' I said. 'Have you ever managed to destroy one?' I asked, something like hope blinking its eyes open inside me.

'Oh yes,' Sybil said, as though we were having a perfectly normal conversation, not talking about destroying demonic entities that devoured people. 'Although I have to say –' she paused, some of her confidence faltering – 'I'm afraid my memory isn't what it used to be. I couldn't tell you exactly when or where I encountered most of these entities any more. That truly is the worst part of the magic leaving me. I feel as though my mind is slipping away from me. Slowly at first, but oh so quickly over these last few weeks.' She smiled sadly.

'Once I would have been able to tell you every detail about every Otherworld encounter. Well, at least I've maintained the archive.'

I nodded. I was grateful indeed for her immaculate record-keeping, especially knowing now that Sybil's grasp on her memories was slipping. 'One of the mimics is here, in London. It stole Austin's voice.'

Austin began writing.

It would have taken all of me, if it weren't for this.

Austin reached inside his shirt and pulled out the gemstone on the chain around his neck to show Sybil. Recognition flickered in her expression instantly. She gave an arch smile, her commanding presence returning. 'Ah, yes. I see your grandfather passed on a little gift from me.'

Austin clutched his fist around the gemstone instinctively, as if she meant to take it back.

'That necklace used to be worn by my father. But it was the one thing Dorian asked to keep. I felt that protection was the least I could afford him given everything he has offered me.' She gestured at the room around us.

'Where did it come from originally?' I asked. It seemed to me that we could use more of them, and yet I felt instinctively that, given its power, it must be impossibly rare.

'The first girls brought it back,' Sybil said. She noticed my quizzical expression. 'Did your mother truly never tell you the story of the first girls in our family that went into the Otherworld?'

I shook my head and Sybil raised her eyes to the ceiling. 'She was trying to keep us safe,' I murmured.

'And are you feeling safe? Do you think Lucille is feeling safe?' Sybil challenged. I demurred, lowering my eyes to my hands in my lap. I was feeling many things, but safe wasn't one of them. Sybil spoke again, this time with the sharper edges knocked away from her voice. 'Knowledge gives us choices.'

'Will you tell me the story now?' I asked. Through all of these events, I had become greedy for knowledge. I wanted to know all of it.

She took a great, steadying breath and began. 'The first pair of sisters are almost a myth to us now. The story has been passed down for so many generations, long predating the keeping of the archive. As a child, the younger sister was stolen into the Otherworld by a monstrous creature, but was remarkably unharmed. The older sister followed her into the brokenness of the Otherworld and stole her back. When the sisters were in the Otherworld, the world was shifting, moving, time passing by. They managed to survive in there, but by the time they returned, everyone they'd ever known was dead.'

I shuddered at the thought of Lucille finally finding a way to escape that place, only to discover that we had all died, that decades had passed. 'But what happened to them after?' I asked, already feeling that there would not be a happy ending.

'They grew up and became strange and powerful, flooded with something of the Otherworld. Those powers are the ones that have lived in our family ever since, making us the best defence against the threats of the

Otherworld. A single pair of sisters in every generation since.'

Austin quietly scratched out a note for Sybil. *When was the last time you heard from my grandfather?*

Sybil looked at him keenly. 'Much longer than is usual for him to go without contact. I have been concerned.'

Austin nodded, crestfallen. The tiny candle of hope he'd been holding, that Sybil might be able to tell him where Dorian was, was extinguished.

He's been missing for the last six months. The necklace was damaged. He didn't have it.

She frowned, her mouth a twist of knowing fear. 'The Otherworld, it ... it stays with you. When you've been there, it wants to keep you. When you get out, it tries to bring you back. Horrors will almost certainly have come looking for him. And if your grandfather didn't have the opal's protection ... then I am sorry. I would fear the worst.'

Austin clenched his fist, and a little muscle in his jaw twitched. His grandfather had been missing for longer than Lucille, and I couldn't see how it could ever get easier, how it could ever hurt less. The confusion, the loss, the not knowing.

'Your grandfather has been a good friend to me,' Sybil continued. 'Someone who truly believes in my purpose. To protect this world from the threats of that broken place. I know that he has not always been kind or patient, but he has always believed in me.' She sighed. 'I think that my parents didn't understand Dorian, truly. He saw going into the Otherworld as the only way he could know for certain that he'd exhausted every opportunity to find his sister. I assume you are aware of what happened?' We nodded, and she continued. 'He was so young when he lost her.'

His obsession with the Otherworld consumed him, Austin wrote.

'He is not the only one.' Sybil's expression was wry. 'When he wrote to me and Emily, after our parents had died, he told me that he was sorry about his heavy-handedness with them, the way he'd resorted to threats and pressured them. After they had parted ways, he had to go back to a life where nobody believed him all over again. It made him bitter. He wanted to find his sister, yes, but he also wanted to have a bigger impact. He wanted to make sure that nobody was ever harmed that way again. Which was why he said I could come here, to Shade's View, why he's been willing to support my work for all this time.'

Dorian and Sybil had found an understanding. She believed that her very existence in the world was to destroy the evil and dangerous things that seeped through from the Otherworld, and he was desperate to understand it, to conquer it, to bring it under control.

My father suspected that he kept a second family with a mistress here.

Austin flushed red as he showed this to Sybil.

She nodded. 'An understandable assumption. But your grandfather was always faithful to your grandmother. He adored that woman, was never the same after she passed away.'

We all fell into silence. Sybil tapped her fingers on the arm of her chair. 'Three mimics, in such a short space of time. That *is* unusual. Have you encountered anything else?'

'Yesterday, at the station, I thought I could feel something malevolent, but I didn't stay to find out what it was. And in Whitby, I thought I saw a sleeping beast with great, bloody fangs. Now I am certain it's what I saw.'

Sybil was beginning to look concerned, her brow furrowing. 'This is alarming,' she said. 'Such a concentration of activity in such a short space of time. I wonder . . .' She trailed off.

'Wonder what?' I pressed.

'You and your sister haven't been trained, the way that the girls of this family usually are. Your mother, she . . .'

Even though Sybil's tone wasn't critical, I found a defensiveness over Mother bubbling over. 'She wanted something different for us.'

Sybil folded her arms across her chest. 'Yes.'

The simple weight of the word hung between us all, and then she fixed me with a stare, as though I were an unusual painting she was trying to comprehend. 'But what is it that you want for yourself?'

'I – I don't know.' It was true. I'd sworn I'd try to use my power to help, but the night in the archive was the first time I'd really felt a thrill at the potential of what I could do, instead of just being scared of it.

'You've felt the strength of your power?' Sybil asked.

I twisted my hands in my lap, anxiety shooting through my body like lightning. 'It's like a . . . a rush of fire.'

Sybil grinned at me. 'It makes you feel spectacular, doesn't it, all that fire gushing around in your belly, heat searing through your hands. Just spectacular!' She was giddy now, and I could tell that this thing that we could do made her feel alive. Maybe I could feel that way about it, too.

'I – I don't know about that,' I said, my voice a quiet, pathetic thing. 'It makes me feel more as if I'm about to turn to ash.'

Sybil's demeanour shifted, all the delight replaced with a deeply empathetic gaze. 'We'll change that. I'll teach you.'

A lump formed in my throat. 'Thank you.'

'You needn't thank me,' she said. 'This is something that has been promised to you since before you were born. And I have a feeling that the reason the Otherworld is growing stronger is because you and your sister haven't renewed the fountain.'

I frowned. 'Renewed the fountain?'

Sybil let out an exasperated sigh. 'I warned your mother there would be consequences. I told her that we couldn't know what keeping you from expressing your powers would do. And now we do. The Otherworld senses the weakness. Its creatures are bolder. You and your sister have a very important job to do. We have no time to waste.'

29

Sybil insisted that my training needed to begin immediately. Time might move differently in the Otherworld, but it was still of the essence. Lucille was in danger every moment she spent in that place undefended. More than that, Sybil said we had a task to complete.

Since the very first pair, every generation of sisters had made a journey into the Otherworld. Just the once, Sybil emphasized, although of course that was another rule she had broken. After they'd been trained in their powers, the sisters would cross through an entrance to renew the structure that was known as the fountain.

The fountain, Sybil told me, was a towering, opalescent structure, and the only thing in the Otherworld that was *not* broken. When the powers of both sisters were brought together in the Otherworld, they were transforming, renewing. Sybil had been taught that renewing the fountain was an acceptance of the powers. Superstition had wound its way around the practice – perhaps renewing the fountain strengthened the powers, perhaps it was an ongoing commitment and promise to protect our world, perhaps, perhaps, perhaps ... But it had never not been done.

But now Sybil had a new theory. Renewing the fountain weakened the Otherworld.

If Sybil's theory was right then until Lucille and I used our magic at the fountain together, renewing it, the Otherworld would keep growing stronger and stronger, with more horrors bursting through, putting innocent people in harm's way.

What was happening was so much bigger than Lucille and me. And maybe that should have made me feel important, but really it just made me realize how far behind I was from where I needed to be and everything that was at stake if I couldn't learn fast enough. My sister and I were a weak fence against a crashing wave, a poor defence against the cascade of horrors flooding out from the Otherworld.

Sybil sent Austin and Mrs Spencer away, declaring that an audience would only make it more difficult for me to focus, and I confess I was relieved. There was no part of me that wanted Austin to see me trying, and failing, to get to grips with the fire that ripped through me.

'The first thing you need to understand,' Sybil said, running a thoughtful finger across her lips, 'is that your power is alive. It lives inside you, and it needs you, but it is not made from you. It is from the Otherworld, and it has taken up residence in your chest.'

My heart sank; it was as I'd feared. 'It feels so incredibly strong,' I said. The sensation of it rising up in me had been so overwhelming. Even talking about it to Sybil made my body squirm and twist in discomfort. And then I admitted the deep fear that had taken root in me. 'I'm frightened that it will destroy me.'

Sybil grimaced. 'Well, it might if you let it. Like any fire, it will utterly consume its source of fuel.'

I couldn't help but picture a piece of paper set aflame, curling into ash. That was what my power would do to me if I couldn't get to grips with it.

'But just as fire is dangerous, it also warms us, and we keep it in grates and use it to our own ends all the time. Your power can become that to you too, if you let it, Alice.'

I nodded. If only I had been able to learn this long ago.

'Tell me what to do,' I said, my mouth set determinedly.

Sybil nodded. 'Your power is a wild creature you need to tame, so treat it as such. Invite it to come out of its lair, the one it's built inside your ribcage. You need to teach it exactly how much it can take from you without destroying you. Both you and it can only learn that through practice.'

Invite it out? I didn't want to invite it out. The panic was rising in my chest, my hands sweating at the thought.

And yet. If I couldn't learn to work with this creature, then I wouldn't last a moment in the Otherworld. I wouldn't find my sister, and we wouldn't accomplish the task we needed to.

Sybil lifted up her palm and fire gathered in the centre of it, conjured from within her with complete ease. With a move of her hand, the fire danced at her direction. I looked on enviously. She made it seem so simple, but I knew this was so many years of mastery. Then she flicked her wrist and the ball of energy leaped into the fireplace and caught hold of the logs there. 'Your turn.'

'But how do I *do* that?' My only experience with the flames had been the sensation of being burned from the inside. What Sybil could do felt impossible, and all my doubts and insecurities started thundering at the door of my mind. There just wasn't enough time for me to learn how to control it the way she could.

'Speak to it! Talk to it and tell it what you need. It might not listen to you at first, but it will.'

I took a deep breath. My heart was rattling inside me. Trembling, I remembered the force of the fire that had almost destroyed me at the station. Unless I could learn to cope with it, then the consequences would be dire and far-reaching. I needed to be brave, more brave than I'd ever had cause to be. Gritting my teeth, I imagined knocking at my own ribs. A tentative greeting.

At first, nothing happened.

And then, I felt it stirring. The same impossible heat that leaped to my defence whenever it sensed the dangers of the Otherworld. It flickered awake, began to catch alight, and I could sense the great, unfurling essence of it.

'It's there,' Sybil said. 'I can see it in your eyes.' What did my eyes look like? They felt hot, as though my tears would bubble and burn. 'Now, guide it to your hands.'

And I tried. I really tried. I lifted my hands up and tried to will the living fire inside me to gather there. But now that it was awake, it was truly awake. And it had its own ideas of what it wanted to do, now it had been invited out.

Like a wildfire taking hold, it began to rush through me all at once. My face flushed with heat, as if I had a fever, and a great shiver shuddered its way through my body. I was sick with it, this rising force.

So then the fear took hold, and I began to panic.

'That's enough,' Sybil said. 'Tell it to stop.' But I couldn't. I was losing all sense of myself as a person with thoughts, with a voice. There was only the fire, rampaging relentlessly. I shuddered and fell to my knees, the burning sensation tearing through me. My teeth chattering, I wrapped my arms around myself as though I were trying to hold myself together.

'Stop,' I said, but it only came out as a whisper.

It was the meekest request, but to my astonishment, the fire listened to me. It stopped its thundering roar with what felt like a sense of disappointment, and then retreated back into its cave. A little at first, and then all the way. I collapsed, weak and exhausted.

'That's a good start,' Sybil said approvingly. 'A very good start.'

I looked up at her from the floor, aghast at her casual tone. Tears sprung to my eyes. 'It didn't feel good,' I spat, each word like a broken tooth.

She shrugged. 'It takes practice. You haven't had practice. We'll try again. And again. And again. When it listens to you, you'll be able to control it. To defend you when you need to be powerful. To light the way for you in the Otherworld. To search out your sister in that place and guide you to her.'

'It can do that?'

'It led Emily and me to the fountain when we needed it to.' Sybil lifted up her frail arms, palms to the ceiling. Those hands were skeletal, the skin loose, and her fingers trembled, but she still seemed to me more powerful than anyone I'd ever met. And then she smirked. 'Can you believe these hands cast fire to crush the windpipe of a great beast? Can you believe they lit the way through an everlasting night in that terrifying world that's not our own? Probably not. But they did. Not so long ago.'

But I *could* believe it. There was a strength of spirit and conviction in her every word that belied her new physicality. She was everything I hoped I would survive long enough to become.

'And now?' I asked tentatively.

Sybil sighed. 'It began five years ago. No doubt it was when you first became aware that there was something different about you. First, I had a twinge in my back, a sharp slicing pain in my knee. Then came the exhaustion. I wrote to your mother and asked her to visit me.'

That trip to London, the one where Mother had left Lucille and me alone for the first and only time.

'We were not in agreement about what should happen next,' Sybil said simply. 'And since then it has been like a stone rolling down a hill. It has rapidly accelerated over the last month. I knew it was the power leaving me when I started to vomit black. I remembered that from my own mother.' She hesitated. 'Is it . . . is it the same for Emily?'

I thought of Mother, the black substance in a pool by her mouth, and nodded.

'She is not well,' I said, and my voice cracked. It was horrid to think that this was happening because of me. Even if I had not asked for it, even if I couldn't refuse it. The guilt shredded me.

'Oh, Emily.' Sybil looked up at the ceiling and blinked. 'I fear that I've already seen her for the last time.'

There was a bone-deep love that Sybil had for her sister. The love she felt for my mother was a tangible, living thing in the room with us, something akin to grief, a loss like no other. They had endured the curse that was thrust upon our family, and it had splintered them from each other. Sybil's letter to Lucille had said *I truly believe that this is the work of sisters*. And I understood, because from the moment Lucille had vanished into the Otherworld, I had longed to bring her home to me.

'I know my time is limited,' Sybil said, a weary acceptance in her eyes. It wasn't that there was no fight in her – I got the sense that for as long as she could, she would roar and rage against death – but it was that she knew that it would ultimately be futile. 'I wanted to train you. You must understand that,' she implored, eyes fierce.

'I understand,' I murmured. It was against Mother's wishes. 'Mother completely hid it from us. Even when I started to change, and she recognized it, she was in denial. Perhaps she imagined she could suppress it if she never acknowledged it. She – she wanted me to be safe.'

'We have not been born to a safe life.' Sybil closed her eyes and let out a stream of breath.

'I wish it had been different,' I said. I wanted a version of this life where there had been less hurt.

Sybil shook her head firmly. 'There's no use in wishing. There's just the way it is now, and the chance to change the future. Trust me.' Her expression softened. 'Your mother could never forgive me, and I can understand that. When your father died, I could not forgive *myself* for the longest time. But . . . I am not made to be soft and loving and healing, the way that she is. I am made for destruction. It is just what I am. I have come to accept it. I was put on this earth to destroy the monsters that threaten our world and the lives of the innocent. That's what Dorian always understood.'

And underlying her words was a truth I was struggling to come to terms with. I was also made for destruction. It wasn't fair. I hadn't asked for any of this. I didn't want it. I watched Sybil's determined expression, the certainty she had in herself. Would I ever be able to feel that way too?

Sybil continued. 'I am so deeply sorry for what happened to your father. I still feel an immense grief knowing the part I played in it. I am not sorry for being what I am, though, and for trying to understand how we can stop the destruction and devastation that the monsters from the Otherworld bring with them. I know that everything I did was to try to protect people. I am a weapon.'

Her words carved through me. Did that mean I was a weapon, too?

'Do you trust yourself?' she asked, her stare boring into my soul. The question was confronting. For the longest time, I had not trusted myself at all. I thought that I was strange and wrong. I'd hidden my true self away from everyone except Lucille. And even though I was growing to understand that this power was something incredible, was something I had been born to, I could not help but feel that I would not be able to live up to the weight of its responsibility. When I'd felt the fire coursing through me, I had not been able to destroy the mimic that had devoured Theodore. It was only my sister sealing the portal that had stopped it from killing me.

'No,' I whispered. I did not trust myself. Not yet.

'Well, you must. That voice inside you, that instinct right at the core of you. That's what the power will listen to. That's not to say that you will be unstoppable or infallible. If you use it too much, and you'll be prone to this in your early years, you will exhaust yourself and it will sicken you, take you to the brink of death. That's why you need your sister. Her healing is the only thing that will enable you to use the full strength of that power that lives in you.' Her expression turned nostalgic, and I got the sense she was stretching back through her memory to reach for a time when my mother was by her side.

'This life will consume you,' Sybil said. 'It's a door warped in its frame. It does not close when you have opened it.'

But she didn't need to tell me that. I already knew.

'Right. Now try again.'

30

Try again. Try again. Try again.

The week that followed passed in a strange blur as Sybil trained me. I knew that every moment we spent was designed to keep me alive when we got to the Otherworld, and so I pushed myself harder each time. I had never worked so hard at anything in my whole life. I practised calling on the power over and over again. It was draining, the constant push and pull of drawing the fire out and increasing my tolerance to its heat.

Austin kept himself busy reading and assimilating as much information from the archive as he could, and then in the evenings sharing snippets with me, things Sybil or my grandmother or the women even further back than that had written about their experiences of using this powerful force. And every time he turned his notebook to me, or handed me an almanac with an open page, a bolt of yearning struck through me like lightning. The way he was so eager to learn about the destiny I'd been abruptly plunged into made me feel closer to him than ever. I found myself longing for him to write to me, more and more. I was hungry for his words.

Each night, I fell into bed exhausted, my body tested to its limits. Austin took to his nest, still prepared at the furthest side of the room from the bed. And every morning, I woke up and felt as though I were sat at the bottom of an hourglass, the sand pouring over me, threatening to drown me as time slipped away.

The moment where I first felt the fire form in the cup of my hand, threads of flames unspooling, I screamed – in delight and in fear. And that was only the beginning. Instead of becoming an overwhelming inferno, I found I could shift it into orbs of light that I would be able to cast ahead of me to light the darkness of the Otherworld's everlasting night. My stamina was increasing, my confidence building, and I started to thrill in the potential of it all – if I didn't think too hard about what would be facing me in that broken place. Just because I could light my own way didn't mean I could destroy the monsters of the Otherworld without the fire consuming me.

But time was pressing down on me. Mother was dying, so many miles away. Lucille was trapped in a night that never ended, and even if her time moved slower than ours, the longer she stayed there, the more chance she'd cross paths with danger.

And then Mrs Spencer brought news that ten people had been killed in an incident near the train tracks heading north out of London.

It looked as though they had been torn to pieces – like paper dolls, wrote one journalist – and nobody knew how that could be possible. It was inhuman, the article said, and, of course, at Shade's View we knew that could probably be taken literally. People were frightened. The monsters were overflowing. And the more time that passed before Lucille and I made our way to the fountain to fulfil the task that had been performed by so many generations before us, the worse it was going to get.

Going to the Otherworld couldn't wait any longer. There was no more time to learn or to train.

I began to formulate a plan, based on two critical pieces of guidance from Sybil.

Firstly, I should use an entrance to the Otherworld that already existed, rather than tearing a new one. I asked her if the latter was worth trying and she shook her head so firmly it looked as though it might snap off. 'To do that, you have to break things,' she said. 'Things that matter.'

And besides, something even worse than a mimic might break through immediately; the Otherworld housed all sorts of monsters. Sybil wasn't confident that I had enough control over my power as it was, and hers was fading fast.

So we decided to go to Austin's theatre, and the dressing room that held the portal to the Otherworld. While there, we could try to destroy the mimic lurking there and possibly even return Austin's voice. But when I confirmed the plan with him, I saw a shiver move through his body, a momentary anxiety flickering behind his eyes. It would take him great courage to return, I knew, and the only thing I could assure him of was that I'd be right by his side. So I clinked my ring against his, our unspoken promise.

Secondly, I should use my power to guide me through the Otherworld. It would lead me to Lucille, and then both of us to the fountain together. In the way that heat can turn sand to glass, the fire of my power and the mending of Lucille's would renew the fountain.

Austin insisted, with capital letters and underlining, that we wait for the next Sunday before we went to the Reverie Theatre. It had to be Sunday. There would only be a matinee performance on that day, which would end around 5 p.m., and then the cast of the show would change out of their costumes, leaving the place locked up and vacated by 7 p.m. with any luck.

Sybil was adamant that she would come too.

'Well, how much longer do I have anyway?' she said with a shrug when I protested that she was too weak. 'It is impossible to know precisely, but I am not long for this world anyhow.' There was a flat acceptance in her voice, a strange sort of knowing that this was likely when and where her life would end. But then she had grown up knowing the sharp edges of this curse, the rules and the reality that, no matter what strength or power it gave, it took and it took in the end.

'You really think you won't come back,' I murmured.

Sybil raised an eyebrow at me, and I felt suitably rebuked for my naïvety. Of course Sybil wouldn't be coming back. It grieved me, even though it hadn't happened yet. In the time we'd spent together, I'd grown so fond of her, despite her stern demeanour and how hard she'd pushed me.

'Now, as you know, this property belongs to his family,'

she said, nodding over at Austin, 'and so this shouldn't be an issue, given that you're already married.' She smirked. 'But all of my items within Shade's View you may consider your own, Alice.'

'Sybil, are you certain that you want to be a part of this journey?' I asked.

She glared at me, as if she were insulted that I had even asked the question. 'This is the way it has always been in our family. Our elder generations have always had a role in guiding the younger ones in this destiny, and it always ends the same. Look at me. I am fading. And I am tired. And I have a choice. I can lay in a bed up those stairs waiting to rot away, or I can go into the Otherworld and use the last of my power to go out in a blaze.' Her jaw was set firm. I got the impression that doing this was her final act of defiance against the Otherworld.

Austin's eyes were full of awe. My chest, too, felt full of admiration. Sybil's whole life had been dedicated to the protection of the innocent, often for those who did not even know that they might have been in peril. My mother thought her dangerous, and that was true as well. Sybil and her power *were* dangerous, but stronger even than the fire she had mastered was her selflessness.

Sybil had told us that the monsters that burst through into our world all had one thing in common. The shadowy entities were drawn to the good and the light that exists in all humans. As the weapon she believed herself to be, she was the protector of that light.

When I imagined a world where people lived in fear, were

torn and devoured by the monsters of the Otherworld, their lights extinguished one by one, leaving our world a darker place, my heart shredded. Grief clawed at my throat.

And I thought of my sister, and how deeply I missed her. All of her. The creative soul and the chaos and the explosiveness. All that light. It had felt, if not easy, then unavoidable, for me to embark on my desperate search for Lucille. I could say without hesitation I would step into harm's way to bring her home, not because of what she gave me, but because I loved her.

Because the word 'sister' was engraved upon my heart.

31

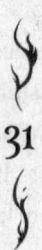

Austin had a nervous energy about him when I found him in the drawing room after waking on Sunday morning. He looked up from the almanac he was reading and his eyes lit up at my arrival.

'I'm still so tired even though I slept all night,' I lamented with a yawn, sinking on to the settee next to him. I stretched out my arms, uncrumpling while I waited for him to write.

You've been working so hard.

'And yet I still don't feel ready.' But then, how could I ever feel ready for the impossible?

Austin had the book open at a page on which something familiar leered out at me. It sent a skewer of recognition straight through me, as though I had been pierced. Loosely sketched there was the bright white of an eye suspended within a horrid sludge, a slack mouth and the shape of a hand, mid-formation. Sybil had an uncanny knack for capturing these supernatural entities in all their horror. He'd found a mimic.

Is that what it looked like to you?

I nodded, and then I squeezed my eyes shut, hunching over as I tried to steady myself. I felt his hand sweep across my back. At his touch, the terrifying image lost its hold on me. It were as if his hand on me was the most natural thing in the world, and yet the sensation was almost breathtaking. I opened my eyes and met his, wishing that we had all the time in the world without the threat of the Otherworld looming over us.

I broke the intensity of our gaze and turned back to Sybil's notes. Her encounter with the mimic echoed much of what I'd experienced, although as we had found to be common, she wrote about it with excitement, as though she was thrilled by the encounter.

Invisible in its early stages, but is able to fully reveal itself, even to those without powers, when it has absorbed enough from its victims to fully imitate them. Incredibly strong. I had to call on my power a great deal to be able to destroy it, and it brought me closer to expiration than I have been in a long while. Thank goodness for Emily and her steady stream of healing, otherwise I think the fire would have ended me this time!

My throat felt thick. Austin's jaw tightened and I could hear the grinding of his teeth. Without Lucille, I would be vulnerable to my power overcoming me, killing me as it passed through me to vanquish the Otherworld's monstrous creations. If Lucille hadn't closed the entrance in the railway station, I would have been destroyed, whether by the mimic that had worn Theodore's face or through my own inexperience with the power inside me.

'I'm scared,' I whispered. 'I'm not sure that I can do this even with Sybil's help.' Preparing to go to the

Otherworld felt like plunging my head under cold water, the instant dread that drenched me, vision blurred, all sound warping, and the strangest sense that none of this was real.

I will be coming too.

I could tell from the look in his eye that there would be no dissuading him. At least the gemstone would protect him with its glowing shield. And, perhaps, if he were there, and I managed to destroy the mimic that had stolen his voice ... perhaps I could capture his voice somehow and return it to him.

The alternative made my gut wrench. There was an equal possibility that in destroying the mimic, his voice might be lost forever.

But at least if he were there with me, I felt there was a chance.

'I'll do everything I can,' I said to Austin quietly.

He raised a quizzical eyebrow.

'To get your voice back. When we find that mimic, I'll strangle it for you. Squeeze your voice out of it. And then I will destroy it so it can never take anything away from you again.' I closed the almanac firmly and slammed it down.

He grabbed my hand and pressed it to his lips, the tempestuous sea of his eyes never leaving mine. I can still feel it now, the softness of his lips and the firm pressure of his kiss against my knuckles. I was tilted off balance by it, dizzy and filled with desire. Our fingers interlaced, every part of me felt alert, alive in a way I'd never felt before. When I looked at our hands, entwined like that, there was a rightness to it that transcended what I'd always been told about what was 'proper'.

'Whatever happens ...' I began, and he lifted his other hand to my face, rubbing a thumb over my cheek. We stayed like that for a moment, our eyes both asking the same question: *Do you feel this too?* And my heart was beating *Yes yes yes*, and then he pulled me close to him and his mouth was on mine, and I felt as though my whole body was dissolving. The kiss was a rush and a crash like the waves in the harbour, eroding all my doubts and my fears.

Then he drew back, and there was almost an apology in the way he was looking at me. But I'd never felt less apologetic about anything in my life.

'I want this,' I whispered, giddy with the thrill of that first kiss. As long as we were together, I was certain that there was nothing we could not overcome. There was no need for words between us as our lips met again, and I melted into him. His hands were in my hair, his lips soft but insistent. The kiss deepened and everything within me sparked like the strike of a match.

I was lost in him.

We had been brought together by a history that stretched back before we were born, a history that had brought us together so inevitably. And perhaps it was ill-advised and reckless, but that kiss made me feel alive and hopeful in a way I never had before, even more than when I wielded fire.

'You can trust me, Austin,' I whispered, as he pulled away, our foreheads still touching. 'I will do everything in my power to restore your voice.'

I did not make a promise, did not dare to even bring that word to my lips, but even so something in his demeanour shifted, and he stood up from the settee, backing away from me. Where our bodies had been pressed against each other, now there was a cool space.

'What's wrong?' I asked, heart skipping a beat.

He reached for his notebook and waved it at me by way of explanation, gesturing that he'd like to leave the room to write. Clearly whatever was troubling him was something he wanted to take his time over. But still, I felt hurt, and unsure as to what had caused this change in him.

My confusion must have shown as, before he left, he marched back over to me and lifted up my hand, the one with the ring on, raising it to his lips and giving it a final, brief kiss. I knew then that whatever happened next, he would stay with me, and if I survived it, we would always be together.

After he had left the room, I touched my lips, still feeling the ghost of his kiss. I smiled. It felt impossibly right. When Austin had arrived at the Honest Opal, dropping into my life like a stone into a pond, his ripples upsetting the tranquil surface of my carefully sequestered life, he had come with self-centred intentions. He had probably been expecting someone more established in this mission, a professional monster-hunter, well hardened to the awfulness of the Otherworld.

Instead, he'd found me. Undeveloped. Unformed. Uninformed.

I must have been such a disappointment to him at first.

And yet ... he had continued to watch me, to watch out for me. He had seen the potential in me. For my part, I could see the good in him, almost like the literal light Sybil described humanity as having. For all that our journey together had no doubt been inspired by his own self-interest, I trusted that now he cared about me and Lucille and this thing that was bigger than all of us, the endless battle against the Otherworld.

After we'd kissed, which had felt like the most right thing I'd ever done, I believed in him more than ever.

And now, whatever I was turning into – whether defender or destructor, I couldn't be sure – I did know one thing: Austin would always have a part of my heart.

32

Mrs Spencer had arranged for a horse-drawn cab to pick us up from Shade's View and deliver us to the Reverie Theatre. It was dark by the time we left the house. Sybil embraced Mrs Spencer.

'There, there, don't cry,' she said, chastising Mrs Spencer, even as her own voice cracked with emotion. 'We knew this day would come soon enough. Perhaps not quite like this, but still ... Maybe it's better this way.' When they'd finished their farewell, I offered Sybil my arm to guide her down the steps, but she batted it away, determined to manage by herself. Mrs Spencer watched us make our way to the cab, standing in the doorway with red-rimmed eyes.

Austin touched the white diamond on the horse's nose, his fingers making a pattern around the marking as it gently snuffled under his touch. I narrowed my eyes inquisitively at him and he gave me a coy smile. Another of his strange little superstitions, like his performance with the salt. So, for luck, I did the same.

We had not seen one another since the morning, and I found I was eager to read whatever missive he had spent so long writing. But he did not give me anything to read, and I wondered if that was an effort to avoid distracting me from the imminent trial I was about to face.

Austin helped Sybil with the step up into the cab, and she positioned herself on the bench inside. There was something regal about her, alongside a look in her eye that told me just how much she despised having to be helped. I kept getting glimpses of the fierce and powerful woman inside. Because I had not known her before, it was easy to imagine that she had become frail gradually, the slow decline that only the lucky experience as a result of the many years they've been gifted. But no: hers was an abrupt unfairness.

Austin held his hand out to steady me as I climbed into the cab next to Sybil, and then leaped in by my side with ease. We were cramped together in the small cab, and after the kiss we'd shared, I felt more aware than ever of his body next to mine. The subtle movement of his chest as he breathed in and out. The heat from his leg pressed up against mine. The slight tap of his toes the only sign that he was nervous.

Whatever it was he'd rushed off to write, he wasn't in a hurry to give it to me. I couldn't read him, and was beginning to feel fearful that he regretted what had passed between us.

Then the cab lurched off. It was certainly a more pleasant experience than the horse-bus, where the fear of being thrown off it was ever-present; at least in the cab, I was securely fixed between Austin and Sybil. Sybil was uncharacteristically quiet, and my own voice felt as though it were silenced by the magnitude of our endeavour. My nerves were worse than ever and I spent most of the journey biting my nails to the quick and checking that I could sense those coiled-up flames behind my ribs, ready to be unleashed. And I found I felt real gratitude that my power was there, lurking within me.

As we approached Covent Garden, I craned my neck to see as much as possible out of the cab's window. There seemed to be a theatre on every street. It was Sunday evening, so they were all closed up, but the architecture was still impressive and awe-inspiring. Each one had steps leading to great, swallow-you-up doors, and they seemed completely enormous compared to our theatre back home in Whitby.

But our destination, the Reverie Theatre, was nothing like the ones we had just passed. It was a squat, shabby-looking little building, painted white but scuffed and worse for wear. The poster advertising its run of *Romeo and Juliet*, the show that had long replaced Austin and continued on without him, was hand-drawn and showed both artistic talent and deep care and effort. So it was not that the Reverie was unloved, more that it was not making the money to keep its building in good repair. While the other theatres had a sense of glamour about them, the Reverie Theatre looked run-down but eager, a puppy from the streets with big, hopeful eyes. I could see what it was about this place that might have charmed Austin, why he might have been drawn to it to make his mark, I thought with a small smile.

While I was helping Sybil down from the carriage, I saw that Austin was lost in his thoughts. Once we were all outside the cab, he drifted towards the Reverie like a ghost, his face stricken. There was something ethereal about him in that moment. It's an image that lingers still in my mind: Austin, a lost soul, helplessly tethered to his theatre.

And there was nothing I could say, no words that might help. I wanted to reassure him, to tell him that he would soon be reunited with his voice. But of course there were no guarantees to any of this. Even though I'd talked about it with Sybil during training, trying to work out if I could direct the flames to tear Austin's voice back from the mimic, it was a terrible unknown with no precedent. Sybil had never attempted anything of the sort. She had only ever been intent on destroying the horror in its entirety. So my hope was just a theory. And I had a feeling it was the hope that was causing Austin so much pain.

Beside me, Sybil straightened herself up, arranged her skirts. She looked up at the sky, thick with dense cloud, and sighed. 'I should have spent longer looking at the stars,' she said, her voice twisted by a wistful twinge. 'It feels more important when you realize it's probably the last time.'

I looked up with her. 'There are no stars in the Otherworld?'

Sybil glanced sidelong at me. 'None.'

A deep dread was winding through me now, tightly squeezing my heart. Days of training, intense and productive though they might have been, did not feel enough.

Austin had swerved the main entrance to the theatre, moving to a side alley and hesitating to check that we were following him. A tiny flicker in his cheek – the tensing of his jaw – was the only sign that he had to steel himself to continue. I offered my arm to Sybil, who took it with fingers that pinched tightly into my flesh.

It was time.

The side door was locked, but Austin knew where there was a key hidden behind a loose brick. He unlocked the door with a clunk, and it swung open. He looked at me, attempting a reassuring smile, and I attempted one back.

Heart in my throat, I followed Austin as he entered the theatre and began making his way along a very dark, thin corridor. Sybil placed her hand on my shoulder so she could follow me. The walls felt close, pressing in as though they might crush us for entering without permission. In the darkness of the theatre, my terror grew, a nasty little creature that clawed at my insides. My eyes slowly adjusted, but my feet remained clumsy on the uneven floor, and it took all my concentration not to trip over myself. Austin knew exactly where he was going, though, and moved through the building as though the floor-plan were etched into his mind.

For the longest time I had imagined going to the theatre, but not like this. I'd imagined filtering in through the auditorium with a bejewelled crowd, like a shoal of glittering fish; I'd imagined a great chandelier twinkling above us and an intricately painted ceiling; I'd imagined the roar of the audience and the feeling that we were all connected through the performance unfolding on the stage. Not sneaking in through a stage door, fumbling along a corridor in the darkness.

Through the gloom, I could see there was a series of doors, most of them partly open. The dressing rooms. One of these would be the one that used to belong to Austin, the place where an entrance to the Otherworld had been ripped in the corner.

This was the moment everything had been building to. The fire inside me flickered in anticipation. I turned to look at Sybil and she patted my shoulder encouragingly. I was so thankful for her grounding presence. She had a fearlessness that I could only hope to live up to one day.

Abruptly, Austin stopped, so suddenly that I bumped into the back of him.

'What's wrong?' I asked, whispering instinctively. The fire inside me flared to attention.

Austin glanced back at me, holding a finger to his lips. On tiptoes, I peered over his shoulder, and my heart jumped to see a figure moving up ahead, a lamp emitting a warm glow.

Somebody was in the theatre.

This wasn't part of the plan.

The theatre was supposed to be completely empty. If we were discovered, our entire plan would surely be ruined, over in a moment. There was no plausible explanation as to why we were there, no lie that could excuse us. Any nightwatchman would surely call the police, suspecting thieves. My stomach twisted, and I held my breath, hoping that the figure wouldn't notice us, for there was nowhere to hide. Almost as if reading my mind, Austin took my hand and squeezed it. The figure was tall and broad-shouldered and had his back to us. Slower now, Austin crept forward until he reached the door he had been looking for. But this one, unlike the others, was firmly closed. Austin's hand tried to quietly turn the handle, but it stayed shut and the lock thudded in the door as Austin attempted to pull it open.

The tiny sound reverberated around the otherwise completely silent corridor.

Sybil gave a tiny groan behind me.

The response was immediate. 'Hello? Who's there?' the voice called from down the corridor.

We were caught.

33

The figure barrelled down the corridor towards us, as purposeful as a train thundering to its destination.

I tensed up, no words to be found. Sybil gripped my shoulder. There was nothing to be done now.

'What on earth are you doing here? How did you get in?' the figure yelled. As he drew nearer, the lamp he held aloft revealed him to be a gaunt-faced young man. He continued to storm towards us, brave in the face of this intrusion, and then he abruptly stopped. He was frowning, and I saw a moment of recognition cross his expression.

'Austin?'

For a brief moment, I felt relieved. This was clearly somebody Austin had worked with at the theatre, a friend. We would be able to explain why we'd come, the friend would be able to help us gain access to the room...

I was very wrong.

The man's face curled into a snarl at Austin, and his hand drew back into a fist.

The punch hit Austin in the face with such force that he crashed backward into the wall with a horrid crack.

His nose spurted blood, his mouth open in a soundless cry of pain.

Instinctively, the flames inside me surged, my body recognizing the threat and responding to my call. I drew the fire into my hand, and then felt Sybil's surprisingly strong grip on my shoulder, pulling me to face her.

No. She shook her head. Her conviction surprised me.

I turned back to Austin to see him grimacing and pulling himself up. There was a defeated look in his eye. He wasn't going to fight back. So perhaps I shouldn't either. The flame in my palm flickered away.

'She died,' his assailant was shouting now, his voice cracking. He lowered his fist. 'She's dead, Austin.'

Austin flinched. The words the man had uttered seemed to wound him more than the punch had. Both of them were blinking back tears, and I had the horrible feeling, immediately and with certainty, that all this had something to do with the promise that Austin had made ... and broken.

She died. Had he made promises to another girl here, in the life before we met?

I turned to Austin. Blood was streaming from his nose and into his mouth, and he was rubbing the back of his head.

'Are you all right?' I asked, my hand reflexively going to his cheek. He nodded, wincing under my fingertips. Burning with questions I knew Austin couldn't answer quickly, I stood in between him and his attacker. 'Who are you?'

'I should be asking you the same thing,' he said, glaring at me. 'You're no one good, if you're associating with that liar.' His eyes were arrows shooting into Austin. Sybil, ever driven by common sense, was attempting to pinch Austin on the bridge of the nose to stem the bleeding while he was scrabbling through his pockets for his notebook.

'Who died?' I asked the attacker, my voice treading gently.

'Oh, what a surprise. He hasn't told you,' he growled, glaring at Austin. 'You didn't want to tell your girl here what sort of a man you really are?' He turned back to me, his eyes still furious. 'He's a liar and a cheat and he uses people. I'm sure he's brought you here to do something for him. That's the sort of person he is. Whatever he's promised you in return, you'll never see it.'

Austin looked at me sorrowfully, shame all over his face. This was the truth then, the heart of everything that had led him to me. He finally pulled his notebook out of his pocket and scribbled urgently.

I'm sorry, Christopher.

'Sorry,' Christopher spat, 'means nothing.'

'What happened? Who has died?' I asked again, urgently. I was desperate to know who she was, who she had been. Someone that Austin had made promises to. What kind of promises I hated to think, my face flushing.

'My sister, Hannah,' Christopher said quietly, and the anger dissipated when he spoke her name, replaced with grief. 'She was sick, and she didn't get the treatment that she needed, and she died.'

'I'm so sorry for your loss,' I said, trying to keep my voice gentle. 'But I don't understand. How does this involve Austin?'

Christopher shook his head. 'I was such a fool. Your friend here, he wanted to be on the stage. But he'd done a bunch of auditions and got nowhere. So he befriended a group of us here at the Reverie, told us he was from a rich family but that acting was his dream. Oh, and Hannah thought he was just wonderful. So charming. And I thought he cared for her in return, but that was foolish of me. He promised me that if I gave up my role in the show and recommended him to my director, he would pay for her medical treatment. But when I came to his dressing room after his first performance and told him what it was going to cost for her to get the help she needed, he wouldn't pay.'

And then it all fell into place for me. Because of course Austin *couldn't* pay. He didn't have the money. Shortly after he'd secured the role, he'd been cut off by his father, and for the first time he had his own lodgings to pay for. Yet whatever the reason behind it, he'd reneged on his promise. This was the person he had been before we met: somebody who would say whatever they needed to say to get what they wanted. And he'd let them down so terribly.

I felt sick to the bottom of my stomach, the horror of what he'd done settling there.

My heart ached. Christopher had tried to save his sister and put his trust in the wrong person. I looked at Austin, who had crumpled to the ground, his head in his hands. His face was painted with regret. Even as he twisted with remorse, the awfulness of what he'd done continued to sink in. He'd used Hannah's situation to further himself, to get what he'd always wanted. And the money he'd promised wasn't his, it was his father's. Perhaps my first instincts about him had been right all along; perhaps I had been stupid and naïve to trust him.

I couldn't look at him any more, couldn't bear the unravelling of the person I'd started to fall in love with.

'Why are you here?' Christopher demanded, the shock of his revelation about Austin still crashing over me.

I blinked. 'The dressing room,' I said, pointing. 'I need you to let me inside.'

Christopher's eyes narrowed. 'It's haunted,' he said. 'People think us superstitious theatre types, but it's true.'

'I don't think that,' I said firmly, though my voice was shaking. 'That's what we're here for. To end the haunting.'

The man raised an eyebrow. 'You can do that?'

'I can,' I said, sounding more confident than I felt. 'Tell me about the room, what's been happening.'

Christopher looked apprehensive. 'There's something in there. It's so . . . cold. Just a real sense of . . . wrongness.' He shook his head, exasperated. 'I can't explain it. It started with him, though. Nobody's set foot in there since Mr Parker here, when he took the role I so graciously stepped aside and secured for him. You know they say a ghost ate his voice? That's what you get, Austin. That's what you deserve.'

'Please,' I said. 'I know that you're angry with him. But I very much need you to let me enter that dressing room. There is a haunting in there, a supernatural entity that only means to devour and cause harm.' I wanted to tell him, *I know how it feels to try to save your sister. You and the locked door to that dressing room are standing in between me being able to try to save my own.* But that felt too cruel to vocalize. The fact I had somebody who could still be saved.

'And you think you're the answer?' he sneered, but he didn't seem wholly committed. It was more like a performance of nastiness, a costume he was wearing to protect himself. There was a sadness in his eyes, and a fear.

So I gathered up the fire inside me and cradled it in my hands. I watched it flicker as Christopher gave a shout beside me, before sending it dancing down the corridor, lighting the way. It bounced down to the end and then I snapped my fingers, calling it back. Sybil made a little sound of approval behind me, while Christopher blinked and shook his head, his mouth hanging open. 'I believe we are the best chance.'

Christopher managed to recover some of his bravado. 'If you want to throw yourself into the path of a devouring monster, then who am I to stop you?' he said. 'But I'll be watching you the whole time.'

'I wouldn't recommend you stay, young man,' Sybil interrupted. 'You will be putting your own life at risk. Do you have a mother? Do you think she would want you placing yourself in harm's way like that, especially after the death of your sister?'

Christopher's firm expression wavered again. He did have a mother. One who'd already lost a daughter. He hesitated. He was frightened. 'You think I want to come in there with you? That room is cursed. But I wouldn't trust *him* –' he gestured to Austin – 'as far as I could throw him.'

'Perhaps you could simply wait out here,' I suggested. 'And you have my permission to search us afterwards, if you so choose, to prove we're not thieves.' It was just a lie to get us inside, of course. Once we'd gone through to the Otherworld, time would pass differently for me and Sybil. Christopher would surely burst in at some point and find us vanished, only Austin remaining, but hopefully, the mimic would be destroyed by then and Austin would have his voice reinstated. At least I knew he'd be able to come up with a good story to explain our absence to Christopher. Who knew how long it would be before we re-emerged, if we ever did.

'All right, then,' Christopher said, narrowing his eyes.

'And when this is over, you can tell the owner of the Reverie that you found a way to banish the ghost in there and the room can be used once more. And then you never need to see Austin again. Isn't that right, Austin?' I nudged him, and he nodded slowly. I could tell that it wounded him to do so, not just the pain in his face from the punch, but also the grief at acknowledging this dream he'd had of being on the stage here was truly over.

'Deal,' Christopher said, and he grabbed my hand, shaking it. 'Unlike your companion, you can trust my word when I give it to you.'

'Thank you,' I said, taking a deep breath, the kind that makes your lungs feel as though you are coating them with steel armour. Austin got up to stand, but he couldn't meet my eye. He looked as though he wanted to disappear entirely. The shame was splashed all over him.

Christopher brought out a loop of keys, and identified the correct one for the dressing room that had once been Austin's. The door unlocked with a great clunking sound.

'Well, be my guest,' Christopher said, extending his hand like a showman.

I went to open the door and felt Austin's hand on my arm. He looked utterly diminished by the revelation of his faults. He held up his notebook.

Alice, I swear to you that I am not that selfish person any more. I made a grave error in judgement. I thought there would be more time for me to raise the money to help her. I didn't realize how urgent it was. I never imagined she might die. And I'll be sorry for it until the end of my days.

I tore my eyes from the paper, a great lump lodged in my throat. 'You should have told me what the promise was,' I whispered, feeling all the hurt and bitterness at how I had discovered the truth. It wasn't me who had been betrayed by him. No, that grief belonged completely to Hannah and those who had loved her. But it stung.

I turned towards the door. The breaking of that promise had had such terrible ramifications, and now we had to face the monstrous thing that had gained strength from Austin's dishonesty. Behind me, Sybil was prepared, unbent to her full height. A strange team we made, ready to plunge into a place beyond our world and bring my sister home.

Gathering my courage, I rolled my shoulders back and thought of the mimic we were about to face. A fire began to spark as I reached for the handle and turned it. This was it. Behind this door was my one chance.

My one chance to save my sister.

Or I'd die trying.

34

The dressing room was cold, a bone-numbing chill that felt scraped from the depths of winter. When I breathed in, the air caught in my chest and then came out in plumes that curled and rose. There was a sense of wrongness in the room, and in response, the fire inside me coiled and prepared itself for battle. I shivered, feeling intensely aware of my skin and its sensitivity.

I held up the lamp that Christopher had given to me, and shadows danced. Along the left side of the room, a rack of costumes was covered in frost. There was a scratched wooden dressing table with a streaked and dusty mirror and a stool with threadbare upholstery. This room held none of the glamour or allure that I had imagined.

In the corner of the room was the tear, a shimmering silver knife wound in the world. The chill was trickling out from it, an unsettling draught that should not be.

And there it was. A shadowy, formless figure. It leant against the tear, and at first I thought it was facing away from us, but then I realized it did not have a face to turn.

A scream was caught in my throat. Because the faceless horror was murmuring something, low and urgent.

'That gallant spirit hath aspired the clouds.'

The voice that spoke was low, passionate, the emotion in it was real, raw with grief, even though the lines were rehearsed. It was the voice I'd heard in my dreams, and it matched him just the way I'd imagined it would.

But the voice also sounded lost, as though it knew it had been stolen away, that it was not in its true home.

'Which too untimely here did scorn the earth.'

I didn't know if my magic could pull Austin's voice out of the mimic, or if destroying the mimic would destroy it too, leaving him without a voice for the rest of his days. But I had to try. Not least because this mimic was standing in between me and the Otherworld my sister was trapped in. Gritting my teeth, I focused my attention on the horror, the fire in me roiling now.

'Trust yourself,' Sybil said from somewhere over my shoulder. My fear melted away in the face of the heat that burned through me. All I had to do was concentrate, trust the thing inside me to know what to do and bend it to my will. 'I'm here if you need me.'

I called to the fire inside and it began to blister its way through me so that even my eyeballs felt hot within my face. It felt like tapping into the most scorching anger I'd ever experienced. How dare this creature think it could snatch Austin's voice away? How dare these monsters come into our world and extinguish our light? It was my destiny to throw everything I had into destroying it, into being a weapon against it. I called the fire into my hands, saw the whirling flames ignite in my palms.

The mimic moved, or tried to, and I could see how poorly formed it was. It had taken Austin's voice, and had arranged its oozing sludge-self into the rough outline of a person, but that was all it was. The theatre had acted quickly, through superstition and fear, and the horror's access to people to steal from had been limited. But that did not make it less strong. I could feel its hunger making it desperate and dangerous.

It surged towards me, and I raised my hands in defence, calling the fire to become whirling, swirling ropes, before plunging my hands straight into the creature. *Hisssss*. The sound was like the immersion of a hot pan into water. There was a scream of pain from the voice that belonged to Austin, and I had to remind myself that it was not him, that he was behind me, with the gemstone around his neck protecting him. I allowed myself a quick glance over my shoulder, reassured to see him bathed in the golden light, his expression something like awe. At me. At my power. Then with my hot and searing hands, I scrabbled at the mimic, hoping there was something tangible I could grab on to, praying that the voice would be in there, like a pebble I could wrap my fingers around and take back for Austin.

Find it, I told the fire. *Find his voice.*

But the mimic was so very hungry. It wanted to devour, and I could not allow that.

More fire. More. All rational thoughts left my mind; I was only fire, a roaring dragon of rage and destruction.

'Hold on to yourself!' Sybil shouted, but she sounded so distant and far away. I was utterly lost in the magic as it took control of me, lashing out against the mimic. The magic moved me like I was a puppet whose strings it was holding. I was burning. It was too strong for me. My eyes felt as though they might melt, the rushing heat a force I could not control.

Then Sybil's hands were on my shoulders, trying to pull me back, trying to rein me in, but I was stuck, still raking through the mimic, grasping for something that felt like a voice, while simultaneously trying to shred it into pieces.

'The magic is too strong for her,' I heard Sybil echo in my ears, as though she were in a tunnel, and all I heard was that I was not strong enough, not good enough. The fire was destroying me. But even once I'd understood that, there was nothing I could do to pull myself back. It was overpowering me, and I could not catch a thought. All I wanted to do was lie down, a great exhaustion crashing over me. I'd failed. The magic was going to burn me to nothing, and the mimic would devour everything it could in the meantime.

Without Lucille and her healing, I could not do this.

But I had tried.

At least I had tried.

And then the mimic began wrapping itself around my hands. It wanted my hands for itself. There was a searing pain, like teeth sinking into them.

Then a stool from across the room came flying past me, but it went straight through the mimic and crashed into the wall behind. I knew it was Austin trying to do *something*. He was trying to fight alongside us. But he could not see what Sybil and I could see, and there was nothing physical enough of the mimic to damage.

'Listen to yourself!' Sybil cried, but there was nothing in me to listen to. I'd spent so many years denying myself that the voice had been quietened too much for me to identify it against the rushing noise of the magic taking charge, using me to destruction. 'Remember what we practised – tell the fire to stop.'

My body felt weak. I was failing. I did not have the strength for this. But I could sense that the fire was still searching for Austin's voice, even as it aimed to destroy the mimic. It felt close, it felt possible. If I could just hold on a bit longer . . .

'Alice, if you don't tell it to stop, you'll die,' Sybil insisted. 'NOW.'

'Stop,' I gasped out. 'Please, stop.'

It took a moment, but then I felt the magic shift, felt it listen. As if noticing for the first time that it was killing me, the fire responded. It began to whirl itself back in, the way it had when I'd been practising, curling itself up in that place behind my ribs. But without it, I was defenceless against the mimic. Sensing that, the monstrous thing tightened its grip on me, causing me to scream out.

'Right then,' Sybil said, and then she was all fire. Her eyes turned orange and yellow and red, the flicker of flames inside her. She swiped, her fingers outstretched, and the mimic burned at her touch. Whatever Sybil had unleashed, it was far, far more powerful than my attempts to destroy the creature. It immediately released its grip on me, my hands undamaged, and it was Austin's voice that once again screamed in pain.

She was going to destroy it entirely, Austin's voice and all. Beginning to panic, I clawed at the thing, desperately searching for anything that might be Austin's voice. But the monster was melting, a thick, shapeless ooze retreating to the entrance to the Otherworld. But Sybil's fire pursued it relentlessly. It did not make it back through the tear, and instead finally became still, a spill of horror on the ground of the dressing room.

'Austin?' I turned to him, breathless. Perhaps it had still worked. Perhaps in destroying the creature, we had freed his voice.

He opened his mouth.

And nothing came out.

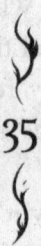

35

Austin touched his throat and tried again. Again, nothing came out and he shook his head slowly. He attempted a smile, but the crushing disappointment was written all over his face.

'I'm sorry,' I said, tears swelling. 'I'm so sorry. I tried.' I went to his side and took his hand in mine. He squeezed it back and then released it, rummaging in his coat pocket for his notebook.

If it had been possible, I know you would have done it.

I couldn't find the words to tell him that I thought it *had* been possible, that I'd felt the fire searching. But I just couldn't hold on any longer. I had done my very best, but perhaps it had always been a foolish hope that the pair of us had been holding on to. I'd had the chance to hear his voice, but never spoken from his lips. Oh, how I wished it were different. Austin's chest rose with a deep breath and when he released it, it seemed as though he was letting go of all the hopes he'd had of being reunited with his voice.

He must have already run this scenario through his mind, contemplated the idea that we would not be successful, that it wasn't possible, for some time. This moment was the final blow, but maybe he had already quietly been growing accustomed to the idea that his voice was not ever returning to him. The dreams he had had for his future would need rethinking; he would never perform a hero's soliloquy on stage to an audience. But I'd fallen in love with him in his silence.

I did love him. I knew it with a new certainty.

Yet I couldn't deny the way I felt about him was blighted by the truth about the promise he'd broken. The awful consequences of his actions simmered in the back of my mind, all that distrust I'd struggled with raising its head once more. I wanted to see the best in him, I truly did. But in the light of what he'd done, that felt difficult.

'You were incredible,' Sybil said, her gravelly voice weary.

I shook my head. 'I wasn't good enough,' I said. 'I couldn't do it by myself.'

'It was very hungry,' Sybil said. 'That made it desperate. You haven't had a chance to learn even a tenth of what you will be able to do one day, and you managed to do so much damage to it . . . and you're alive.'

'Because of you.' My voice cracked. 'You saved me.'

'Not *just* because of me.' Sybil smiled. 'You will be able to do this, Alice. You're having to learn at an impossible rate, with a mentor on her last legs and no healing. You are remarkable.'

That word again. But it seemed as though everything was stacked against me. Even going to the very ends of myself had not been enough.

'Your sister is waiting for you.'

There was a twinge in my chest, like a pluck on an instrument. Lucille. She was still inside the Otherworld, waiting for us to bring her out. I looked at the entrance, that shimmering strand of impossibility, a seam joining our world to the place where my sister had been lost. We had only just begun.

'Come on,' Sybil barked. 'Get up.' At some point, I'd fallen to my knees. Getting to my feet felt like an insurmountable challenge.

My aunt turned sharp. 'I said get up.' She pulled at my arm, which flapped by my side uselessly. 'Lucille needs you. I won't be able to get to her on my own. And you need her. You're drained and her healing will facilitate your recovery. Otherwise you'll be languishing. Weak. We have to go in there and then you can both go home, together. That's the way it should be.'

The entrance. It was mesmerizing, almost beautiful, if you tried not to think of the awful things that came out of it. My heart pounded when I thought about plunging through. Beyond was the unknown landscape of the Otherworld. There was never going to be a moment where I felt ready. In fact, I felt catastrophically unprepared.

'I can't do it,' I whispered.

Sybil took a painful step towards me, wincing as she did. 'You have to. This work is never easy. It comes at great personal cost, as you've discovered. But it's what we are made for.'

I knew she was right.

Next to me, Austin clinked his ring against mine, his hand warm and comforting. My heart tugged at the gesture. I willed away the anger I was still feeling towards him, given that we had to say goodbye.

'All right. I suppose I will see you in a little while,' I said to Austin. Who knew how long it would be. What for me might feel like the work of moments would be so much longer for him. How would he explain our disappearance to Christopher? Where would he go? To his parents?

I wondered about when I eventually came back, where that would leave us. What if he considered our time together finished? Despite the kiss we'd shared, doubt was beginning to creep in. Hadn't I failed him? The reason he'd sought me out, the one thing I had to offer him, I hadn't managed to accomplish. And hadn't he failed me, too? Proven himself untrustworthy and dishonest?

I saw he was writing, his tongue slightly sticking out as he scribbled.

I'm coming too. I said that whatever happens I would be by your side, and I meant it.

I stared at him. 'Come with me? Into the Otherworld?'

He nodded firmly, a smile on his lips. If he felt nervous, it didn't show. But perhaps the shielding glow of the opal filled him with reassurance. It certainly made me feel better about him accompanying us, knowing that whatever we faced, he would be safe.

At least, relatively. I looked at Sybil and she shrugged.

'If you choose to go with us,' Sybil said, directing her words at Austin, 'then you must accept that you won't be the same after. Once you've been in there, you'll see all of it, the way we can. The monstrous beings, the entrances... all of it. Alice's mother only saw them after she'd made the journey with me to renew the fountain when we were younger. And it happened to your grandfather, too. He was... different, after he'd been to the Otherworld.'

Austin didn't look to consider this at all. He just nodded again, his expression determined. I'm not sure there was anything that Sybil could have said in warning that might have stopped him.

Maybe I want to be different.

His words sent a shiver down my spine. 'You don't have to do this,' I said to Austin. He could still turn away from it. Cut his losses and try to start afresh. Return to his parents. Learn accounting like his father.

I know.

He was fearless.

For a moment, I allowed myself to imagine that we might be able to do this together, after bringing Lucille home. When we returned to the world, I would have a choice to make about how the rest of my life would look. Relinquishing that life to this work, the dread and the destruction of it, felt more bearable with the idea of him by my side, after having long ago come to terms with a much more lonely notion of what my life would be. But all the affection I had for him was now tangled up with the horrible way he'd treated Christopher and Hannah to further his own dreams. The false hope, the broken promise. He hadn't killed that poor, sick girl but what he'd done was still undeniably dreadful. And it had taken so much for me to learn to trust him in the first place.

But then, I could believe that regret was gnawing at the core of him. And the Otherworld had taken something precious from him. Why shouldn't he join forces with someone born to fight its dark forces?

'All right,' I said, my voice tightly strung. There was nothing more to be done, except to cross into the Otherworld. I had the sense that once I did, I'd never be able to look at our own world the same way again, that it was all about to shift, the way it had done the first time I'd seen a horror.

I slipped my hand into Austin's, and his fingers interlaced with mine. Then we stepped towards the icy chill. Beyond the shimmering entrance of the Otherworld, there was only inky blackness.

Taking a last deep breath, I gripped Austin's hand tightly and passed through the entrance.

But where there should have been ground beneath us, there was nothing. We were falling, falling to who knew what, and I felt certain we would be dashed to pieces, like a shipwreck upon the rocks.

36

The Otherworld was full of broken things. Austin and I were spat out from the entrance to our world, landing with a crash in a heap, still clutching each other's hands. Aching and bruised, I let go of Austin and scrambled to an upright position. My skirts tangled around my legs, my boots struggling for purchase against a mountain made of brokenness.

I flinched as I realized the horror of what I was resting on – shattered glass, fragments of bowls, a splintered bone, a great fallen oak tree, torn paper, a cabinet with the door hanging off, a skull with a spiderweb of a fracture spreading out across its crown, a glinting and broken golden necklace. Small, insignificant breakages, and bigger, more devastating ones too, each one weakening the barrier between our world and this place.

Beyond the immediate spotlight of our entrance, the Otherworld was blanketed in darkness in all directions. Shadows were rising and falling, creeping and crawling over the heaving landscape of brokenness. No stars watched us from above; there was just an endless shadow cloaking this world. And it was so very, very cold. But the entrance emanated warmth, reminding me of the library at home, and my heart ached.

Beside me, Austin sat up, holding his arms out in front of him. He was glowing. But this wasn't the magical protection of the gemstone. No, the light was coming from inside him. When he turned to me, his mouth open in surprise, he reached for my hands. They, too, were glowing. In this place, we were both illuminated, lit up from within. No wonder the monstrous creatures were drawn to our world, to us, like moths to a flame.

We were warmth and light in a place that had neither of those things. When the entrances to our world ripped open, they must have been a taunt to the creatures that dwelled here.

My eyes began to adjust, until I could see variations in the shadow, the peaks and trenches of the landscape taking shape, lined by what might be dwelling places, squat little shelters. I didn't like to think what might be residing in them. In among the jagged piles of snapped and shattered things, there was almost a pathway carved into the ground, but even that would still be a challenge for Sybil. I was only just beginning to understand the scale of the place. Who knew where Lucille might be in here, if distance condensed like time did.

I was apprehensive to draw out my fire, having felt it so dangerously rampaging to destroy the mimic. But this was what I had been practising and training for, and I knew that this at least was something that I could manage. At my command, the fire puddled in my palms, and I flung it out ahead of us in orbs. They lit the way and made me gasp in horror. The Otherworld was truly a dead place, endless and barren, undulating like hills, scattered with more and more and more broken things.

Surveying the misery of the wasteland, it was impossible to feel anything but a great tidal wave of hopelessness. The desolation was everywhere.

And all I had to offer this place was more destruction.

After a few moments, Sybil passed through the entrance, more gentle than the way Austin and I had barrelled in, landing in a practised way despite her aging body. She, too, had a subtle glow to her.

'This place,' I said, shuddering. 'It just feels like . . .'

Sybil grimaced in response. 'Despair. Yes, I know. I thought the same the first time I came here,' she said, as though she could read the pages of my thoughts like a book. 'The only thing that saves me is remembering that we are the light. Just look at us. We are the light. That's why the Otherworld tries to cling to us. It means something. It matters.'

I looked down at myself again. The glow was persistent, unwavering.

But within moments of righting herself, Sybil began to vomit, the same sticky black substance that I'd seen erupt out of Mother. When I went to help, Sybil raised a hand, warning me to keep my distance. She wiped her mouth. Her face was drawn with the exertion of destroying the mimic, and something essential had drained out of her. I thought that if she had to call on her fire even one more time, it surely would kill her.

She shot a glare my way. 'Don't look at me like that.' I hated seeing the magic draining away from her. It was a haunting fate.

'It's not fair that this is happening to you,' I said weakly.

'Don't feel sorry for me. I have always known some version of this was coming, from the moment my sister told me she was expecting a baby. And do you know how I reacted both times she had that news for me? I squealed with joy. I'm just sorry that the wounds in our family mean I haven't had the chance to guide you, prepare you, the way I would have liked to over so many years. But I have loved you since before you were born, and I will love you after I leave you.' Sybil reached out a hand for mine and squeezed it tight. Our fingers were stiff, frozen from the chill. 'Your mother and I couldn't hang on to each other in all of the grief and the sorrow. You find your sister and you keep her tight. And when you're giving the darkness hell, you remember me.' She shivered despite herself, trying to cover her discomfort with a smile.

My eyes pricked with tears. I hoped Sybil couldn't see them within the gloom of this place; I knew they'd make her furious. But I had come to care for my aunt so much. She surely deserved a better end than this one.

Sybil then turned to Austin and gave him a hard stare, the one I knew so well from training. 'And you, young man. Remember that you don't have to be who you have always been.' He nodded, the shame letting go of some of its grasp on him, so that he seemed to stand a little taller. I felt the strings of my heart twinge. She was saying goodbye.

'Sybil, do you want to go back?' I asked.

Sybil frowned and her eyes were defiant. 'Absolutely not. I told you, I won't survive this magic leaving me either way. So I will be as much use as I can until that moment.' Sybil cast her gaze around us, getting her bearings by the light that I'd cast out. 'I don't recognize this place. But your magic should still be able to find Lucille. If you cast it out and send it to search for her, it should lead the way. And from there, we can get you both to the fountain.'

'If she's still alive,' I said pointedly, the bleakness of the place overwhelming me. Any sense of hope seemed difficult to excavate from the sands of my soul.

'Enough of that,' Sybil said. She poked me in the centre of my chest. 'Listen to yourself. Do you feel as if she's gone?'

Taking a deep breath and closing my eyes, I tried my best to listen. All I could hear was the beat of my heart. But that was enough. Lucille was here somewhere. I just needed to find her.

When I opened my eyes, I gathered up the magic and took a deep breath. I was going to ask it to find her. If it didn't respond now ... Well, then I suppose I finally had my answer.

But to my unspeakable relief, great ribbons of flame tentatively, then more firmly, unspooled from my hands, threading out ahead of us along the pathway that was etched into the piles of broken objects. It *was* a path. A guide. It was unmistakable. Unlike the fire that had poured from me previously, this felt calmer. Alert, certainly, but a seeking force rather than one of sheer destruction.

A new hope broke loose in my chest. This was what it had all been for.

I turned to Sybil and Austin, both of them lit up. And, suddenly, it began to feel possible that I might bring Lucille home, that we might use our magic together to stem the rising tide of the Otherworld.

'Lucille,' I whispered, stretching my hand out as if it were as simple as plucking her out of the darkness and putting her in my pocket. It would surely take us hours to find her, picking our way through this land of broken things and praying that we didn't come face to face with any of the monstrous things that this world housed along the way.

I watched the dancing tendrils of flame wind forward, out into the everlasting night. And then, somewhere very, very far out in the distance, I thought I could see a stubborn little light. The tiniest of glows. My heart leaped. My mouth dropped open.

'Look! Over there. Do you see that?' I asked urgently.

Austin gave my shoulder a reassuring squeeze, nodding *Yes*.

'Yes, that'll be her,' Sybil said, sounding both pleased and relieved. 'I knew your magic would search her out. It'll be able to do the same thing with the fountain when the time comes.'

So simple, in principle. But traversing the landscape of broken things was like being asked to climb a sheer cliff face. On top of which, my whole body felt consumed by the coldness of the Otherworld, as if the very air was trying to crawl inside my skin and leech away the warmth that kept me alive. My teeth began to chatter painfully, although that might have been the shock.

Without hesitation, Austin slipped off his coat – that warm, luxurious grey coat that I had so envied when I had first laid eyes upon it – and began guiding my arms into the sleeves. With a grateful smile, I shrugged it on, feeling the weight of his notebook in the inner pocket knocking against my ribs. Wearing his coat felt like his arms enveloping me, defending me against the painful chill of the Otherworld. He looked at me. And for a moment, I wanted to kiss him. But then my conflicted feelings rushed in to spoil the moment.

Our romance was haunted by the past. It always had been.

The discordant emotions must have been written all over my face, because he tapped the coat as if to ask for his notebook. I handed it over and he wrote to me.

You don't feel the same about me any more.

'No, it's not that. I – I . . .' I stumbled over my words, because the way that I felt about him was so much more than I could express.

I know what I did was wrong. If I could take it back I would.

I nodded. I did believe that he could have made a mistake and have learned his lesson. It was just going to take me some time.

I'm different now.

'We can ... we can talk about this later,' I said firmly. He handed the notebook back to me and I tucked it into the coat pocket. I turned to Sybil. 'We have to keep going, don't we?'

Then I fixed my gaze upon the fiery trail leading towards my sister, that stubborn glow, and I decided to be stubborn too. Stubborn in my hope, and resolute that I would bring Lucille home.

And the three of us pressed on into the darkness, following the tendrils of my magic.

37

We picked our way down the slope carefully, Austin with his arm wrapped around Sybil to support her. I tried to stop myself noticing what broken items my feet were passing over, not wanting to think of the heartbreak or the sorrow or the pain they were connected to in our world. There was just so much of it, and I wanted to close my eyes and close my heart and shut it all out, to concentrate on the job at hand. It was only later, once I'd returned to our world, that I figured out that the heaviness that pressed in on us from every direction was all the broken things we couldn't see, the dreams and the promises that lingered in the air.

There was no conversation between us as we concentrated on our steps, on our breathing, on the numbness spreading through our fingers and toes. The lost, despairing feeling scraped away at my insides. And then I would fix my eyes on the light that was my sister, growing ever so slightly with each step, or I would take a sideways glance at Austin and the ethereal glow of him in this place, and I would try to hold on.

The light mattered, and it still matters, and that is still the thing I tell myself in the middle of the night when I can't sleep, when I wake up from dreams of the Otherworld and light a tiny stub of a candle to comfort myself, or go to the window and look at the stars – the stars! What tiny wonders that we get to witness, if we remember to turn our eyes to the skies. The light counts for something, and it's always there – even in our world where it's hidden beneath our skin.

Sybil quickly grew weary and breathless. Much as I could tell she was trying to suppress the pain, navigating the uneven ground was difficult for her, and her face went pale with a sheen of sweat on her brow. Even in my hardy boots, it was easy to lose my balance. We were traversing a tricky pathway, which seemed to be made of a cluster of broken crockery, when I slipped on the edge of a cracked serving dish and rolled over my ankle. The pain was sharp, immediate, and I crashed on to items that looked as though they had once been somebody's best crockery, pristine and foiled with gold.

Austin was at my side instantly, helping me to my feet, rummaging through the pockets of his coat that I was wearing to find a handkerchief to staunch the bleeding coming from a deep slice in my palm. He tenderly stroked my hair as I tried to stem my tears as the red of my blood soaked through his monogram. My exhaustion with it all was growing. And while I was biting back my sobs, struggling to gather up the pieces of my strength, drops of my blood splattered on to a plate.

The blood. That's what drew the creature out from its hiding place.

The first I knew of it was the sound. The clink of the plates. But neither Austin nor Sybil nor I were moving. We were not alone any longer.

I froze, gripping on to Austin's arm. 'What was that?' I whispered.

Clink.

Something shuffling, beneath the surface.

I conjured an orb of fire in my uninjured palm, directed it to see what was moving among the broken crockery. 'Sybil?' I squeaked.

As ever, she was calm, stoic. But there was fear in her voice. 'I don't see it. Just be ready.'

My imagination roved wildly, conjuring up images from the almanacs – wide, gaping mouths and piercing, slicing limbs. I turned to look at Austin. The gemstone had already leaped to his defence, casting its protective radiance around him. All that told me was that there was something to be frightened of. I skittered backward, pushing myself up the slope.

Unsettled from its position, a dainty cup slid down from behind me and came to rest at my feet. And then a small but monstrous tentacle burst up from beneath it. We instinctively froze. The tentacle flailed, a grasping, searching thing, and then paused, twitching as if to sniff the air. Then it seemed to sense what it wanted. Drawn to my blood, it slithered, snake-like, towards the drops on the crockery, making a horrid sucking noise.

It couldn't see us, I realized, but that made it no less sickening, this creature that wanted to feast on my blood.

'What do we do?' I whispered, gesturing to my hand. It was still bleeding freely. If we tried to run, the beast would hear and pursue us, and I would be leaving a trail for it to follow.

'Destroy it,' Sybil said grimly. 'You can do it. Just make it quick.'

I turned back to the tentacle, and was repulsed to see it was covered in hundreds of tiny, eager mouths. Each was lapping at the crockery, but those drops would not sate a great, yawning hunger for very long.

Indeed, the tentacle raised up once more, the plate licked clean, twitching like the nose of a little rat. And then, with a fierce speed I couldn't have imagined, it went for me, wrapping itself tightly around my arm before I'd even had a second to react. I cried out, and it began squeezing my arm so hard that my fist opened up involuntarily, dropping Austin's blood-soaked handkerchief upon a teapot with no handle. I tried to pull away, but the pain was instant, sharp and horrific as I felt the bite of all those tiny mouths on my skin, the blood-sucker already beginning to drain me. I was suddenly aware that it could all be over in seconds, that this creature could devour my entire life force in moments, and yet the pain was blinding me. I struggled to react, trying to pull away, but its grip was so tight I could barely think.

Instead it was Austin who leaped into action, jumping on to the thick ropey tentacle and trying to pin it. It pulled us both down on to the ground in the process, and the collision was enough to sharpen my senses. Focus. Concentrate. Or die in this dark place with no stars.

I swiftly called for the fire to come into the palm of my good hand, and the effect was tremendous. Its power filled me, and with one single tight squeeze, it burned straight through the tentacle, severing it immediately. The part of the tentacle still wrapped around my arm went limp, and I gasped for breath, pulling the suckers from my flesh with a great wince of pain as the tiny teeth detached one by one. I threw the disgusting thing as hard as I could, casting it into the shadows.

My hand felt so weak, and now the great slash in the centre of my palm was accompanied by small, circular wounds from the creature. I clutched it to my chest, cradling it like a baby, suppressing the tears that threatened to spill.

Austin produced another fresh handkerchief, equally delicately embroidered, and pressed it tightly to the cut, trying to stop the bleeding. His eyes were tender and his hands were gentle.

'I'm all right,' I said, in response to his searching, concerned gaze. 'I'm all right.'

But then I noticed that the other severed end of the blood-sucker was still thrashing around where it protruded from the ground.

That was when I began to contemplate, with a cold chill that set deep in my bones, what was beneath the surface – what the tentacle might have been attached to.

The one thing that Sybil had been so keen to impress upon me was that I needed to start listening to myself. After years of overriding the quiet voice inside me, allowing fear to drown it out, trying to suppress the fight in me, I needed to *listen*. That was what Mother had tried to say to me as well. Her words echoed in my mind.

Remember to have faith in yourself, the way you did before you learned to be frightened.

And suddenly, I was absolutely certain that, whatever monstrous thing had been awoken beneath the surface of this land of broken things, I was powerful enough to destroy it. I looked to Sybil and she nodded encouragingly.

The tentacle was still writhing around, and I saw that the end of it had swollen, like the bud of a flower before it blooms and emerges. And indeed, at the end of this swollen, squirming thing was a new tip. No, I realized in horror: *three* new tips, new tentacles sprouting, bursting through its flesh.

That was all I needed to welcome the fire again. It gathered in me like a rolling force, shrieking through my body. It was sharp and hot and endless, moving through my seized-up fingers, shooting out in flaming daggers. With blazing fingers, I grabbed on to the tentacle and it sizzled in my grip. But that wasn't enough. Pushing further, I directed that fiery energy down, down, down, so that it would flow through the tentacle, down into whatever creature was beneath the surface.

It was a more controlled fight than I'd managed before. The blood-sucking creature was horrifying, but it was nowhere near as strong as the mimics had been. And although I could feel the power of the fire brewing inside me, I knew that this time I wouldn't be consumed. I was in control. I told it what to do and it listened to me.

In seconds, the three sprouting tentacles were seared and lifeless, and I felt sure the fire had consumed whatever lurked beneath us too. I asked the fire to retreat and, this time, it responded immediately, tucking itself away somewhere near my heart. It was as if we were growing to understand each other, as if it were learning my limitations, or as if I were growing stronger and more resistant to being consumed by it.

'You did it,' Sybil's gravelly voice affirmed. 'Well done, Alice. I told you you could. That was all you.'

I smiled at her, my eyes overflowing with tears. I *had* done it. The destruction that had flowed through me had been controlled, had saved me, had saved all of us, and I had not allowed myself to be swept away by its power.

I'd dragged myself from the safety of the Honest Opal into this world of monsters, thinking that the magic that tore through me was a curse rather than a gift. Now I was beginning to understand how it could feel thrilling and meaningful. I was learning how to survive this destiny that had been mapped out for me.

And Austin was right at my side, his face lit up with pride. I turned to him and fell into his arms, which wrapped around my trembling body as a rush of relief flooded through me. For just a moment, I allowed myself to relax in the safety of him, and he gently pressed a kiss into the top of my head. Against his chest, I could feel the steady beat of both his heart and mine. I pulled back to look at him. 'I did it,' I said, my voice just a murmur of wonder.

Again, he patted the place where his notebook rested in the pocket of his coat I was still wearing, and I retrieved it for him once more.

I knew that you would.

And my heart opened to him again the tiniest bit. The aching yearning to kiss him rose once more. It was almost painful.

But we couldn't linger in the Otherworld. Not when every moment in there was passing so much faster on the outside. Mother would be deteriorating. Monsters devouring innocents.

I thought that it could wait. That when we returned from the Otherworld, we'd have so much time.

Now I wish I had pressed my lips to his once more while I had the chance.

'Come on,' I said, sighing, letting a steady stream of breath out as I stomped past the burned tentacle. The danger we'd been in started to truly sink in. My hand still throbbed with pain where it had sliced open when I'd fallen. I didn't want to think about what the tentacle might have tried to do if it had more chance to feast on the open wound. And who knew what the rest of it looked like now, burned in its burrow.

It felt like just a tiny taste of the dangers the Otherworld might bring our way. Just because I'd managed to use the magic to destroy this one creature didn't mean I was any match for some of the more powerful monsters that lurked in the darkness ... yet.

The idea of facing another mimic still felt like more than I could handle. We needed to go faster. I was about to echo this sentiment to Austin when he flashed up his notebook to show me something he'd written.

I feel so useless.

I shook my head. 'You're not useless. I am very glad you're here,' I said. 'All you need to do is stay safe.' He gave a small smile in response, tapping the opal necklace, but I sensed that his thoughts were weighing heavily on him.

He handed me the notebook and I tucked it safely away in the coat pocket. Then Austin gestured in the direction of the entrance we'd emerged through, our way back to the Reverie Theatre. It was far behind us, its glow strong and unwavering but much smaller now. We had already come a long way, but it barely felt like a matter of moments. Time and distance had turned strange. There was nothing to do but press on.

I thought of Dorian and the way he'd refused to give up on his sister. When he knew she had been lost to this place, he had promised his support to Sybil so that she could continue her work. His ongoing obsession was easier to comprehend now I had arrived in the Otherworld, experienced its bleakness.

It made you want to do something, to take action in any way you could.

I understood now why Sybil was happy to think of herself as a weapon – because it was unthinkable that such a place should encroach on our world, threaten to devour us, extinguish the light of people who were unsuspecting, defenceless.

In that moment, I knew I was going to spend the rest of my life fighting it.

The flames I'd cast ribboned their way out into the darkness, leading the way to that stubborn little light that was Lucille. We grew closer, ever closer.

Fixing my eyes on the light ahead, I shivered and pressed on with as much haste as was possible, aware of the urgency with which we needed to move, before other creatures found their way to us. We kept having to stop to help Sybil navigate the uneven parts. But after a little while, I noticed that the light was progressing towards us in return.

My heart soared. It could mean only one thing: Lucille was coming to us. She must have seen our lights, known what it meant.

Keep going, I urged her, wishing she could hear my heart. Perhaps she could.

'Look,' Sybil croaked. She cast out a flame and it danced ahead of us, illuminating the most spectacular construct I'd ever seen.

Jutting out from a great pile of broken doors was a tremendous monument, at least twenty feet tall, made of glittering stone that reflected the lights we'd cast.

The fountain.

What was most striking about it was the way it was cracked in two. Sybil had told me the fountain was meant to be the one thing in the Otherworld that wasn't broken. But that crack through the centre revealed a great crater that swirled with darkness. And something stirred inside. Then, with a great eruption, splatters of an awful, sludgy substance were propelled from the centre. And from that spillage, something squirmed and moved and then scurried away.

'I always wondered what it was,' Sybil said. 'Why it was important that we come. I think it's a birthplace. I think it's bringing new monsters into existence. It wasn't open like this when I came here with Emily. This is what you and Lucille need to remedy. Forget healing, forget destroying; when your powers blend together, they make something new. You can do the impossible.'

I turned to look for Lucille's light. She was steadily making her way towards us.

But then I heard footsteps coming from my right. Somebody else was approaching us, too.

I paused, grabbing hold of Austin's shirt sleeve. He had also heard the steps, and whirled round to face whatever was coming towards us.

A figure emerged from the shadows, arms stretched out.

'Austin!' said a warm, aristocratic voice. 'Grandson!'

38

For a moment, joy broke over Austin's face, alight with relief at the sight of the grey-haired gentleman. The question that had been tormenting him was finally answered. And, for just a second, I felt that joy as well. We had found Dorian! Austin's grandfather, missing for so long and presumed dead by all his family, and Austin the only one holding out hope of finding him.

Against the odds, in this miserable place, we'd stumbled across him when it had seemed almost a certainty that he had perished.

How foolish of me to have had such faith, even fleetingly.

'And my dear friend Sybil!' The figure turned to her, and his smile slipped across his face. It was uncanny and wrong.

Sybil remained very still behind me.

Austin began to move towards his grandfather, his own arms wide. And then he stopped completely still, looking back at us for reassurance. His eyes became wide and fearful and he stumbled back a step, his arm reaching out for me. Once more, he was bathed in the glow from the opal.

We had all had the same realization.

This was not Austin's grandfather.

Of course it wasn't. Perhaps it looked like him, talked like him, moved like him, but it wasn't him. It was an imitation. This was not Dorian Parker, because he had no light.

'Oh, Austin, you're not scared of your grandfather, are you?' My heart pounded a beat of fear. This mimic was doing a very good job of impersonating a human; it must have devoured Dorian completely to get it so close, and be very powerful. It dawned on me with horror that to be able to create such a convincing performance of Dorian, to know Austin by memory, it must have also feasted on his mind.

Yes, it was very convincing.

But still, it couldn't hold it together fully. The smile was very wrong now, had begun to slide off the face completely.

I thought of the apothecary's wife, and what she might have seen before she lit the fire. I thought of the mimic that had worn Theodore's face in front of Lucille. And I thought of the first and only time I'd heard Austin's voice, encased inside one of those horrors. The creatures of the Otherworld were all monstrous, but there was something especially awful about these mimics, which wore the trappings of our loved ones as they tried to devour us.

Austin looked sorrowful and his lip quivered. He must have known this meant his grandfather was long gone.

Consumed by this creature that now stood before us, taking on his appearance, mocking Austin.

'Don't be frightened, my boy,' the mimic rasped, and I could tell there was a part of Austin that was still holding out hope that this was all some terrible mistake. The expression on his face was one I hadn't seen before.

Before he could be drawn in any further, the fire began to swirl within me.

'*Don't*,' I said sharply, the heat of the fire making itself known in my voice. 'Don't believe it, Austin. It's not him.'

Even though defeating that tentacle-wielding creature had given me confidence in myself and my abilities, I knew that my strength was waning, that my body could barely take any more without any healing. It was the same for Sybil, but worse. I thought of Lucille, her light coming closer to us, and I willed her to go faster, to get to us with haste.

The fire was in my fingertips now. It burned with such ferocity that I thought it might slip from my grasp. *Hold on*, I reminded myself, and although I wanted to tell the fire to retreat a little, not to overwhelm me, I also knew that this mimic was the strongest I'd ever faced, and I needed to use as much of the fire as I could possibly bear.

Then, without warning, I dived towards the mimic pretending to be Dorian, aiming my flames straight for the face that was haunting Austin, the ghost of his past.

The mimic screamed and thrashed, trying to retreat, but I would not stop. The face quickly melted beneath my hands, turned to a sickening sludge. The fire raged through me, and for a moment it seemed as though it was working, as though I was strong enough.

But this mimic had more reserves to draw on, and the face reformed itself around my fingers, grinning wildly.

I gasped, and risked a glance behind me at Austin. He'd picked up a broken plank of wood and was holding it as a weapon. Before I could tell him not to, he swung at the mimic's back, and to my surprise it buckled beneath the blow. Where the mimic we'd seen in the Reverie dressing room had been too fluid and unformed to take damage that way, this one had built itself a body, and bodies can be hurt. I glanced at Austin, saw the agony on his face. It must have felt as though he were fighting his own grandfather. He was still shielded in the shimmer of the gemstone, and a deep gratitude for that protection rippled through me.

Taking advantage of the damage Austin had done, I allowed myself to get lost in the rush of the magic again. The fire flowing from me felt a lot like hatred. I went to the end of myself, fire ripping through me as I plunged towards the monstrous thing, roaring. Still, the mimic tried to pull itself back up.

And then I felt Sybil at my side, and saw her all ablaze.

'Sybil, no!' I shouted. Oh, because I knew this was inevitable, but I wasn't ready for it. She'd told me that she was coming with us because she'd rather use the last of her powers to stand by my side and fight against the horrors of the Otherworld. This was her purpose. But surely she would expend everything she had, and I wasn't ready to say goodbye. 'You don't have to do this.'

She looked at me, and there wasn't an ounce of regret or hesitation. 'I think we both know that I do.' She winked, and then gently pushed me aside, out of the path of the mimic. From her outstretched hands there spurted great, crackling flames. It was extraordinary, and it seemed endless.

But then almost as soon as they had begun, the flames sputtered out. Sybil stared at her hands, her mouth slack with shock. Her eyes squeezed shut and I watched the tension in her face as she tried to rekindle her power, but instead what poured out from her was black and sludge-like.

My whole body shook with shock and fear, but I couldn't let her efforts be in vain. I pressed my own fire further than I ever had before, shooting it out from my palms, sending it at the mimic like I was throwing stones.

There was no power left in Sybil now, only decay. And as she kept pouring herself out beside me, my heart gave another leap, because now I saw she was ... dissolving. That was the only word for it. She began to dissolve into nothingness. The magic had deserted her, and she had drained all her energy away until there was nothing left of her – no body, no physical presence at all.

She had given everything of herself.

I squeezed my eyes shut, horrified at what had just unfolded. I knew our time together was always going to be cut short by the cruelness of the magic ebbing away from her, but the unfairness of it still stung.

We'd only just been brought together. She'd changed my life.

I whirled my head to look at Austin, and his face was stricken too. He was staring wide-eyed at the monstrous thing that wore his grandfather's form, and he looked so lost and frightened.

And then the mimic laughed. It was not a human laugh. It was a bitter, hollow sound that made me shiver.

Then it set its sights back on me.

Sybil told me to remember her. Well, I think about her all the time.

I read her almanacs. She lives inside them now. I read them, and I read about the Otherworld, the monsters she defeated and the people that she saved, and also her journal entries about how she lived her life. I have learned so much from her wisdom and courage – about how to fight, and how to live – and so much about her that I feel as if I were by her side on all of those pursuits.

I think often about the last time I saw her face and those fierce eyes that burned.

Sometimes it is easy to imagine her in Shade's View, waiting for me. It's just a musing I indulge in from time to time, imagining what she might say, how she would guide me. And sometimes, in the dream, the archive is filled with candles and light, and Mother is there too, the pair of them together once more. Sybil is painting, Mother is cross-stitching. And something is mended, something that was never mended when they were both alive.

But in that moment, the moment where her magic had deserted her so fully, that moment where she had given all of herself to help me, I did not have a moment to grieve her.

Even though we knew it was coming, even though she'd been prepared and accepted that this was how it would end, she was willing to give everything she had left fighting the Otherworld.

And so must I.

The mimic lunged at me, the hands wrinkled and covered in veins, a facsimile of the ones that had belonged to Dorian Parker. It was strong, too strong for me, and I screamed out again in pain – the pain of the mimic's darkness latching on to me and the pain of the fire burning through me.

I couldn't last long, and it knew it.

Then I felt Austin behind me, his steadying hand on my shoulder. I turned to tell him to step back ... and then, the pain stopped.

Everything around me was covered in a golden glow. It was the most at peace I had ever felt, as if somebody had quietened the whole world, as if my heartbeat had slowed, as if the fire within me had been quelled.

My hands dropped, undamaged, protected by this enveloping radiance.

Instantly, the mimic wanted nothing more to do with me. I felt it sweep past me towards something else.

My thoughts returned slowly, with an organized calm to them.

I was safe. Nothing could harm me in this bubble.

Nothing could harm *me*.

But Austin ...

The realization arrived like it had been dropped into

my mind. My hand scrabbled at my throat and I felt it. A golden chain, a gemstone at my chest. No.

I whirled to look at him, and he smiled, lifting up his hand to show me the ring encircling his finger.

He mouthed something, and then he ran.

No, no, no.

My heart clenched tight in fear, the scream stuck in my throat.

Austin was running away from the fountain, clapping his hands over his head to call the mimic to follow him.

And follow him it did.

39

The mimic was pursuing Austin, and I knew he couldn't outrun it, couldn't go faster than that supernatural body. Terror and panic flooded through me and I began to sprint after them, feeling torn in two as I put more distance between me and my sister, between me and my purpose at the fountain.

But I was always going to go to the ends of myself for him.

Tearing the chain that Austin had so delicately fastened around my neck, I screamed for the fire to come back. Austin needed me to be stronger than I'd ever been. He'd been willing to throw himself in harm's way to draw the mimic away from me. Now, I would do it for him.

I saw the mimic swarming ever closer towards Austin, a hair's breadth away from him. It started to shift and change. The hands and arms transformed into something utterly inhuman. Great slicing scythes extended out from it, almost like monstrous wings. This creature was so powerful because it wasn't just humans it had been devouring. No, it had been lurking here, also feasting on its own kind long before it had crossed paths with Dorian. This was so far beyond anything that I had thought possible.

And then in one awful swiping motion, it lashed out its claw and raked it down Austin's back.

I gaped as I ran.

Time slowed as he fell to the ground.

I howled, a pained animal sound that I have not made before, or since, as he crumpled.

The creature flipped Austin over and sliced at his stomach, and then it opened its mouth and kept opening it, the jaw hanging so low that it barely looked attached. This was it, the moment it would devour him.

'No,' I screamed. '*No!*'

The fire ripped through me, uncontrolled, and I tried to cast it out of me just as fast in great whirling plumes that swarmed the mimic, and ran as rapidly as I have ever run, my very breath on fire in my chest. With every part of my strength, with every bit of energy I could muster, I knew I would destroy myself ending this monster if I had to.

Once, I had been a little girl who wanted adventure, who felt bravery coursing through her veins before she ever had a reason to need to be brave. Before the nightmares, before the horrors, before the beach. I'd lost her. I needed her. And her quiet voice piped up inside me. *You are braver than you have remembered.*

Where I had been at the end of my strength, I scraped the inside of myself for something more, and I asked the fire to bring as much of itself out as it could. I gave it permission.

The fire roared in response, and the small voice inside me got firmer and started to direct it. I wouldn't let it be stronger than me. The monster and the magic both.

I was incandescent, and I would blaze at the mimic until there was nothing left.

I defeated it. I destroyed it. What was left of the mimic was pooled in an inky spill on the ground.

But I am afraid this is not the sort of story where evil is defeated and all is well.

Austin.

At the sight of him, my flames failed, sputtering out. I scrambled towards the place where Austin lay, pulling myself towards his crumpled body. Despair washed over me, as if the very starless sky of the Otherworld was collapsing over my head. I clenched my fists tightly around him, feeling all the injustice and anger balled up inside them.

If he hadn't given me the gemstone when he did, I would have succumbed to the mimic.

He saved me.

But at what cost?

Desperate, crouching by his side, I touched his face, turned so pale now. He was so cold, and his breathing was ragged. I didn't dare to look at the mess the mimic had made of his poor body. His eyes met mine, and he looked so scared.

'Hold on,' I told him. 'Austin, please. Lucille will be here, and ...'

His hand reached for mine and I clutched it, brought it to my lips. His own mouth moved, as if he were trying to say something, but of course no sound came out. I wish I knew what he'd wanted to say.

'Please,' I whispered, as if begging could change it, as if my words alone could restore him, bring him to his feet, save him. I wanted to curl up next to him. What did it matter that I had managed to gain control of the fire, if I managed to defeat the horror, if he was lost?

I hung my head over him, my tears dripping on to his face, his chest.

Austin's breath was slowing. A manic feeling rose inside me. I would do anything to save him. And yet, the only power that I had was to destroy. I closed my eyes and tears streaked down my cheeks as I held his hand and stroked his hair.

'Alice? Alice!'

My eyes snapped open.

It was Lucille, her hair erupting over her shoulders with no ribbon to tie it back, her dress grubby and torn at the knee and her face tear-streaked. She ran towards me, her arms stretched out.

My heart swelled at the sight of her.

My sister.

The light that shone from her was bright and warm, and my arms ached to embrace her, just to feel that she was truly real.

'Please.' My voice was ragged with pain. 'Save him. You can heal, can't you? Heal him.' My whole body was trembling as I reached to grab her, to pull her close.

Lucille crouched down beside us, her face a mask of fear. She looked at Austin. He was fading away, the light in him dimming. Lucille shook her head. 'I don't know what to do. I don't know what to do. Alice, I don't even know who this is, what are you –'

'Just try, Lucille. You have to try.'

But she was frozen, completely unsure of what to do next. Nobody had taught her how to use her powers either. While I'd been training with Sybil, she'd been trapped here, time barely moving. Of course she didn't know what to do. But then, she'd managed to close the entrance at the station through instinct, hadn't she? So I grabbed her hands and placed them on Austin's stomach, the place where his shirt was torn open, where he was . . . I swallowed hard, trying to keep my breathing under control.

Austin's eyes fluttered closed.

'We're here, Austin,' I said, holding his hand tightly. He wasn't squeezing back. 'We're not giving up.'

Lucille's eyes were wide and tearful.

'Try, Lucille. You have to try!' I begged her.

'Alice, I – I really –'

'Please!' I screamed.

So Lucille ground her jaw and squeezed her eyes shut. Strands of light began to wisp out from her hands – like my fire, but gentler, so much gentler – and they slowly wound their way to Austin, dancing over his wounds, trying to knit them together.

But they were deep, and there was a spreading darkness in them that was fighting her healing power. I could see it.

Please, I thought. *Please, please, please. Don't take him from me. Please.*

Then I noticed that he had stopped breathing.

'No,' I said. 'No.'

The fire inside me raged. This was not happening. I couldn't let this happen. I had to do something. Hadn't Sybil told me that our powers combined could do the impossible?

Perhaps this was it.

And I had to know that I'd tried everything.

So I put my hands over Lucille's and welcomed the fire. *Join with Lucille*, I told it. *Do whatever you can. Do **something**.* The flames ribboned out from me once more, entwining with Lucille's mending threads and setting them alight.

She looked up at me with fearful eyes, and I sensed in that moment that the thing she was most frightened of ... was me.

'We have to try together,' I said, completely resolute. 'Together, we can transform things. It's the only thing left we can try.'

She nodded, still fearful, but accepting my lead.

And together, our magics melded and whirled around Austin.

I truly believed it would save him.

I had to, or I would have given up there and then.

But what happened next was something I could never have imagined.

His wounds knitted together, but not as flesh.

With our powers rippling over him and through him, he began to transform. Sparks began to fly up and down his limbs, across his face, until the magic faded away to reveal his body.

His whole body, which was glittering, sparkling stone.

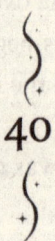

40

Did you think that this story was about me and how I learned to become a fearless destroyer of the demons of the Otherworld? No, I'm still very much unfinished in that regard.

It takes a long time to grow into a power when it was hidden from you, when you fought it for so long, and when your only guide is lost to you. The Otherworld will break through, time and time again, and as the darkness seeks to consume the light, I will grow stronger and braver.

I have not given up in my fight against the horrors. I have many more stories, and will have many more stories to come in my life.

But this story?

This is the story of a boy who learned to be selfless, when all he'd known before was self-interest. This is the story of a boy who dreamed of the stage, who wanted to play the tragic hero, but became one instead.

And I am the girl simply trying to find the strength to write about him.

I wish I'd heard his voice from his own lips, instead of cruelly mimicked. Sometimes, I close my eyes to see if I can remember what that voice sounded like, but it grows more distant every time I try. I can still conjure up the image of his face, the expressiveness he wore so freely, but even that has begun to blur, as if obscured by a steamed-up window. Perhaps if we had been traditional sweethearts, I might have had a portrait of him, but instead I have to try and rely on my memory.

I still wear the ring he gave me. And sometimes I'll clack it against a wall, just to remember what it was like when he was standing next to me.

The one thing that does not fade is the words he wrote. His notebook is my constant companion. I've read it cover to cover countless times so that the conversations we had are etched upon me.

And after it was over, I found a new letter to me, folded up. The one he wrote after we kissed. Those words are the last ones he gave me. I have a dream sometimes, where I open the notebook and there are new pages, new words to read. It is only a dream.

I have tried to find moments of light to fight the darkness. The spring and its blooms are not yet here, but I walked in a park and felt the fresh air in my lungs. I took myself to see a comedy performance at our local theatre, and I even laughed and looked up at the stars as I left. I savoured a mouthful of chocolate. I did it all alone.

I keep living. In spite of it all.

Grief is a strange thing. I've experienced more grief in the last few months than at any point in the rest of my life. In the Otherworld, my heart broke, split down the middle into two, conflicted parts – half that delighted at finding Lucille, and half that was lost to the darkness of that place. The half I brought home with me is a weight in my chest that I lug around with me. It aches, it leaks, it grieves, calling out for what I've lost. And I survive, but I am not the same. The other half of my dark heart, the part of it that fell in love, the part that belongs to him, is still trapped there in the Otherworld, my love encased in shimmering stone.

41

'What did we do?' Lucille gasped, snatching her hands away. She stared at them as if they horrified her.

I ran my trembling fingers across Austin's glittering stone cheek. It was hard and cold to the touch, somehow made even more perfect.

We'd transformed him.

I shook my head. I'd been so sure that it would work, that our magic could do the impossible. And it had – but not like I'd wanted.

He was encapsulated in magic, it felt. And then I saw that there was still a light emanating from him. His light, dimmer than ever before, but not totally extinguished. It was a beautiful and horrifying thought. My eyes brimmed with fresh tears, my heart crushed by an invisible hand. Austin's transformed body lay upon a bed of broken things.

And above us, an entrance to our world cracked open.

Now I was one of the broken things, too.

Every part of me was trembling, and I was heavy with exhaustion. I'd gone too far, let the fire run me ragged, and truly, I began to feel as though I were dying. Not just of my grief, but the effects of using my powers to such extremes. I tried to breathe, but it was difficult and laboured.

Lucille's features pinched in concern. 'Alice, what is wrong? What is happening now?' I went to embrace her, and collapsed in her arms, my legs and arms completely weak. I was shaking all over, my body giving up.

'I need you,' I murmured. 'You need to heal me.'

She winced, uncertain, and then laid her hand against my forehead, the way Mother had always done when we were young and unwell. And then a tranquil energy flowed out of her, so supremely soothing. Something inside me was knitting back together, mending in response to her power.

'Oh, I missed you so much,' I said, my strength beginning to return. Lucille frowned. She could never understand how it had felt for me when she'd been gone, because to her, it would have felt like a fraction of our world's time since she had passed through into the Otherworld. And I had been so changed in that time. My whole world had shifted since the last time I'd seen her. And even though I knew she'd hidden the truth from me and kept the secrets she'd begun to uncover, I knew that she'd only ever been trying to keep me safe; any anger I might have felt evaporated in the wonder at having found her.

When she withdrew her hands, my body restored, the joy at being reunited with her ebbed in the face of the anguish that had space to resurface.

Austin.

I burst into tears. Great, wracking, heaving sobs.

'Oh, Alice,' Lucille said, but I could barely hear her. I'd found her. But I'd lost him. She couldn't understand what it meant, that it was only because of him we'd been brought back together. But there would be time to explain later, once we were safely returned to our world.

I moved away from Lucille, and ran my hands over the cold stone of his face, of his hands. Even his ring had turned to that same, sparkling stone.

I couldn't stay with him forever, even though there was part of me that wanted to. At some point, I'd have to leave him there in the Otherworld and return to my life, the life that had already been blown apart, which I had thought Austin and I would piece back together again.

'I don't want to leave him,' I said, my voice cracking.

'We don't have to go anywhere yet,' Lucille said. 'I'll stay with you here as long as you need.'

I shook my head. 'We can't. We have to renew the fountain.'

'The fountain? What do you mean?'

I gestured at the great structure, the birthplace of monsters.

'Again,' I said, sounding just like Sybil. 'We have to do it again.'

42

The fountain was a mighty structure towering over us. Beneath it, I felt like Lucille and I were dolls from a doll's house, so small and insignificant. It glimmered with every colour I'd ever seen, along with some that I hadn't. It was breathtaking, and yet the beauty of it was marred. There was a giant break through the middle of it, like a cracked tooth. It hurt to look at.

'Mother and Sybil came here before we were born,' I told Lucille. 'And every generation of sisters before them, ever since the first pair came into the Otherworld. We should have come to renew it a long time ago. It's never been left open for this long before.'

'What is it?' She was staring up at the fountain in awe and trepidation. Her eyes were so wide, her mouth open. I could tell that, inside, her thoughts were racing. I understood, because all the same emotions were running wild inside me, my mind struggling to catch up with the shock of what we'd been immersed into.

'Before you found us, Sybil said she thought it was a birthplace. There've been more breakthroughs to our world, and they've been increasing.' I dreaded to think of how many horrors had been unleashed from the fountain, growing hungry, longing for entry to our world.

Lucille shuddered. 'It's horrid, isn't it? All these terrifying things that want to hurt people, and no one knows they're in danger.'

'I want to do everything in my power to fight that,' I said. 'Time moves differently in here, so I've had longer to think about it. And this is what I want to do.'

I couldn't ask her to be so certain. Not yet.

'I knew there was a reason for what was happening to you.' She looked at me, her eyes earnest. 'I didn't realize that I was part of it, too. I was trying to protect you, to make it go away.'

'So was Mother,' I said thickly. She felt so far away. In a different world, even in a different time. I hoped that she wasn't in pain. 'She wanted to free us from the responsibility of it.'

'But she's wrong,' Lucille said, impassioned. It was such a relief to see that spark from her once more. 'We can't turn our backs on this.'

I nodded in agreement. Even though the horror of the fight with the mimic was so fresh, the pain of what had happened to Sybil and Austin so intense, there was a part of me that glowed in quiet appreciation for Lucille's presence next to me.

My sister.

The gap she'd left in me sighed closed. I went quiet in wonder at having her next to me again. This was what I'd been fighting for all this time. I watched every inhale and exhale she took, grateful for each one. She was alive. And that had never been a guarantee. It still wasn't.

But, for now, at least, we were together. Reunited. And there was a rightness about it.

Even if she would never know how lost I'd been without her, how agonizing the weeks had been. For her, it had been mere moments. But she seemed to sense, instinctively, the way she always had, that something inside me was broken, and she reached for my hand and held it tight.

'This is the work of sisters,' I said, Sybil's words reverberating through me, her gravelly voice an echo. 'We have to do this together.'

'I'm with you,' Lucille said. 'Just tell me what to do.'

'Tell your magic what you want it to do. You want it to mend, and I want my fire to burn, and together, we make something that can transform.' The image of glass blowing into a new creation rose in my mind. But it was quickly followed by the picture of Austin, captured in our magic.

I'm sorry, I thought. *Even if I'll never be sorry that I met you.*

Lucille took a deep breath, my hand still in hers. I felt my palm warm with the golden threads of her power, and matched it with the fire of mine. They merged together, making something extraordinary, something indescribable.

And together, we guided it towards the fountain, the place where monsters were born. With all the strength we had, we renewed that cracked structure and transformed it until the dark matter threatening to spill out was stemmed.

From the combination of our powers, we had created something new. And perhaps we couldn't undo what had already been done, the steady birthing of monsters that had been worsening in the years this place had been unknown to us, but through that act, we'd accepted our destiny.

And together, we stumbled through the brokenness of the Otherworld to find our way back.

43

Time had unfolded so strangely in the Otherworld. Although so much had happened, it felt as though only moments had passed since I'd left the Reverie Theatre, Austin's hand in mine. When I passed back through the entrance, blinking and startled by the light, I was confronted with the sights of the destruction we'd wrought on the dressing room and the dead mimic we'd defeated pooled on the floor. It was daytime, although what day, I didn't know. The sun streamed in through a dusty, streaked window, lighting up the dressing table where Austin had left an open copy of his *Romeo and Juliet* script.

Lucille looked around, astonished. Even though I'd explained that time and distance moved differently in the Otherworld, that the entrance we would leave through would bring us out in a different part of the world, she was still understandably disoriented to emerge into a London theatre when she'd left our world from the station in Whitby.

She saw me running my hands over Austin's dressing table and came to my side. 'He meant a lot to you,' she said. My eyes stung and my throat was choked. I knew that if I could ever find the words to explain him to her, then she would understand. Of course she would. She'd lost her childhood sweetheart, hadn't she? Lucille was grieving Theodore, she knew the agony of having someone ripped away, understood the way I'd keep turning it all over in my head thinking about how it could so easily have been different. And yet even though I knew that she was the one person whose sorrow mirrored my own, my grief felt like its own unique creation. A pot moulded from clay that had his fingerprint smudged upon it. I didn't want to share all of it just yet.

'You were wrong about him,' I said, thinking back to that conversation we'd had about Austin when he arrived. 'He wasn't just a young man who wanted to gather up ghost stories. I think he was just trying to understand himself, understand how he'd become who he was.'

Lucille nodded. 'Isn't that what we're all doing?' She winced. 'I'm sorry I kept everything from you. I was trying to protect you from it all. I always thought that was my job, you know? I don't know when it started, but even when we were little, I used to try to stop you from climbing the stairs because I didn't want you to fall.'

'I understand.' I rested my head on her shoulder, marvelling at the solidity of her next to me. There had been an emptiness when she was gone, a gnawing anxiety that was now quelled in her presence. 'You don't need to apologize about any of it. We're in this together now.'

'You ... In there, you were so ... so powerful,' she said, wildly gesturing with her hands. It was just one of many things I'd missed about her, the way her hands flailed so much in her exuberance that I couldn't stand right next to her when she was impassioned about something. 'Your eyes were on fire and your hands were flaming, and . . . and yet you reminded me so much of when you were younger. I'd forgotten that you used to be so fearless when you were small. I don't know where that part of you went.'

I bit my lip. One day I'd tell her about the day I'd nearly drowned. One day I'd tell her about how I'd found my strength again – Mother's words, Sybil's encouragement.

'That's the part that can control the magic,' I said simply. Lucille nodded like she understood. Only, it seemed to me that she'd never silenced that part of herself to begin with. When her magic had told her to close the entrance in the station, she'd listened to it. She'd been able to follow her intuition. It had taken me a little more time to learn to do that. Once, I'd thought that I was invisible without Lucille. But really, I'd allowed the world to frighten me, I'd hidden myself away, hidden myself so well that I couldn't even remember the hiding place. Until now. I'd brought Lucille back from the Otherworld. I'd done it.

But at such a great cost.

Lucille got to work sealing up the entrance back to the Otherworld. Her magic was thread spooling out from her fingers, as though she were a spider creating a web, weaving together the fabric of the world. It sounded like the plucking of strings, beautiful and haunting at the same time.

As she put the finishing touches to it with a little flourish of her wrist, my gut wrenched and I found myself wanting to pull it all apart. It was wrong that it should be so wrapped up, like a present, with whatever particles of Sybil were left languishing inside, left to fade away, and with a frozen Austin laid upon the broken things. The awfulness of it was a bitter taste in my mouth, a scream that hollowed me out from the inside. I'd got what I wanted. I'd brought my sister back safely.

But I could never have imagined what I'd lose.

As I sobbed, Lucille wrapped her arms around me. I wanted to crawl into a bed and sleep for a thousand years, but I needed to go a little further still. We had to go to Shade's View and gather what belongings we could, arrange with Mrs Spencer to send the journals and the other contents of the archive to the Honest Opal, because now there was no Sybil and no Dorian, the house rightly would be reclaimed by Austin's father, and we didn't even have Austin to explain our connection to the house or the things inside it. Then we had to navigate the travel back to Whitby and finally arrive home, and a fear gripped me that we'd get there only to suffer even more grief and loss. Mother had been so sick when I had left. Time had continued to pass in our world. We might walk through the door of the Honest Opal and discover that Mother was already dead, already buried.

It felt like I'd been on a great expedition, reaching the summit of a peak, only to realize that I still needed to walk all the way back down again. There was no option but to just keep moving forward, even though every second took me further away from the time I'd spent with Austin.

But Mother might still be alive. We had to try to get back to her. I'd asked her to hold on for us.

Gathering myself together, and with Lucille by my side, I went to the door of the dressing room.

But it would not open. We were locked in.

44

'We could try to climb out of the window?' Lucille suggested, but it was too high, too small. I imagined climbing on her shoulders, trying to squeeze myself through, and decided against it. We were just going to have to gamble and try to get the attention of somebody in the theatre.

I started by knocking against the door, hoping that somebody would respond. But when that didn't work, I had to escalate things. Bashing the door with a heavy fist, while Lucille flinched beside me, I shouted out, calling for somebody to come and unlock the door, hoping someone would hear me.

Eventually, we heard footsteps approaching, and there was a clunk as a key was turned in the lock. When the door opened, it did so very slowly and hesitantly, a wide pair of brown eyes appearing in the gap created. A young woman with curls piled elegantly on top of her head, dressed in an Elizabethan gown, a costume. When she saw Lucille and me, she let out a squeak of surprise and fumbled with the key, dropping it on the ground. I went to pick it up for her, and as I handed it over, she flinched from me.

'We don't mean any harm,' I said, lifting my hands up, although I was aware that I was covered in something viscous, wearing a blood-stained dress and sporting an injured hand. No doubt I looked utterly frightful, and Lucille certainly was bedraggled as well – never mind that we had just apparently appeared in a locked room. She must have thought us ghosts, and then I felt rather impressed with her for being the first one to respond to my bellows and knocks.

'What are you here for?' Her voice was strong and the words perfectly articulated, and I could picture her on the stage. 'What is it that you want?'

'We came a little while ago,' I said, being vague to cover the fact that I truly had no concept of how much time had passed in our world since I'd taken Austin's hand and dived into the Otherworld. 'We spoke to Christopher about the trouble you were having with this dressing room.'

The girl frowned, looking at me and Lucille in turn with discerning eyes. 'He's been ... superstitious of late. Even more than usual.'

'I fear that might be my fault,' I admitted. 'We came to investigate the cold draught in here, the reports of strange noises and the incident with one of your actors.'

'You mean Austin Parker? The one who ran off? The story was that a ghost stole his voice away.'

I slapped a serene smile across my face as if it didn't injure me to hear his name. 'Well,' I said, trying to bring a lightness to my voice that I didn't feel. 'My sister and I are in the business of solving problems like this for people. Hauntings.'

'Oh, like mediums?' The girl raised a suspicious eyebrow.

'More like ... exterminators,' I said, aware my smile might have looked more like I was baring my teeth.

'Or maids!' Lucille interrupted. 'You know, cleaning up the mess.'

'I see.' The girl kept her hand on the door, as if she wasn't sure whether to release us or slam the door shut and lock it again. 'Well, I'd imagine Christopher will want to settle this business then, if you came on his request. He's just getting into costume for the matinee performance at two.' So, we had been gone at least a week, but maybe more than that. What would that mean for Mother? Would she have been able to hold on that long?

'Yes, well, if you could just take us to him and then we'll be on our way.' I tried to continue to smile.

'Strange that he locked you in.' She wore her suspicion boldly, but opened the door a little wider to let us follow her. Putting her head into the dressing room, she took a glance around. 'Oh! It's not so cold in here any more.'

'Quite,' I said. 'Supernatural activity has been ended, you see. That's what we do. Very happy to help.' I hated the way I sounded like a travelling salesman. But this was how our lives would be, I realized now. If Lucille and I were going to perform this service and become guardians of our world, then we would have to learn to drop breadcrumbs of our work so that those who needed us could find us.

Giving a shrug, the actress took us along to another dressing room further down the corridor.

Christopher's eyebrows drew up in shock when he saw us. He was dressed in his Elizabethan doublet and ready for the stage, a wooden sword hanging from his belt. 'You're back!' he exclaimed. 'I waited all night for you and when I finally looked inside the dressing room in the morning, you were all just gone! And now you show up here three weeks later.'

Three weeks? Even though I had known this would happen, I felt like I had been struck. The image of Mother confined to her bed rose in my mind and my stomach knotted itself in worry, the thought that she might be gone already, that we had taken too long in the Otherworld. But Christopher was in front of me, demanding answers, so there was no dwelling upon it.

'You won't have to worry about that dressing room any more,' I said. 'It's safe now.'

He took in my dishevelled appearance and then noticed Lucille. 'Who's this?'

'This is my sister, Lucille. She was in the place where the entity plaguing this theatre originated from.'

'I see. And where's Austin? And that old crone you were with?'

'They –' the words were strangling me – 'they didn't make it back.'

'Dead?' Christopher's mouth gaped.

'Something like that,' I murmured. I felt Lucille's hand on my shoulder, the flow of her goodness and healing passing into my body, soothing the pain. I brushed her hand away. I wanted to feel this. I didn't want her to take the grief away from me.

'I . . . I can't believe it,' Christopher said, stumbling over his words. All of the hatred he'd looked at Austin with that night in the theatre had vanished.

'For what it's worth, I don't believe he was a bad person,' I said. 'Just . . . selfish. At least when you knew him.'

Christopher nodded, but there were tears springing to his eyes. 'I was counting on him. That's all.'

'Hope can hurt,' I admitted, and then a bell rang.

'I have to go,' Christopher said, wiping his cheeks hurriedly. There were streaks in the powder on his face. 'The show must go on.'

'Yes.' I gave a wan smile. 'Yes, it must.'

45

Lucille kept looking at me as though she didn't recognize me, but maybe it was just that she didn't recognize this version of me, the one who was capable, assertive. That had always been her role. But she was dazed by the busyness of London, the sheer number of people moving and roaming, the thick fog that clung to us as we moved, the terror of being on top of the jolting horse-bus as I navigated our way to Shade's View by public transport, paid for with the small handful of coins Christopher had insisted I take as payment for services rendered to the Reverie Theatre. I even let him know how he could reach us, should he or anyone connected with the theatre be troubled by the supernatural again.

It seemed we were in the family business.

Shade's View had not changed in the least since I'd last seen it what felt like mere hours ago, but was actually weeks in the outside world. Lucille followed me up to the door, seemingly at a loss for words. In fact, she'd been quiet the whole journey back. She must have been stunned into silence.

Mrs Spencer answered the door. Although I'm certain there was a pang of grief when she saw that Sybil hadn't come back, her face broke into a wide smile when she saw that I at least had returned, that Lucille was with me, that we had been successful. We had done what we set out to achieve. That was what Sybil had wanted.

'Let me get a bath started by the fire,' Mrs Spencer said, ushering us in and taking in our dishevelled appearance. 'And I'll make tea. And porridge too?'

My stomach grumbled in response. There was nothing I would like more than the comforting warmth of porridge and tea. Lucille nodded hungrily. As we entered the spotless hallway, Mrs Spencer looked at the two of us and cleared her throat. 'And ... are we expecting Mr Parker?'

My throat tightened as I shook my head sharply. I'd bring myself to tell her later, but I just couldn't say it again, over and over. *He didn't make it, he didn't make it, he didn't make it.* It was an endless hammering in my mind, a painful strike every time. I couldn't bear to find the words for what had happened to him.

Without even hesitating, Mrs Spencer continued with her professional performance as caretaker, nodding swiftly but not probing any further. She went to stoke the fire and pull out the great tin bath, and got to work boiling water to fill it up. Lucille and I sat next to each other on the sofa, and I took her hand in mine. This was what I'd been desperate for, ever since the moment I'd realized she was gone: that we would be beside each other once again. And yet, a great chasm had opened up between us, one that we had to learn to bridge.

'You go first,' Lucille offered when the bath was prepared. I wanted nothing more than to plunge myself into the steaming water, to wash away the blood and grime and the darkness of the Otherworld that felt as if it were clinging to my skin. I took off Austin's coat and a great, gulping sob escaped me as I folded it up and placed it down. Lucille took my hand to steady me and helped me with my dress, preparing me for the bath as if I were a child, and helping me to submerge my weary body into the water.

'Can you tell me what happened when you went into the Otherworld?' I said, curling my knees up to my chest and allowing the heat to soothe my aching muscles. I wanted something to take my mind off my grief, even though I knew it wouldn't be a happy tale.

'I didn't mean to leave. I mean ... I *was* going to leave at some point. I was planning on coming here to meet with Sybil, to learn about us. But it wasn't meant to happen like that. I wasn't meant to just ... disappear. I'd gone to the railway station to work out which would be the right train, that's all.' She rubbed her forehead with her fingers as though plagued by a headache. 'I was planning on coming up with some sort of story for why I needed to go, because I didn't want you to worry.'

'I knew you wouldn't leave without letting me know. That's why I wouldn't let it drop. We had police detectives involved, a search party in the streets. They thought that you'd drowned yourself. And then when Theodore didn't turn up to his wedding, they thought the pair of you had eloped, but I knew you wouldn't do that without telling me. But one thing I don't understand is why you took your diary with you, if you weren't leaving?'

She bit her lip. The fire crackled beside us, the water ebbed around me. 'I was keeping Sybil's letters inside it so you wouldn't find them. Maybe I should have told you what I'd learned.'

'I wish you had,' I admitted. It all could have been so different if Mother and Lucille hadn't been so protective. But then, I could understand why it had felt essential to Mother, after what she'd lost. And Lucille had only been responding to my own reticence and fear, my own choices sparking her urge to guard me, to shield me. It was all a cascade of dominos that had begun generations ago, long before Lucille and I were even imagined by our parents. 'But it might all have ended here anyway.'

She sighed. 'I'm sure you're right. And I suppose we can't know. But I keep thinking, if Theodore hadn't been there that day, what happened to him . . .' Her voice cracked and she shook her head. 'He saw me on my way to the station, followed me. And we were talking in the antechamber, and he was telling me that he didn't want to marry that girl, it had all been arranged by his father, and in such a rush, and he was sorry. And the whole time I could feel this terrible, bone-aching cold. At first I thought it was just how I was feeling about losing Theodore, and then . . . then I felt so incredibly strange. Like I had something wriggling inside me, and I was trembling and ... Well, now I know it was the magic.'

'Had you ever felt it before then? The magic, I mean?'

She shook her head. 'I promise I would have told you.'

And I winced as she said that. Don't make promises, I thought. Promises can be broken. Whether on purpose or by accident.

Lucille continued. 'Theodore asked me to run away with him then, and I started to think that perhaps we could come here to get married, and then I could meet Sybil at the same time. But then I was filled with fear. Just this awful sense that something was wrong, that we were being watched, this great dread. And then Theodore was thrashing around, but he couldn't scream, because, because ... his mouth, it ... wasn't there any more. It was like he was wrestling with some invisible monster, and I reached out to try to help him, but it was like he was just being erased in my arms, and then I could see this glimmering rip in the stone wall, like a window into darkness, and I just flung myself and Theodore through it, trying to get him away from whatever it was that was killing him.'

She paused to breathe, her eyes all wide and terrified. It was as though it were happening for her all over again. Her arms were stretched out. Now she had begun, it was as if she couldn't stop. 'And then we were ... there. It was so dark, and he was dead, and I was so alone. And I knew I'd made a mistake. The wrongness of that place pressed down on me. And I just sank to the ground and cried. I cried until I heard your voice. I knew you were in trouble but I couldn't get to you. And that awful monster was hovering in the entrance, and I could see it now, the evil of it and the way it was trying to arrange itself into Theodore. And I couldn't get to you, but the magic in me was thrumming and erupting out, and before I knew it, it was spilling out of me and the entrance closed up. I saw you, and the monster was with me, but at least I knew you were safe.'

I reached for her hand, tried to comfort her. 'What happened next? What happened to the monster? Did you run?'

She looked at me, puzzled. 'You destroyed it, Alice. As soon as it came through the window to the Otherworld, it melted.'

I ... destroyed it? I blinked at her in disbelief. I had thought that I was too weak, that it was only Lucille closing the entrance that had split the mimic in half and saved Austin and me.

But I had already defeated it. I had had the strength all along.

'You saved me,' she said quietly. 'And then I was lost and alone in there and you came to bring me home. I only hope I was worth it.'

Whatever happens next, I want you to know that I am forever changed because of you. Even if it is not possible for you to retrieve my voice, please know that you have my utmost gratitude for being willing to attempt it. I have to admit that my motives for tracking you down in the first place were entirely selfish. I did not know exactly who I would find, but I hoped so desperately for a person who wielded power to destroy the creatures of the Otherworld, for a person who would get my voice back.

The script led me here, but I also thought it could be a weapon.

When my grandfather was writing it, he meant for it to strike fear of exposure into the heart of those with the power. Before I met you, I would have done anything to get what I wanted: lied, charmed, threatened.

I'd already done it before, you see. I'm ashamed to tell you this story, but I want you to know everything. I promised money to a friend of mine for medical treatment for his sister. In return for his role in Romeo and Juliet. *I wanted a way in to acting and truthfully I always intended to get him the money to help her from my father.*

But when my friend came asking for the money, the treatment was far more expensive than I'd imagined. I just didn't have that much. I'd been cut off financially and I was responsible for paying for my own lodgings. I had started to feel insecure and needed to hold on to the little amount I had. I was too embarrassed and stubborn to ask my father for help. I just needed some more time, to save up my wages from the theatre a bit more.

So I broke my promise. And you know what happened next, when the promise broke.

But I do intend to make amends, to ensure that girl gets the treatment she needs. And that means swallowing my pride and asking my father to intercede, because I've used the end of my own money on my deposit at the guest house, and the inexpensive rings to protect your reputation, and our travel here. But I couldn't live with myself if anything happened to her because I didn't keep my side of the bargain. It's the very next thing I must do – make good on my promise.

I am not proud of the person that I was when I came to your door.

But then I met you, and you have transformed me.

I've watched you step into danger, unflinchingly, to save your sister. You provided a place for a humiliated young woman to gather her thoughts. When the mimic lunged at us in the railway station, you thought of me, you looked for me, when I cowered beneath the protection of my grandfather's gemstone.

And along with this, you've trusted me, believed the best in me, in a way that nobody else has done before. Do you know what a gift that is? I'm worried that once you read these words, you won't think the same of me.

Alice, you are brave and selfless, and you have inspired me to be better.

Whatever happens, I am forever yours,

A

46

I found the letter in the pocket of his coat. He'd wanted me to know everything, but he'd been too frightened of what I might think, that the truth about his broken promise would change the way I felt about him. And, momentarily, it had. I'd withdrawn from him. If only he'd given me the letter before, we might have had a chance to resolve everything before the events that unfolded.

But if I were to begin thinking 'if only', I would never stop.

All the parts of our story that led to his being encased in our magic, turned to glittering stone in the Otherworld, were also the parts that had brought us together in the first place.

Perhaps the 'if only' I should wish is that I never met him.

After I'd read the letter, his last words to me, I sobbed all night long in the bedroom we'd shared.

The following morning, Mrs Spencer was attempting to organize a plan for Sybil's wishes regarding the archive before we departed. 'We must arrange for all of it to be sent to you in Whitby,' she said, 'and we must do it before I inform

Mr Parker that the resident of the house has passed away. Once I do, the family will want to seize the property and its contents quickly, I'd imagine.'

She'd given us more information about the arrangement she had with the Parker family. Originally a member of Dorian's staff at his summer house in the countryside, he had organized for her to head up the household here at Shade's View when Sybil had moved in. When Dorian had disappeared, Mrs Spencer had received a letter from Austin's father stating that he did not wish to know the details, (presumably concerned that Dorian had been supporting a mistress and extramarital child, given the length of the arrangement, as Austin had told us), but that he would honour whatever agreements were in place, in line with his father's wishes. He sent her salary promptly every two weeks, along with a small income for Sybil. Now that Sybil was gone, she would have to let him know, and perhaps return to work in the summer house.

We agreed that I would take Austin's suitcase, that his father should never know that he came to Shade's View. I ached for Austin's family, for his parents and his brothers and sisters, who would never know where he had gone, for his empty seat at their table at celebrations. And the same mystery surrounded Dorian, their enigmatic patriarch. Perhaps they knew enough of his stories of the supernatural and the Otherworld to draw their own conclusions. Perhaps they'd rather not open that door.

Sometimes I imagine one of them might show up at the Honest Opal, seeking answers. But for the time being, there was no need to invite scrutiny into something that could not be explained simply. I didn't even know whether anyone in Austin's family even knew he had lost his voice or that he was planning a trip out of London.

We thanked Mrs Spencer for the way she'd taken care of us and made plans to return to Whitby the next morning. I headed up to the archive to see it for the last time, Lucille trailing behind me up the stairs. When she entered, she let out a small exclamation at the sight of it.

'Do you think Dorian and Sybil did the right thing, going into the Otherworld the way they did?' Lucille asked once she had had a chance to browse the shelves.

'I don't know,' I said. 'If they hadn't, then maybe our father would still be alive.'

'Tell me everything you know about what happened to him,' she said, urgently. The next few days and weeks would be a push and pull like this, the pair of us trying to even out our lumpy understanding of everything that had gone before us. It was like solving a jigsaw together. And we agreed that from that day on, we wouldn't be secretive where the Otherworld was concerned.

'I think we've only seen a tiny fraction of what the Otherworld holds.' I could feel it tugging on me, inviting me back in. Or maybe it was only me wanting to be close to Austin. 'I think we've barely scratched the surface of understanding what's in there.'

'That sounds like dangerous talk,' Lucille said, her protective nature kicking in again.

'This is what we have to figure out,' I said. 'For the

rest of our lives, we have to learn how to deal with this responsibility.'

She took my hand and squeezed it. 'Together,' she insisted. 'Always together.'

I looked into her eyes and felt relief once more that she was back by my side.

Sybil had written two letters before she left, one for our mother, and one addressed to Lucille and me. We agreed to read it together once we'd made our return to the Honest Opal. And I hoped against hope that Mother would be alive to read hers. Everything from the archive would follow us in time.

We took our leave of Shade's View not long after, both eager to get home to Mother as soon as possible. I'd tried to prepare Lucille for the eventuality that she might already have passed while we'd been gone. Lucille had shaken her head in disbelief, and I tried to explain the progression of the desertion of her magic.

What hung between us, unspoken, was the idea that the same would happen to us one day. Was it dependent on whether one of us had children for the magic to flow to? Or would it happen anyway, the magic seeking out the next generation regardless? It was impossible to know. But I was certain that we would face it together.

The train delivered us back to Whitby, and I wrapped my arm around Lucille as we walked along the platform, steadying her. Austin's coat was wrapped around me to fend off the chill of the air, winter fully taking its grip. As we moved towards the stone antechamber at the entrance of the railway station, the pair of us clung to each other, the ghosts of our loves alive in our memories. I was suddenly very aware of the opal gemstone on the chain around my neck, tucked under my dress, resting next to my heart.

This place would never be innocuous to us again. Lucille paused by the stonework, and reached out to touch the place where she had stitched up the world. She flinched at the feel of it – coarse and uneven, a permanent reminder, a scar that only we could see. We stayed there for a moment as all the other passengers of the railway went about their days. Our wounds were not something we wore on the outside.

Lucille took a deep breath. 'I was so horrid to Mother the last time I saw her,' she said. 'And then I've been gone while she deteriorated.'

I put a hand on her shoulder. 'You didn't know,' I said.

'But I did. We all know, don't we, that our time alive is limited. Why don't we remember it, every second of every day? We all know that one day, our loved ones will breathe for the very last time, that their hearts will stop beating. Why can't we just love each other every day?'

Her words hurt more than she could have known, as I thought of all the things I had never had a chance to say to Austin.

'It might not be too late,' I said, although I hadn't been able to find even a pinch of optimism since we'd emerged from the Otherworld. 'I asked her to hold on for us, and she said she would.'

Lucille blinked tears away, and then we rushed back home, back to the Honest Opal, our feet pounding, our breaths chasing, our hair caught in the wind, luggage bashing against our sides. The door was locked when we arrived and we knocked hard and heavy, and while we waited, I explained to Lucille that I'd cancelled all guests, that Dr Binding was the only one who remained to look after Mother.

When he answered the door, he looked delighted to see us, Silver turning circles around his feet, almost tripping us up. 'Girls!' Dr Binding exclaimed, his arms wide in greeting. We sank into his strong embrace. A gleam in his eye, a beam on his face. 'You've returned!'

'It's so good to see you, Dr Binding. Is Mother ... is she ...' I asked, tentative, unable to finish the question.

'She's in bed,' he said, and I heard Lucille gasp beside me in relief. 'She's awake right now, but she can't get up any more. Things have ... progressed since you left. I wasn't sure you'd make it to see her.'

The tears were instant. I dropped my luggage and grabbed Lucille in a tight hug. She could say whatever she needed to say. I was painfully aware that while I'd had the chance to say a goodbye, just in case, Lucille had almost missed that opportunity.

We raced up the stairs and burst into Mother's room, with all the exuberance of children on their birthday. Mother was in the bed, but she was a shrunken, diminished version of herself. The skin on her cheeks was loose, her lips thinned, and her eyes vague and watery. There was the smell of decay in the room. 'Oh, my darlings,' Mother said, and even her voice sounded as though it had been eroding. She reached her arms out for us, and we both climbed up on to the bed, one sister tucked into each arm. And the comfort that landed on me was feather-light.

She was our first home, the place where both of us had begun.

Lucille made her apologies, and Mother assured her that her love was unconditional and had never been in doubt. Mother read her letter from Sybil, and wept, and then Lucille and I read the one addressed to us and swore again to one another that we would face the future together. I held Mother's hand; the papery skin felt so fragile, as though it would tear if I wasn't gentle enough. From beneath her nails, the black substance leaked out, coating her fingertips. It was crusted around her nostrils, and her gums were affected, too, undeniable evidence of her impermanence. These moments we had with her were temporary, precious.

We stayed there all afternoon and long into the evening. Dr Binding popped in to administer some pain-relieving medicine to Mother, and at points she drifted in and out of consciousness. When night had drawn in, and Mother had settled into a deeper sleep, her breathing steady and peaceful, Lucille and I went to prepare some supper.

Dr Binding came to find us in the kitchen, as the stew we were making bubbled away on the hob. Where his face had been bright and full of delight when we'd first arrived at the Honest Opal, now it was rearranged into sympathy.

'My dears ... she is gone,' he said, his voice thick with sadness.

'Who's gone?' Lucille asked, as baffled as I was.

'Your mother. She is at peace now.' The gentle, practised words of a doctor.

'What do you mean?' I asked. 'We were just ... we were just there with her. Moments ago.'

Dr Binding's tone was soft. 'It happens that way sometimes. People will wait until their loved ones leave the room for a moment to slip away. But she held on for you. To see you one last time.'

I had thought that my heart couldn't break any more. But as I experienced grief tear through me anew, I felt certain that if it wasn't for Mother's wards of protection on the Honest Opal, a great rip to the Otherworld would have opened up right there and then.

Dear Alice and Lucille,

This is the work of sisters. The responsibility of our gift, this double-edged sword that we wield against our will, is to aid each other. One to heal and mend, and one to destroy and defend.

Read the journals, read them all. There is wisdom going back generations encapsulated within their pages, and I hope that my words are a small comfort when you both feel as though nobody else in the world can understand who you are.

There is more to the Otherworld than we know and understand. Maybe you will choose to try and learn more. Myself and Dorian have long had suspicions that it is not a senseless darkness, that not everything within it seeks to harm our world. Or maybe you will seek only to protect those who are haunted by the malevolent forces that break through.

Whatever you choose – choose it together.

Sybil

47

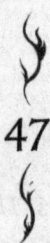

So much of what I've documented in this account is vividly etched in my mind. Memories full of intensity and strangeness and horror and luminosity.

But those yawning, aching days after it ended were mired in grief. They're already hazy, more difficult to distinguish. They felt like when Lucille rinsed out her paintbrushes, all of the colours blending together into muddied water the colour of disappointment. They felt like the pressing down of the unseen broken things in the Otherworld. They felt like they would never end.

We had a funeral for Mother. The contents of the archive arrived from Shade's View, and we got to work organizing the journals in the hidden basement room. One day, Dr Binding said he needed to return to his practice, and we found that we could cope without his steady presence. And on another day, we started to talk about when we might open for guests again, remaining indecisive on that matter but beginning to worry about money.

My dreams were a stage for Austin. Every night, he appeared. Sometimes we were together at Shade's View in the archive, and sometimes we were in the audience at the Reverie, side by side in the dark, waiting for the curtain to rise, and sometimes I could feel his hands on me. But other nights, it was horror and pain and a deep panic that I could not shift that seeped in and turned my dreams to nightmares. He would transform into darkness, the mimic wearing his face. I woke in the clutches of the nightmares, my sheets tangled around me like seaweed.

And Lucille, Lucille slipping into bed beside me, stroking my hair the way she always used to, soothing me.

'He's gone,' I cried.

'He's gone,' she murmured. Agreeing, speaking of her own grief, too.

The pair of us held on to each other like we were drowning, like we were going down in a shipwreck. And I decided to begin trying to excavate some moments of light.

And then one day I woke up, and the year was ending, and the people I'd lost were not the first thing I thought of. I had been dreaming about Isobel and her wedding dress, and I wondered what had happened to her in the time since she'd gone back to her parents' house. I thought about what she called her curse, but I felt certain now was a monstrous Otherworld creature that had attached itself to her family, with its own strange conditions for feeding.

And I thought: maybe now.

Lucille was tucked in bed, and the sight of her sleeping there was a comfort, healing those mornings where I'd woken up to see it empty, not knowing where in the world she had gone, when she was not in this world at all.

Leaving Lucille sleeping, I got dressed and headed outside into the bright December morning, my breath billowing, dragon-like, and Austin's coat shielding me from the cold. Isobel lived in a very fine house a short train ride away. Knocking on the grand front door, I came face to face with a housekeeper who barely disguised their confusion at my asking for Isobel, but went away to find her with instructions to say that it was Miss Alice Everglass from the Honest Opal.

Beautiful and elegantly put together, Isobel crossed her arms when she saw me, but her lips also quirked into a smile. Immediately I noticed the engagement ring on her finger; it glinted and sparkled in the winter sun.

'You're getting married!' I said.

'I am,' she said, and the anxiety rippled over her face. She lowered her voice to a whisper. 'And the worst part is, I think I love him.'

'I think ...' I began, and then had to pause to take a deep breath. 'I think I can help you.'

When I returned to the Honest Opal, feeling invigorated by the beginnings of the investigation into the origins of the monstrous thing that haunted Isobel's family, I knew I had to speak to Lucille. I had pursued my idea with impetuousness, and I needed to make sure that she was willing to begin this adventure with me. But I felt certain that she would.

With my new lease of energy pulsing through me, I went back to our bedroom. Lucille wasn't there, but I was confronted once more by the pile of wood that had once been our set of drawers languishing in the corner of the room.

I hung Austin's coat up on the back of the door. Laying all the pieces of the drawer out on the floor, I began to work out how I could piece it back together. Now I only needed to get Mother's adhesive. And then I got to work, methodically reconstructing the drawer, piece by piece.

That was how Lucille found me, half of the way to a functioning chest of drawers. She sat down beside me and quietly helped. When I told her about Isobel and the sum of money she'd promised if we could get rid of the spectre once and for all, Lucille nodded with a deep certainty that told me that she felt it would give her as much purpose as I did.

I think we are both searching for meaning in it all.

When we'd finished fixing the drawer, I caught a glimpse of Austin's coat out of the corner of my eye, and for a moment I almost thought he was standing there. And somehow I knew that I was ready to begin writing this account. I draw to the end now and hope that I have done justice to his story, to our story. The year will change soon, and with it the century, and who of us can know what the future will hold?

At least I know I have a purpose.

The magic inside me is destruction, but that won't stop me from fixing what I can.

And maybe, one day, I will be mended, too.

Acknowledgements

A book comes into existence with the support of many people, and this one is no exception.

My deepest thanks go to:

my agent, James Wills, and the team at Watson, Little,

all the team at Penguin who have supported the creation of this novel and getting it into the hands of readers, including my editors, Naomi Colthurst and Jenny Glencross; the copy-editing and proofreading team, Melissa Mackey, Shreeta Shah, Victoria Hegedus, Deborah Warner, George Maudsley and Mollie Schofield; and the Design, Marketing and Publicity teams, Lauren Maxwell, Michael Bedo and Rebecca Mason,

New Writing North,

the North East Novelists – Anca, Charles, Eirinie, Hazel, Lauren, Lucy, Naomi, Rebecca and Seth,

my oldest writing pals – Laura and Danny,

my friends and family,

my husband and little ones,

and you, the readers.

Also by H. F. Askwith

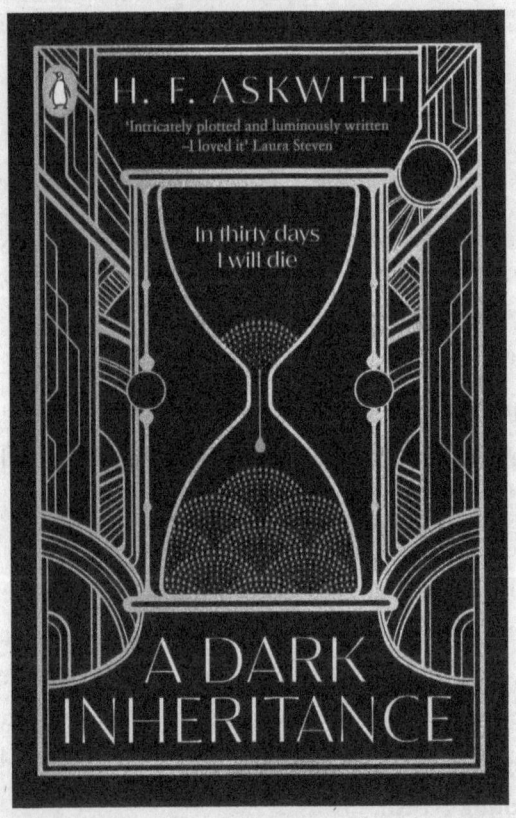

Felix Ashe is sure of only one thing. In thirty days, on his eighteenth birthday, he is cursed to die. So when an opportunity to break the curse appears to present itself, it's impossible not to heed its dark call.

Soon long-buried secrets will take Felix to the darkest underbelly of Jazz-Age New York, to the far-flung wilds of the Yorkshire moors – and bound to everything is a deadly secret society who will either be Felix's downfall . . . or his one chance at redemption.

When Helena is sent to be a governess at the isolated, mysterious Archfall Manor, she feels confident she will know how to deal with the esteemed but eccentric Cauldwell family who own it. But it quickly becomes clear that the Cauldwells are hiding more than Helena could ever have dreamed of.

But the Cauldwells aren't the only ones keeping secrets. Helena has some very important ones of her own – and soon she begins to wonder whether dark powers beyond her control might be forcing her to twist the fate of the family – and her own destiny – forever.

Read on for an extract from
A Cruel Twist of Fate . . .

February 1846

TERROR AT ARCHFALL MANOR!

Sighfeyre Isle, the tidal island that is home to the enigmatic and extravagantly wealthy Cauldwell family, has been cut off from the mainland for four days. Now that the storm has abated, it has been revealed that unspeakable horrors have unfolded within the Cauldwell ancestral home of Archfall Manor during this period of isolation. A number of bodies have reportedly been recovered, and foul play is suspected.

It is not the first time that the Cauldwell family name has been drenched in mystery – Mr Thomas Cauldwell's daughter, Mrs Caroline Temple, has been thrice widowed, and eighteen years ago the elder Cauldwell son, Edwin, disappeared. Although his body was never found, the family reported him dead. These incidents continue to cast a long shadow . . .

1

The day the debt collector came, I was making cinder toffee. The sky was solemn and fateful, shrouding another grim January morning. A grey and miserable daylight strained through the window as I stirred the sugar and the syrup into water in a heavy-bottomed pan. They combined, melting into a gooey, oozing and dangerously hot sludge. I stopped stirring and put my spoon on the worktop before reaching for the jar that contained the white powder, which created an effect that was almost magical when I sprinkled it in. I grabbed a little tool I'd fashioned myself from wire, designed to whip air into my mixtures, and I whisked quickly, beating the mixture as it bubbled, frothing and foaming and taking on a lighter hue, the sandy colour of the coastline in summer. It was transformed.

I always thought there was something about making sweets that was like being a conjuror – take these humble ingredients, combine and transform them, create a treat that provokes the sensation of delight. What is that if not magic?

Before I lifted the pan, I blew away a loose strand that had escaped my plait. My hair, copper-coloured and as thick and strong as wire, required wrestling into submission every morning, and even when it had been fastened it managed to irritate me no end. This was the part where I needed to be careful – my grip was tight, but the pan was heavy, and it would only take one second, one nudge, one slip. Most people don't realize the dangers of working with sugar: not only does it burn, it sticks. You try to wipe away the sugar and you take your skin with it, leaving you raw, revealing the layer beneath . . . I was still waiting for my blistered finger to heal after the previous week's splatter of lemon caramel.

The constant threat of scalding kept me focused, despite the rowdy noise from the busy street outside. Our tiny, ramshackle sweetshop was just a short walk down from the towering Durham Cathedral but being in such a prime location came with a hefty rent and, crammed in among all the other businesses jostling for space, I knew we were barely breaking even.

I began to decant the toffee mixture into trays. It was during this precarious operation, with the surge of sugar requiring all my concentration, that the bell to announce a customer chimed. The toffee was a swollen, puffy thing as it spread across the tray with a life of its own. It breathed in, creating pockets of air in its skin as it cascaded from the pan.

'One moment!' I called, shepherding the liquid with care, scraping the rest of the contents into the tin. Our customers often liked to browse, anyhow.

But this was no ordinary customer. He lifted the wooden hatch of the counter and slipped through, strolled into the kitchen as if he were in charge.

'You can't come back here,' I snapped. 'I'll be out to serve you when I'm finished.'

'I'm not here to rot my teeth,' he said, and his voice was as silky smooth as the centre of a violet cream. His tone, though, was as sharp as a sherbet lemon.

He had shoulder-length hair the colour of coal and a dusting of dark stubble over high and well-defined cheekbones. I couldn't help but envy him his thick tweed coat with its cape over the shoulders – the winter had been biting and showed little sign of relenting any time soon. Despite the warmth of his clothing, his eyes had shards of ice in them. The palest of blues.

He was blocking my way out, and my whole body tensed. A taut muscle in my neck started to twitch. I no longer felt merely irritated by the interruption, but deeply unsettled.

'If you're not here for confectionery, then you've walked into the wrong shop,' I said through gritted teeth, trying to sound braver than I felt.

'Oh, I'm not mistaken,' he said. A smile slid across his lips, which were thin and almost disappeared as they stretched. It was not a kind smile, and my skin started to prickle. He laughed, and it was a robust sound, the laugh of a man who settled down in a comfortable bed and slept every night with a full belly.

'What do you want then?' I snapped, placing my hands on my hips even though inside I was shrinking, like one of those birds who puff up their feathers as a defence. My nerves were frayed. 'I'm not interested in riddles. Can't you see I have enough to do?' I gestured wildly at the kitchen – it was full of the clutter of a morning spent crafting sweets.

'No riddles,' he said. 'I'm here to collect your debt. It's court-ordered now. Your landlord has had enough of waiting.'

My stomach sank. I knew that some months we had struggled when business was poor, but I didn't know Mam was in debt. My gut plummeted further when I thought of the money I'd been stealing from our shop's takings in return for late-night lessons in reading, writing and arithmetic from Josephine, a tutor at the boarding school. I was investing in my future, I'd told myself. But at what cost?

'So?' the debt collector asked. 'Do you have the money?'

'How much is it?'

I steeled myself to hear the answer, but no amount of preparation could have made the blow easier to receive. The sum was staggering, and, given the meagre profit we made at the shop, clearing it by selling sweets alone would be impossible.

'I don't . . . I . . .' The words stuck in my throat.

'I didn't think so. In that case, what do you have for me?' He appraised the row of pans, picked one up and weighed it in his hand as if to determine its worth like a piglet at market.

'You take that and we won't be able to pay the rent, let alone put anything towards the debt. How am I meant to make sweets without utensils?'

The man bared his teeth. 'I don't think you understand. You won't be making sweets here for much longer. This is the end of the road.' He pulled out a document from his pocket and slammed it on the worktop. 'One month to pay up. One month before your ma is hauled off to the debtors' prison, and the bailiffs take every last thing. I'm merely here to collect enough to keep you in business until then.'

I stared at the hand holding the paper. The fingers were bonded together by what looked at first glance like an elegant piece of jewellery, but bile rose in the back of my throat as I realized that the polished silver bar wasn't there for decorative purposes. The raised ridges were designed to turn his fist into a weapon.

'I'll check the cash drawer,' I said, defeated, trying not to think how we'd pay for food. 'Let me past.'

He moved, and I shuffled out from behind the worktop. I had a vision of clobbering him round the head with the cast-iron frying pan hanging on the wall, skewering him with the poker that stoked the fire, tipping the cinder toffee mixture all over him . . . But the pictures were momentary. Any bravery I'd felt had melted away for good.

About the author

H. F. Askwith is the author of three YA gothic fantasy thrillers – *A Dark Inheritance*, *A Cruel Twist of Fate* and *Half A Dark Heart*. She is a Northern Writers' Award winner and has an MA in Creative Writing. When she's not writing, she loves solving puzzles, playing board games with her family and running.